D1602823

Seeing Gray

by

C.E. Brown

Cover Art by *Jennifer Greeff*

The Wild Rose Press, Inc.
PO Box 708
Adams Basin, NY 14410-0708
Visit us at www.thewildrosepress.com

Publishing History
First Edition, 2024
Trade Paperback ISBN 978-1-5092-5530-6
Digital ISBN 978-1-5092-5531-3

Published in the United States of America

Dedication

To my family, friends, and everyone who helped in this process— thank you for believing in me.

Prologue

Giggling, I pushed the tiny shield into the dirt, shoving until it was almost covered. After sprinkling a little grass on top, I hid it with a leaf. Backing up to the middle of the yard, I glanced at the kitchen window. Mom had finally left. As I removed the heavy pendant from around my neck, I called out, "Okay, everyone, gather up."

My stomach fluttered as brightness flared, and a dozen pixies whizzed into a tight group behind the branch that would be my starting point. Only two or three inches tall, they peered around the yard at all the nooks and crannies I'd created. Their translucent wings were almost invisible, moving as fast as a hummingbird's. Large black eyes centered on me, and I rushed to speak, knowing it could be hard to keep their attention.

"This month's hunt is for an epic item. It will help you in battle, and it sparkles too." I had turned a gold coin into a shield by drilling holes, adding a rubber band, and then gluing on some silver glitter in the shape of a starburst. I was pretty proud of it. Whoever won it was going to love it. Hopping with giddiness, I grabbed my blue flag made from an old pillowcase and held it out. "Are you ready? Get set." I paused for dramatic effect then yelled, "Go!" before swiping the flag down.

Wings flittered everywhere as the pixies searched the yard for the hidden prize. Their tiny bodies swerved around each other as they dove under rocks, stick swords swinging as they battled to check the prime hiding spots. On the ground rested a small shoe made from a thick green leaf. I picked it up and set it on the deck. I made an effort to look all over the yard instead of at the hiding spot, not wanting to give it away, even though I was dying to see if any of them were close.

"Zoey Marie Talbot! You put that back on this instant!"

Wincing, I turned away from the bright, swirling bodies and faced the furious wrath of my mother. Her long skirts swung as she raced down the stairs. I shrank as she scooped up the necklace I'd dropped on the ground and forcibly shoved it over my head, catching on a few strands of hair.

"Ow, you got my hair." Turning to the side, I pulled the caught strands from the twisty chain. A few dark pieces fell to the ground. As the medallion settled against my chest, an invisible barrier fell over everything. The pixies' laughter disappeared, and the bright world dimmed. I tugged at the cold, hard chain. "We're in the backyard. Do I really have to wear it all the time?"

Even I could hear the whine in my voice, but I couldn't help myself. The world was so much brighter and fun with it off. And I was going to miss out on seeing who found the shield. I had a whole victory ceremony planned. I wanted to scream and stomp my feet but knew from experience that it would do no good.

"Yes. You are unregistered. You can't be playing with pixies. Humans can't see them. If anyone knows you have the Sight, we could get into big trouble."

I looked around at the drab greens and browns of the yard. "Why don't I register? I know Grammy died, but that was forever ago. Things could be different now. Why don't we try—"

"She didn't just die, Zoey. They killed her. They wanted her Sight and killed her to keep it from others. They will do the same to you."

The same old story. And I was half convinced Mom got it wrong. Why would anyone care if someone could see through spells? It was such a useless gift. Not like breathing fire or walking through walls.

Clenching my fists, I said in a strangled voice, "They won't kill a kid." At eleven, I wasn't quite a kid anymore, but I doubted my mother would disagree.

Mom stood there, staring at me with her stormy blue eyes, unmoved. Looking over the yard, feeling sure that the pixies were watching, a well of fury burned in my stomach. I'd spent all day planning this, and now it was ruined. The pixies were my friends. They would never hurt me. I placed shaking hands on my hips, and said, "I think I should get a choice. If I want to register, why can't I?"

Sighing, Mom sank heavily onto the back steps. Resting her head in her hands, she said, "You're right. You should have a choice." Straightening, she turned to face me. She took my hands and pulled me down beside her. "How about this? When you turn eighteen, if you still want to register, your father and I won't stop you. Some get their powers late, so it won't be too odd if we explain it right. But Zoey, they do kill children. I've seen them do horrible things. The Others are not human. They do not have our compassion or conscience, so for now, you will wear the necklace and pretend to be human. Do we have a deal?"

"Wait, what? You're going to let me register? Let

me visit the Other realms?" My heart fluttered with excitement.

"When you turn eighteen—if that is what you want. I strongly disagree with that choice and hope you'll change your mind by then, but it will be your choice." Mom looked around and frowned, seeing the maze I had created in the backyard. "But Zoey, until then, stop playing with the pixies. They are not friends. They do not think the same way we do. If they are asked to report on you, they will."

Mom stared out at the backyard and said in her *you better obey me* voice, "Leave Zoey alone. I know you mean well, but you are only encouraging her. She does not know about your world."

I wondered if the pixies were giggling or hiding in the bushes. *I'll ask them their opinion tomorrow.*

But the next day they were gone. And then again, the day after that, and then the week after that. I stopped taking my necklace off. There was nothing left to See.

Chapter 1

SIX YEARS LATER

The afternoon sun beat down, making my T-shirt sticky with sweat. I peeled it away from my back and fanned my hot skin, taking a break from weeding. Okay, one of many breaks. I hated weeding, but Mom had promised to buy me a new pair of jeans if I helped. I had extra money from working at the antique shop with my parents but didn't want to spend it on clothes if I could help it. I grabbed the water bottle from the edge of the wooden planter bed and gulped the lukewarm liquid. Closing my eyes, I attempted to block out the rushing sound of the nearby freeway while I soaked in the heat of the sun.

"Zoey, you going to help or what?"

I looked up.

Mom was kneeling next to a second planter bed on an old towel. She pulled up a weed and threw it into a large bucket. "We're almost done. There's a chocolate cupcake in it for you if you can give me five more minutes. On top of the jeans you want."

My mouth watered, and I sat up. I could almost taste the warm, gooey chocolate. "On it." I dug into the loose soil, pulling up the weeds with renewed vigor. Mom got up and went inside. Grinning, I took off my necklace and peered around. Shield was there, his little wings flitting quickly as he hovered nearby. The gold and silver shield he'd won so long ago was a little worse for wear but still proudly displayed. I'd given the tiny pixy his name six years ago when I finally saw him again after our interrupted hunt. It turned out that the pixies were required to return to the Fae Realm a few times a year. They'd taken Mom's scolding that day as a sign it was time for a visit but had found ways to get my attention after they'd returned a few weeks later.

Flying closer, Shield tossed a bit of pixie dust on the ground I'd finished weeding, and I was momentarily mesmerized as the plants there became a little fuller, a little taller. I knew the plants that grew there would be better than all the rest.

"Want to play?" Shield's voice was a sweet tenor that made me think of music.

"Not today. I need to help Mom." His shoulders drooped, and the others grumbled quietly behind him. I hated to disappoint them, but it was getting harder and harder to find free time. "How about tomorrow?"

Bright sparkles glittered around him as he nodded, his large eyes lighting up with joy.

Hearing the steady thump of footsteps, I put my necklace back on before Mom could see. The golden hue of the citrine in the center reflected the sun, sending a wave of yellow dancing across the fence, before flitting away like a bee as I shoved it under my shirt.

As always, the change in view depressed me. Everything became dim and dreary. Finishing the last of my section, I brushed off my hands and sat back, looking around our large yard—the latest of many. We moved every year to keep ourselves from being noticed by the big bad Mythical Council. This time Mom swore we'd stay until I finished high school. One more year of hiding, and then I could register. My stomach fluttered at the thought. Weekly lectures on how awful and dangerous the Others were hadn't swayed me the way Mom had hoped. My fascination only grew.

Living out in the suburbs for the last few years, I didn't See a lot of visitors from the Other realms—Celestial, Fae, and Demon. Few got visas to live in the Human Realm, and those who did didn't want to waste their time checking out the suburbs. I didn't blame them. When I did See the occasional visitor, I wrote everything I discovered in a secret journal. If my parents found my journal, they'd freak. The last sighting had been a strange short man with pointy ears, sharp teeth, and a long white beard. It might have been a dwarf or a gnome. I wondered if they were as curious about me as I was about them.

Noticing I was done, Mom nodded toward the shed. "Put your stuff away. Give me a few minutes to finish cleaning up, and then let's go get that cupcake."

My stomach rumbled at the thought of the rich, melt-in-your-mouth cupcakes from the shop a few streets away.

Shoving my shoulder into the shed door, I pushed it open and let it drift closed behind me. Humming to myself, I put my mini rake and shovel on the shelf and wheeled the yard debris bin to its corner. Then I stopped.

Silence.

I wiped sweaty palms on my shorts. I could hear nothing. Not the birds, the neighbor's yappy dog, nor the constant white noise from the nearby freeway. I turned and pushed open the door. An odd odor wafted up, making me want to gag. For a moment, I couldn't process what I saw. I stood there, staring. Mom was dangling a few feet off the ground, legs kicking and fingers scraping at a man's hand as it held her throat.

"Mom!"

The man holding her was tall, with thick, muscled arms showing through his tight T-shirt.

"Run," she choked out.

I rushed through the shed door. Grabbing a large shovel off the ground, I swung it with all my might at the attacker's head. I felt the impact from my fingers to my back. The force I'd used should have caved in his head, but it bounced off without leaving a single mark. I stumbled but kept my feet, jaw dropping as he cracked his neck. The sound echoed in the artificial silence.

He dropped Mom, and she crumpled to the ground. I could barely process the movement before he swung a beefy fist into my stomach, throwing me across the yard. I slammed into the side of the house, and my head rang with the impact.

I needed to See. Ignoring the sharp pain in my side, I sat up and yanked off my necklace. Heart pounding, I couldn't move. My limbs were too heavy. The monster in front of me was covered with sharp spikes. He had large curving horns, deep black skin, and eyes that glowed a fiery red, blazing like an inferno. He wrenched Mom up by her shirt, the fabric bunched in his fist. From his other hand, sharp black talons extended, skewering her. The long claws made a squelching sound as he pulled them free.

I jumped to my feet, dizzy but running, screaming.

I hit something solid, pain spreading across my face from the impact, and fell back on my butt from the force of the collision. Nose bleeding, I jumped back to my feet, pounding against what I could now see was a faint shimmery barrier.

He stabbed her again. Once, twice, three times. All I could do was watch as I pounded my fists bloody against the barrier. I was screaming so loudly my throat ached. He pulled her head to his mouth and whispered something in her ear, then let her fall to the ground. Holding my gaze, he put his claws up to his face and licked them, his tongue the same deep black as his skin. The monster laughed, a harsh braying that made my skin crawl. He headed toward me, and I spun away, tripping over my own two feet and falling hard on the ground.

That was likely what saved me. He had thrown a knife where I had been, and it flew over my head, embedding itself into the side of the house.

A loud sound penetrated my shock. My neighbor, Mrs. Nelson, was yelling something. I looked up. She was in her favorite purple housecoat, clutching a phone to her ear. Sirens wailed in the distance. The demon snarled. Turning around, he stepped into a cloud of dark smoke and disappeared.

I crawled to my mother's side, hands pushing at her chest, trying to stop the bleeding. Blood was everywhere. It soaked through her shirt, turning the pale-blue flowers a vibrant red. It was like a watercolor gone horribly wrong, the red spilling into the other colors, obliterating them. I couldn't even tell where the stab wounds were. I pulled my shirt off and wadded it against her, crying. "Please don't die, please don't die."

Her hand stroked my hair. "I'm so sorry…" Her voice faded to a whisper, and she coughed up blood.

I pushed harder on her chest. "No, don't talk. You're going to be fine. I can hear the sirens. They'll be here soon."

She went on like she hadn't heard me, eyes focusing on something past my head. "I wanted you to…normal life." She coughed again. This time the cough lasted longer, and she started gasping. She grabbed my hand, fingers crushing mine, and said, "They are looking for… I've only had it a few hours…" I could see her gathering herself.

"Shh, it's okay. Please don't leave me."

"You can't give it to them. Trust no one. I love…" Her head drooped.

I hugged her close, putting my head to her chest. "I love you too." There was no heartbeat. I pressed closer, thinking I had somehow missed it, but still nothing. Putting her on the ground, I started doing compressions, never having been so glad for a stupid course Ava talked me into because of a cute boy. As I did compressions, more blood leaked out. I wasn't sure if I should be stopping the bleeding or doing compressions. Stopping, I pressed my shirt in tighter. And then switched back to compressions.

"Mom! Wake up! I can't do this without you. Mom!" She lay limp. "Please, wake up." I don't know how much time passed, but at some point, red lights swirled and firm hands pulled her out of my grasp. They were covered with iridescent scales and ended in long, sharp claws. I jumped back, screaming and crying. Those same hands tried to grab me. I scrambled away from slitted green eyes, and my legs trembled as I crab-crawled backward. "Get away! Help!"

"It's okay, it's okay." The voice was soft and sibilant, with hisses sounding at the end of each word.

"Help! Mom!" My heart pounded so hard it

drowned out all other sounds; a persistent drumming beat. The world became fuzzy, sounds faded, and then everything went dark.

****

Opening my eyes, I blinked away sticky film and saw white walls, fluorescent lights, and a bag hanging on my left dripping a clear fluid. My mouth was dry, and a rhythmic beeping sounded next to me. My chest was wrapped tightly. Everything ached, but it was a muted ache, far away. It was dark out, but the room was lit with a dim glow and I noticed a woman in hospital scrubs fussing with one of the machines.

"Where am I? Is Mom okay?" My voice was weak and raspy.

The woman turned and smiled that reassuring smile all nurses seemed to have. "Sorry to wake you. You're at the hospital. Take these, and you can go back to sleep." She handed me a couple of white pills. I took them and the paper cup of water and swallowed. The pills caught in my throat, and I gulped more water. I stared. She had wings. Glittery and blue, they would have blended with the night, but the light caught them and outlined their beauty. The woman's eyes were violet. Not just the irises, but the entire eye. Like a bug. I smiled and tried to stay calm, but my heartbeat gave me away, pattering madly on the monitor next to my bed.

"It's okay, honey. Your daddy stepped out for a minute, but he'll be back soon. I know it can be scary in the hospital at night. Do you want me to stay here for a bit?"

I swallowed more water until the cup was empty and then handed it back. "No, thank you. But can you turn on another light?"

"Sure."

She walked through the semi-darkness and turned on another light at the end of the room. The added illumination didn't fill the room, but made some of the creepy shadows disappear. It also made her odd appearance even more obvious. Did she have feathers for hair?

She seemed to be waiting for a response, so I said, "Thanks."

"If you need anything, my name is Molly. Just push that button there, and I'll come to check on you. Try to get some sleep. Your daddy will be back soon."

I smiled shakily and pulled the covers higher. We must be at the downtown hospital. There were never this many nonhumans in the suburbs. Normally I'd have been fascinated and itching to write everything I saw in my journal. But today, for the first time in a long time, I didn't want to See.

I tried to keep my eyes open. I wanted to talk to Dad and find out how Mom was, but they drifted shut, the pills pulling me under. Thinking about feathers and wings, I curled up under the blankets. Drifting off, I saw visions of two curving horns and skin dark as night. I heard the harsh laugh as the monster licked the blood from his talons and told me I was next.

****

The next time I woke, the room was lighter, and a large hand grasped mine. I looked up into Dad's warm brown eyes.

"Hey, you're awake. How're you feeling, pumpkin? Okay?" Dad looked haggard, like he'd aged ten years.

I nodded. "Mom?" My voice was a whisper.

His eyes filled with tears. "I'm so sorry, sweetie.

She didn't make it." He pulled me close. Sobs racked my body as I cried in his arms. Shaking, we clung to each other. His familiar used book scent was comforting, but nothing could dim the pain of knowing Mom was gone. Taken from us forever. By him.

I laid my head against Dad's shoulder, an unfamiliar fire burning in my gut, overriding the deep ache of loss. "Did they catch the demon?" My voice sounded odd. Intense. Angry. Not like me.

Dad was stroking my hair, and his hand stilled. "What?"

"The demon." I practically spat the words. "The thing with the horns and sharp teeth."

Dad pushed me away so he could see my face. "Honey, listen carefully. You can't tell anyone what you Saw. It was just a man. He didn't have horns."

"But I Saw…"

His voice was harsh and guttural, his hands tight on my shoulders, almost painful. "You Saw nothing, you hear me? She hid you to keep you safe. That monster killed her. When they killed your grandmother, I never believed…" His voice cracked. "But they could kill you too. Do you understand? Not. One. Word."

Shocked at his fierceness, I nodded.

He pulled me in tight, crushing me against his chest. "We will honor your mother's wishes. That is one thing we can still do for her."

Biting my tongue to keep from arguing, I asked instead, "Do we know what she had that they were looking for? Mom said she'd had something for only a few hours." My mind swam with the possibilities.

"I don't know, and I don't want to know. We will pack up her stuff and leave it alone. Leave that whole world alone."

The room grew hot. I pulled away and leaned back in the bed, dizzy as the white walls spun around me. He didn't want me looking for what she'd had. He didn't want me telling anyone what I'd Seen. They'd never catch her killer without an accurate description, without involving the MEA, the Mythical Enforcement Agency.

I swallowed, numb. He wanted to let Mom's killer go free.

To keep me unnoticed. Safe. I stared up at him, hot rage coiling inside me. I didn't think I'd be able to do that.

Chapter 2

TWO MONTHS LATER

I strode out the front door of the red brick high school, down the stairs, and headed straight for my bike. I walked with purpose, chin up, backpack slung over my shoulder. If you looked confident, most people wouldn't question where you were going. Or so I hoped.

The security guard was busy chatting with a small group of girls. *Typical.* No one stopped me. There were a few kids taking pictures outside for a photography class, but they ignored me. My hands shook as I undid the lock on my bike.

Breaking away from her class, a skinny girl with a camera bouncing against her chest walked toward me. She stopped a few feet away. "Skippers like you are going to be dropouts. Plan to work at your daddy's store for the rest of your life?"

I looked up at the petite waif wearing enormous boots and said, "I have a 4.0, Gracie. I think I'm fine. Besides, I have an appointment."

Examining her pearly pink nails, she asked, "Where's your pass?"

I pushed off with my bike, gave her the finger, and sped away. Old me would have been horrified. New me didn't care. Everything changed with Mom's death. I never knew one event could change someone so much, but there it was. I was a different person. The same things I used to care about didn't even register with me anymore. I mean, I cared a little. But searching for Mom's killer consumed me.

Thinking of him made the fire in my stomach burn, and I pedaled even faster. I would find him and make him pay.

It took about twenty minutes to ride down to the waterfront where the sighting had been. I enjoyed the cool wind in my face as I pedaled, calming the rage that was so quick to surface lately. The city was made with bike riders in mind, and I flew through the streets. When I got there, I locked up my bike and headed over to an overgrown area by the bridge, grass and tall weeds vying for space.

The ground was muddy, so I slipped and slid as I crawled under the fence and down the steep embankment to get a better view.

After the hospital, I had torn the house apart, looking through everything of Mom's. I'd found nothing I thought someone might murder her for, so had switched my focus to her killer. When Dad discovered evidence of some of my searches, he completely flipped out.

He'd made me change my email address and had banned me from the internet. Well, he'd tried and failed miserably. I needed a computer for school, so that lasted all of a day. Despite his overprotective tendencies, I had set up an alert system for one of my favorite blogs. Someone had sighted what they thought was a troll under this bridge. Since sightings were pretty rare, I skipped school and snuck over here to see if I could See it.

The description of a troll didn't match what had killed Mom, but I wouldn't be able to rule them out until

I Saw one myself. Unfortunately, the descriptions I'd found weren't always accurate. I was still wearing my necklace, but when I found a decent, less muddy spot to sit, I pulled it off and waited. The amulet was cold and heavy in my hand. With it off, the magic from it glowed with deep reds, greens, and blues.

I'd been doing outings like this for the past few weeks. Trying to catch sightings of different beings and drawing and writing about them in my journal. I'd found a pattern around where this troll was sighted. A lot of comings and goings. It could be a portal.

Under a bridge seemed like an odd place for a portal, but what did I know? I tried to stamp down the bitterness at how clueless Mom and Dad had left me. After Mom's funeral, I had thrown myself into finding out what had killed her and had discovered how little I knew about the other races.

Despite my misgivings, I'd followed Dad's request and had kept quiet that Mom's killer wasn't human so the police wouldn't contact the MEA. During my police interview, I only gave the description of his human glamour. Since glamours could be changed, they would never find him. There would never be justice. Fury filled me, flooding my system and making me want to yell and kick things. I took several deep breaths and tried to visualize something nice. I squeezed my hands into fists, nails digging into my palms.

Rainbows, kittens, cookies.

It didn't work. My heart still raced, and I wanted to scream. I probably needed therapy, but I couldn't talk with anyone. Not about what I'd Seen. The therapist Dad had forced me to see a few times was nice and all, but human. I was still unregistered, and Dad refused to let me take that next step. He said it was too dangerous. I wasn't even sure he was going to accept that I would register once I turned eighteen. That had always been the plan. I didn't want to argue, so I hadn't brought it up.

I had asked the pixies about the demon that had killed Mom. They'd refused to say anything except that I shouldn't get involved. *What kind of help was that?* I'd bugged them until Shield told me it could be a death sentence for all of them and to please stop asking. I wanted to know, but not enough to get them hurt. He'd said I needed to ask one of the Greater Fae because they had more freedoms, whatever that meant.

Dad and I had moved out of our suburban house to the apartment above the shop. Neither of us had wanted to stay in our old house after what had happened. He had been willing to drive me to my old school, but it would have been almost impossible with the shop hours. So, I'd had to change schools and be the weird new girl whose mom died. I could have gotten my license and driven myself to my old school, but I used to change schools every year anyway, so I was used to it. Besides, it made it easier for me to focus on finding Mom's killer. No friends equaled no distractions, and being in the city made it easier for me to track down leads. I'd tried to get Dad to let me homeschool, but he was worried about the isolation and made me endure social torture instead.

Sitting down, I could just make out the jogging track on the other side of the river. This side was quiet, with no path, no people. Seeing nothing out of the ordinary, I flipped open my laptop and wrote out the answers for my US History homework. After that I closed my laptop, stowed it, and pulled out my sketchpad. I had to do a still life for Art and could finish that up here. I may have skipped class, but I hadn't been lying to Gracie. I was a good student and was going to keep my grades up. I drew the long lines of the bridge over the gently flowing lines of the water. The tufts of grass and weeds peeking up through the cracks in the concrete wall. I looked up to draw the next part and two glowing yellow eyes stared back at me.

My heart stopped. Hidden in the shadows was a large shape. No, not large—massive. Hunched over, it was a tight fit under the bridge. The two yellow eyes were set in a mud-brown face with a huge potato nose. Floppy ears topped the head, and an immense belly protruded, as well as two curved tusks. I opened my mouth to say something, and no sound came. I swallowed. A low growl came from under the bridge, shaking the ground I was sitting on. I slipped and slid a few feet before catching myself, my side now covered in mud and my foot stuck in a squelching pile of goo. I hoped it was mud. It smelled awful. I somehow had kept hold of my notebook, but my pencil was long gone. I scrambled up the hill half crawling, fingers digging into the grass, terror making me shake. When I was at the top of the hill, I ducked back under the fence and then stopped, notebook pressed to my chest, and waited. No sounds came from behind me. Hands trembling, I shoved my notebook into my bag, grateful it had remained slung over my shoulder.

No pursuit, no more growls. *Should I go back?* I debated, but the growl made me think that might be a bad idea. He or she had clearly not wanted me there. Was I breaking some sort of rule and invading its territory? The troll had just appeared. Had they come through a portal? Maybe they were just passing through.

So, trolls. They exist. Check. I'd have to draw it when I got home and record what I knew. *God, I wish I wasn't such a scaredy-cat.* Before Mom died, the sight of the troll wouldn't have terrified me. I used to love to See strange creatures when I caught a glimpse. Now, anything larger than a cat sent my heart racing into overdrive and made me break out in a cold sweat. Not a full-blown panic attack, but close. *Damn it.* Gritting my teeth, I reached into my bag and grabbed the brownie I'd saved from lunch. Everyone liked brownies, right? I ducked under the fence, put my bag on the ground, and crept back down the hill.

"Hello?" My voice was too quiet, like the squeak of a mouse. Clearing my throat as I inched along, I tried again. "Hello? Um, my name is Zoey. What's your name? Do you speak English? I have a brownie, if you want it."

"Go away."

The rumbling, masculine sound made my legs tremble. I had to stop moving or risk sliding back down the hill again.

Taking a major guess, I asked, "Can I go through the portal?"

"Do you have a token?"

I shook my head and then, thinking he might not see, said, "Not yet, but…"

"No token, no passage. Go away, or I will make you go away." There was a loud thump on the ground. I glanced up. He held a long club covered with spikes. My throat went dry.

"I'm sorry. I didn't mean to offend you. I'll go get a token. Thank you…Um, what was your name?" I wanted to kick myself after the inane question fell from my lips.

The troll wanted to kill me, and I was asking stupid questions. *Get a grip, Zoey.*

He hadn't answered, so I started inching my way back up the hill. I stopped and then threw the brownie toward him. Thankfully, it landed close to his feet. "I didn't mean to offend you. That's for you."

As I inched my way back, I was determined to grill the pixies on portals and tokens when I got home. I couldn't believe they let me get this far without saying anything. Going too fast, I slipped again and face-planted in the mud. Fingers sliding into the pudding-like muck, I crawled my way to the top of the hill, wet and muddy. Standing, I wiped myself off as best I could. Grabbing my backpack, I heard a deep rumble and then the faintest growl of sound. "Carrion. My name is Carrion."

Carrion? *What a horrible name.* Was it supposed to instill fear? Looking back, I couldn't see the troll, but I nodded my head respectfully and said, "It was nice to meet you, Carrion." Hearing nothing else, I shivered. It was getting chilly. I glanced at my phone and the time. It was later than I thought. School was out, and I still had to get home.

Not waiting to see if the troll ate the brownie, I shoved the helmet on my head and started pedaling toward home. I hoped I didn't accidentally poison the troll. Who knew what trolls ate? With that unnerving thought, I pedaled faster, just in case.

Chapter 3

It was close to rush hour, and traffic was rough. I hit every red light, was wet, and smelled worse than a skunk. Pulling into the alley next to the store, I opened the half functioning gate into the courtyard and took the back stairs up to the second-story apartment. I really needed a shower. I hung the bike on the wall and, opening the door, glanced at the clock in the foyer. I winced. I was also late.

I took my muck-covered boots off and left them outside. I'd hose them off later. Walking through the main living space, I turned toward the kitchen.

Dad was leaning against the counter, arms crossed. One of his eyes was twitching. Not good. "So, where were you? What was so important you skipped your fifth- and sixth-period classes? And why are you covered in mud?" He held out a hand. "No, I don't want to know the answer to that last one."

How did he know I skipped already? The calls rarely came in until later.

"I had something I needed to do." Even I knew it wasn't an explanation. But what could I say? "*I was researching a monster sighting in my search for Mom's killer?*" He'd have us packed up and out of here by tomorrow. No thank you. I thought back on what he'd said. He didn't want to know why I was covered in mud. I realized he might think I had a boyfriend. He likely thought we'd been rolling around on the ground together. It was such a funny thought that I couldn't stop the snort of giggles that burst out.

Dad's dark brows furrowed. "This isn't funny, young lady. This is your education."

Reining in my snickers, I said, "I'm sorry. Look, I did all my homework. See?" I held up my notebook and computer before placing them next to him on the white tile counter. He flipped through the notebook, ignoring the slight smear of mud on the cover. "I needed to be by myself for a bit."

Dad raised an eyebrow skeptically, and I clarified. "I was by myself. Doing homework. I couldn't be at the school anymore, that's all."

He put the notebook down, expression softening. "I know this has been hard on you, and I'm trying to be understanding, but you can't skip school." He straightened. "You are grounded for two weeks."

"What? Why? I did my work. If you'd let me homeschool or do online school, this wouldn't even be an issue." *This is so unfair!* My mind whirled with anger. Being grounded would make it harder for me to chase down leads. I'd have to sneak around even more than I already was.

"Why?" Dad asked. "Because I can't have you wandering all over downtown by yourself. It isn't safe. You could get mugged or…" Fist banging on the counter a few times, he let out a frustrated growl, then appeared to collect himself. He took a deep breath. Then another. "Go get changed. You're late for your shift. I'll go relieve Jamie and cover until you get downstairs. I love you, pumpkin, but you are grounded. Stop skipping school."

"Argh!" I stormed off to my room and slammed the door. Then I opened it and slammed it again. The stuffed bear on my bed gave a little jump with each satisfying bang. I was a straight-A student who also worked. Most parents would be thrilled, but no, I had to have a tyrannical father who required me to follow every stupid rule.

I used to. The problem was that I couldn't anymore. I had a killer to catch.

****

Knowing that Dad would cover at the shop and needing time to cool down and clean off, I took a quick shower. The pounding water loosened my muscles and calmed my rage. Dad probably wouldn't even remember I was grounded in a week. Everything would be fine. Pulling my wet hair back into a loose bun, I swept a few escaping dark strands to the side, pulled on some jeans and a new T-shirt, and then went to hose off my shoes. Picking them up from the back porch, I held them as far away from myself as I could, careful not to touch the dark-brown globs clinging to the bottom. Whatever I'd stepped in stank. It clogged my nose and made me want to gag at the same time. This stuff better come off. No way I was getting new boots. Money was too tight.

Breathing through my mouth, I inched down the stairs. The back of the shop had a courtyard with two benches and a small fountain that bubbled a bit but otherwise was broken. The area wasn't huge but had tall hedges on every side, along with a rundown fence, providing a private space for us. Two large wooden beds housed whatever plants Mom had been growing at the house. Dad had taken great care when he brought them with us. Shield and a few of the other pixies had come too, but the green space at the shop wasn't as nice, so I wasn't sure how long they could stay. If the green space didn't meet their needs, they tended to spend most of their time in the Fae Realm. This had happened before. Unfortunately, I was already Seeing them less and less.

The yard was quaint but oddly decorated. It had small, black gargoyle statues throughout the garden. Some people collected gnomes. I had figured the previous owner had a thing for gargoyles until I Saw them move and realized they were alive. They were about a foot and a half tall and growled anytime I tried to talk to them, so we stayed out of each other's way. I may want to learn more, but I wasn't stupid. Mom had said Others were dangerous at least a million times. Talking to one who was growling at me seemed like a bad idea. And they kind of gave me the creeps. Some people feared spiders; I was terrified of dolls coming alive and stabbing me in the middle of the night.

Unfortunately, the courtyard was where the hose was. Dad would kill me if I brought these boots into the house without rinsing them off first. Gathering my nerve, I took my necklace off and stuffed it in a pocket. Knowing they'd be looking anyway, I wanted to be able to See them if they moved.

I reached out a hand and brushed the soft leaf of a mint plant, the bright scent soothing. Thankfully, it also helped to cover the smell of my boots. I took a deep breath. I could do this. Squaring my shoulders, I walked past the two squat forms at the entrance and went straight to the side where the hose was. Grabbing it, I reached around to turn on the water and black eyes stared back at me. I shrieked and dropped the hose. I hadn't noticed the small gargoyle next to the faucet. Dark eyes, pointy nose, and long ears gave the gargoyle an almost elvish cast. I reached for the faucet, not taking my eyes off the statue. When my hand was on the faucet, the gargoyle opened its mouth and said, "That stinks."

I stumbled back, dropping the boots and falling on my butt. Scrambling to my feet, I was turning and running for the entrance when I heard a low rumbling sound.

"Wait. Sorry. Please. Don't leave. Shoes. Troll turd. Awful." The stilted words came out slowly, but they *were* words.

I stopped. Turned around and went back. "You can talk? Wait, I stepped in troll turds?"

"Of course. We talk. Yes, troll turd. Stinks. Useful. In potions." The gargoyle stretched and changed position. I leaned against the house, suddenly feeling lightheaded. Watching them move was like every horror story I'd ever heard. The strange statues in my garden were alive and were going to attack and kill me in my sleep. I would never sleep again. Somehow the idea of moving stone gargoyles was more concerning to me than the big troll.

"How many of you are there?" Did I need to lock my window or burn the entire garden?

"Here? Seven. I am Len."

I was going bat-shit crazy. I was talking to a statue in the garden.

"I will. Tell you. How to. Prepare. And sell. Troll turd."

I looked at my offensive boots. "I can sell this?"

"Yes. Troll turd. Gross. But. Sell well. If you. Collect. And sell. Most do not. Hard to get. The stink out. Sells by weight."

"Wait, what? These turds will get me money?"

"Mmm. Yes. You scrape off. Keep and sell. But don't. Keep here. We will. Spread word. So you can. Get rid. Of it." An odd murmur of agreement came from my left. I turned and saw another, then another. I was surrounded.

I backed away, one step at a time, leaving the boots on the ground. "I'm going to see if I can find something to put that in. Um. Bye." I turned and ran.

Once back in the apartment, I wasn't sure any amount of money was going to get me to go back out there. Pacing back and forth, I gave myself a stern lecture and reminded scaredy me that I needed answers. Talking to supernatural creatures that were being helpful was about as good as it got. I just needed to ignore the fact that they were one of my worst nightmares. Talking dolls…*Eek.*

I grabbed a few small containers, took a deep breath, and then headed back out. Most of the gargoyles were hidden, so I was able to make myself walk outside. Only a few sets of eyes to worry about. I got to the boots, scraped some gunk into a few containers, and then sprayed off the rest.

"We helped. Yes?"

"Ahh!" I dropped the hose, and it sprayed me, the cold water a shock. I turned it off and started wrapping it back up, taking deep breaths to calm my racing heart. "I won't know until I try to sell it." The still form stared at me. I paused. "Did you want something in return?"

"Yes."

Please don't say your unborn child. Note to self, ask if payment is required *before* taking advice. I took a deep breath and asked, "What do you want?"

"Can you. Keep the. Golden beast. From. Pooping. In the garden?"

The golden beast. My mind raced. "You mean Reeses? The neighbor's golden retriever? I'd be happy to try." I licked my lips. "Could I ask you a question?"

He nodded. An odd creaky sound accompanying the movement.

"Did you know my mother? She died, but she used to love to garden, so she would have come out here often."

Len nodded again, the sight of it eerie in his squat, angular form.

Swallowing, I asked, "Do you know who killed her? And why someone would kill her?"

"We. Do not. Speak of. Stuff like. That here." His voice was low, and it took a while for him to force all the words out. "Your mother. Kept you. In the dark. You should. Stay there. War. Is coming."

I hung the last of the hose up, more forcefully than necessary. "You think I should let her murderer go? Because it was an Other? I can't do that."

"We know. Nothing. The small book. Might help. Bella. Brownie. Saw in. The special place." He pointed to an area at the far end of the garden. I walked around the broken fountain to the spot indicated. There was nothing there but dirt.

"Dig."

Well, okay. Kneeling, my knees getting damp from the ground, I brushed aside some topsoil. At least it was loose and moved easily.

Nothing.

"More." Len was closer, but thankfully he stopped a few feet away.

Digging deeper, about a foot down, my hand brushed against something hard. Using my fingers to push the soil away, fingernails now outlined by darkened nail beds, I saw a latch. A lockbox?

"Be careful. What you. Say. Who you. Talk to. She was. Not careful. She is. Dead."

"You mentioned a war earlier? What did you mean? What war?" I looked up, and he was gone. There was no way he moved that fast. Was it some type of magic?

"Len? Len? Anyone?" All the gargoyles were gone. The courtyard was eerily quiet. I had learned that Mom kept a book—*a journal?*—and that I might find answers there. And it was likely in this locked chest. Or hidey-hole, or whatever this was. It was a place to start.

The door slid open, and Dad poked his head out, his dark graying hair rumpled from the long day. "Zoey! What are you doing? It's busy. Get your butt in here."

I sighed and, after kicking dirt back over the latch, grabbed my now mostly clean boots. When I lifted them to my nose, there was still a slight smell, pungent and rank. Lovely. Just what I needed.

****

Inside, I shoved the small containers in a plastic bag. Then I put them in a second plastic bag and shoved them in a drawer. I did not want that stink getting out. I washed my hands three times, hoping the orange-scented bubbles masked any lingering foul odor, and then walked over to Dad to see what he wanted me to work on tonight.

He stood stooped over a pile of mail, opening letters with a wooden letter opener that sported a stylized eagle on the end. There were so many neat original items in the antique shop. While I didn't want to work here forever, I could see why Dad loved it.

He glanced up. "Ready to work?"

"Yes, sir."

He gave me a tired smile. His hair had turned grayer since Mom had died and his eyes didn't light up like they used to, but he tried. We both did. "All right, go check the drying herbs and package the ones that are done. Then come take over the register so I can go over the estate sales for the weekend."

"Got it." I grabbed some small bags and the scale and headed toward the back room. Casper jumped off a shelf and onto my shoulder. "Ahh!" I untangled the purring little guy and gave him a big hug. "Crazy kitty." I kissed the white ball of fluff and cuddled him before placing him on the ground. He weaved between my feet, trying to trip me up as I headed to the back. I'd found the kitten last month in the shop and had put him outside. That night he'd shown up in my room, and he'd been there every night since. Dad finally conceded that we owned a cat and bought the proper supplies. I did not know how the little guy got in and out so easily, but I felt better that he'd be there at night in case the gargoyles got in. Of course, he only weighed five pounds, so he was not exactly an intimidating deterrent to gargoyles. Yet.

Putting the scale down, I checked the herbs. The lavender looked done, so I weighed out little bags and started tying them off.

"Zoey." I looked up at Dad's voice.

"Yeah?"

"Come out here for a minute."

I tied off the last one, finger catching in the twine. Sucking on the abused finger, I headed to the front. "What's up?"

"This young lady says you have troll dung." His

voice sounded strained. "What is that? Do you have some? She said she is absolutely sure."

I looked over Dad's shoulder and saw a small, blonde figure. The customer lifted her head, and I gasped. There stood Gracie, arms crossed, glaring at me.

"I'll take care of it."

"Okay, but don't think we're not talking about this later."

I nodded, gritting my teeth. I needed a confrontation with Dad about the troll like I needed a root canal. Not. At. All. I looked over the counter at Gracie.

"You want troll dung?" I couldn't keep the incredulous tone out of my voice. Was Gracie part of the mythical world? She seemed so normal.

"I asked for it, didn't I?" She was eyeing me like a tiger about to pounce.

"I have some. How much do you want?"

She wrinkled her pert, freckled nose. "Two ounces, please."

"Coming right up." I went to the drawer, pulled out two containers, and added them to an extra plastic bag. Gracie nodded her thanks, took the baggie, and handed me a hundred dollars.

"This enough?"

I tried not to gawk at the money. "Yes, thank you for your business." Closing the register, I looked up to ask her a question, but she was already closing the door behind her.

Leaning back against the counter, I grinned, feeling a lightness I hadn't felt in a long time. I had found an additional source of information, and she went to my school.

****

31

"So. Troll dung. Is that some sort of name for drugs?"

The last customer had left, and Dad had cornered me in the kitchen before I could hide in my room. Stupid snack craving. I put the bag of chocolate-covered pretzels down on the counter and attempted to reassure him. "Absolutely not. I do not use drugs, sell drugs, or have anything to do with drugs."

"Did you happen to meet with a troll, then?"

"It's not what you think!"

He leaned against the white tile counter, arms crossed, foot tapping out an angry, staccato beat. "So, you weren't skipping school to meet with a mythical creature trying to track down information about your mother?"

"No! Well, yes and no. It's complicated."

"Look, I know I don't know a ton about the Others or their realms, but I do know your mom worked very hard to keep you hidden from them. I trusted her one hundred percent, and although I don't know why, I do know that she thought staying away was the best way to keep you safe. Stay away, Zoey!"

I slammed my fist down, narrowly avoiding the pretzels. "I was just looking!" Only a little lie. I had just gone to look. The talking had been purely circumstantial. "What is the harm in looking?"

"What happens when you find them? When you find the demon that killed her, what then? I want them to pay too, but not at the risk of losing you. I need you to stay safe. If I catch you doing something like this again, we're packing up and moving."

"But—"

"No buts." Dad shook his foot, a white ball of fluff

clinging to it. "And get your cat off my foot! How'd he even get in here? Should have named him Houdini." Casper was playing with Dad's sock, little claws and teeth wrapped around the previously tapping foot, clinging like a barnacle. His little tail was wagging furiously, and I could hear his purr from a few feet away.

I bent over and picked up the little fur ball, moving him away from Dad and tossing a small toy mouse for him to go chase.

Dad came over and gave me a hug, squeezing a little tighter than normal, as if he could keep me safe if he just held on tight enough. "I love you, pumpkin. More than you can possibly know. And I will do whatever it takes to keep you safe, even if you hate me for it." He let go and kissed the top of my head. "Now get some rest. You have school tomorrow."

He left, and I crunched a pretzel, the taste like ash in my mouth. Mom was buried here. As well as any clues I might find about her death. It was a lot to risk, but I couldn't give up my search. I just needed to make sure I didn't get caught again.

Chapter 4

Rolling out of bed, the blue and green checkered comforter snagged on my foot and tripped me so I sprawled face first on the floor. Lying on the hardwood, foot still tangled in the blankets above, I took a deep breath. *This is just a false start. Today will be a good day.* I could talk to Gracie, get some answers, and then it would be the weekend. A nice, long weekend since we had an extra day off for teacher conferences. Thankfully, Dad hadn't signed up for any conferences, Mom had always done that, so I didn't need to worry about what my teachers were saying. I just needed to make it through today.

Unfortunately, falling on my face this morning was pretty much a harbinger for how my day would go. I couldn't focus in class, and I got called out in French. I didn't even know the question, let alone the answer. To make my day even better, I'd forgotten my lunch, and it was pizza day, so the lunch lines were ridiculously long and not worth the effort. I only had an old apple buried in my bag from who knew how many days ago.

Stomach grumbling during my last class of the day, US History, I tried to speak to Gracie, but she was doing her best to avoid me. Despite us having a seating chart where we were supposed to be seated next to each other, she successfully sat as far from me as possible. Gritting my teeth, I turned and glared at her in the back of the room. I'd corner her eventually. She couldn't avoid me forever.

A window popped up on my tablet. I looked down. A private message from Gracie. — *Leave me alone!* —

My fingers flew over the keyboard. *—I just want to talk —*

Gracie responded lightning fast. — *No! Not at school. Are you crazy?* —

I chewed my lower lip. — *What about after class? Please?* —

She ignored me. I wondered if she Saw what I Saw. She had to know Others existed, which meant she was likely registered. For the most part, only Mythics—people who were part Other—knew of their existence, and Mythics had to be registered. What did she want the troll dung for? Every time I glanced at her, she was looking anywhere but at me, avoiding my gaze.

When the final bell rang, I rushed out with everyone else and saw Gracie's petite frame disappear around the corner. I slammed my fist into a metal locker, the sound muted by the hundreds of other lockers opening and closing. Of course she hadn't waited for me. I'd allowed myself to hope she'd stop and talk with me after class when she hadn't responded. Stupid, really. Just a great way to end an awful day.

Passing through the crush of bodies, I slammed into someone and heard, "What's that smell?" Did I still smell like troll dung? Yes. Yes, I did. But it wasn't that bad, damn it.

I took a deep breath. I would try again with Gracie next week. It would be fine. I briefly debated bombarding her with messages, but I wanted her to talk to me, not hate me, so I gave up the idea. Kicking a few lockers, I took another deep breath and attempted to channel my frustration. It didn't work.

Jumping on my bike, I sped down the street as fast as my feet could pedal. Dodging school buses and cars on my way out, buildings whipped by and horns honked. I ignored them. The wind streaming behind me cooled my flushed face and took the edge off my irritation. Five minutes later, I came to a block where people were selling tacos, sandwiches, homemade jewelry, and other odds and ends. The clustered booths were jumbled together like a mini Saturday market.

Slowing, I smelled the soft scent of roses and approached a cart with bouquets of flowers. Every week, I replaced the flowers on Mom's grave. I stopped at the stall and picked out some white lilies and pink tulips. For whatever reason, Mom had hated roses, so I tried to give her a variety of anything but roses. Not that she could smell them anymore, but it made me feel better to get flowers I thought she would like. Grabbing the small bundle, I headed toward the lady with cornrows manning the register. As I paid, I noticed the vendor two booths down. The booth had a garish sign with a sun and moon. A psychic.

I hesitated. Mom and Dad had steered me away from anything having to do with magic, but was there any harm? It's not like I was doing magic myself. I'd had more luck finding answers in the past couple of days than in the last few months. I was getting close to something; I could feel it. I just needed a little direction.

Before I could change my mind, I wandered over and asked, "Excuse me? How much for a reading?"

A middle-aged redhead, her curly hair held back by a colorful bandana, grabbed a price sheet and said cheerily, "We're having a sale today. Everything is fifty percent off."

I pulled out some cash and handed it over.

She grinned, nose ring glinting in the sun, and beckoned toward a young boy, who took over the register. Then she pulled me back toward a small tent, pushing aside the ratty cover and waving me inside. I crouched under the flap and entered the dim interior. A bright orange and red rug took up most of the space. Off in the corner were crates stacked on top of each other. Peeking out were bones, crystals, and carved figurines made out of stone. There was an empty bird cage sitting open next to them. *Creepy.* In the center was a simple folding table and two chairs. She lit a candle on the table, and multiple bracelets slid over her wrists. Watching the flickering flame, I hoped the tent wasn't flammable. Death by fire was pretty much the last way that I wanted to die. She pointed to one of the folding chairs, and I took a seat on the hard plastic. I slipped my necklace off when she turned to get something and was not surprised when I didn't See any magic on her. I quickly shoved the necklace in a pocket as she turned back around. Just another charlatan making stuff up.

She sat down and placed a stack of cards in front of me. "Shuffle the cards."

The cards had elegant black and white flower designs painted on the back. "Do I need to think of a question or anything first?"

She shook her head, her red curls bouncing and her multiple necklaces swinging together with a soft clink. "No, just shuffle. The cards want to tell you something. They will tell me what they want you to know."

Well, that was some vague mumbo jumbo. I reached

for the cards and wrinkled my nose as a waft of spicy incense from an ornate brazier in the corner filled the space. Weren't these people worried about fire? As I shuffled the cards, I caught brief flashes of the underside, and the images on the cards started to move. It had to be how fast I was shuffling. It was an illusion of movement. I slowed down my motions and sighed with relief when I didn't See anything. Then my breath caught. As I was holding the cards, a black knight started dancing. I blinked and shook my head. On the next shuffle, I Saw the king of cups riding a horse, moving up and down. I stopped shuffling.

Warm hands wrapped around mine and held the cards in place. "Shuffle more. I will tell you when to stop."

Should I tell her? No, I wasn't supposed to See anything. I couldn't react. I shuffled, hands tingling, which made the cards feel weird. The cards kept moving. I stopped looking at them, focusing instead on the dark walls of the tent. My back was sweating. I needed to get out of there. I tried to put the deck down, but it leapt back into my hands. The action made my chest tight, and I tried to put the cards down again.

The lady grabbed them from me. "Feisty tonight, aren't you," she mumbled, but her eyes were bright with curiosity. "Let's see what the cards want to say." She placed the deck down in front of me. "Choose three cards and place them here." She pointed to the table, a bright glow radiating from her fingertips. I stared at her hands, heart pounding, and realized I'd made a grave mistake. She had the gift. She was going to See what I was. I needed to leave. Now.

Shaken, I got to my feet so fast I knocked over the

chair. "Thanks, but I forgot I had to be somewhere. I gotta go."

Before I could leave, she grabbed my arm, keeping me there. She moved my head from side to side, looking for something. "You're not registered."

No way. Was I already too late? I did not wait all this time to be outed by what I'd thought was a charlatan psychic. "What are you talking about? Don't touch me." Pulling away, I tripped over the fallen chair, banging my knee on the ground, and hustled out of the tent, feet getting tangled in tent flaps as I rushed out onto the busy sidewalk.

"Wait."

I ignored her. A stately woman carrying a child backed away from me, and I looked down, face flushing. My hands shook as I jumped on my bike and headed to the cemetery, pushing hard to get away as quickly as possible. I'd wanted to know, and now…Well, I didn't exactly learn anything except that tarot cards were real and super creepy. *I've definitely had brighter moments. Never again.*

One pedal, then another. Riding up the hill burned my thighs, and the workout helped me calm down. She may have mentioned me not being registered, but she didn't know me. Yes, I bought flowers from the vendor next to her most weeks and would have to find a new place, but she didn't know my name or where I lived. I always paid the flower vendor in cash. It would be okay. I didn't need to tell Dad. We wouldn't need to move again.

As I pedaled away from downtown, the thickening trees blocked the sun, making parts of the ride dark despite the early hour. The shadows cast by the branches reached out like the claws of a large bird, chasing me up the hill. Up ahead, near the top of the rise, was the cemetery. I rode straight to the section with Mom's grave, crossing through an older section first, the mausoleums draped in shadow, with odd statues keeping watch. The tall structures and crumbling tombstones made me shiver.

Tossing my bike onto the soft grass, I pulled out the flowers, only a little crumpled from the ride, and arranged them in front of Mom's gravestone, taking away the old. Brushing debris off the area, I sat down, breathing in the scent of fresh-cut grass and lilies. My shoulders sagged as I told Mom about my day and all my horrible mistakes. The place was deserted and her grave was near the edge of the cemetery, so I didn't need to worry about being overheard. With no judgement or commentary, the time passed quickly as I imagined what she'd say in response to everything that had happened this week.

I was telling her about the tarot card reading when a sharp cry pierced the air. My head jerked up, skin prickling with goosebumps. Out of the darkness of the nearby trees, a man came barreling out, blood pouring from his neck as he attempted, in vain, to staunch the flow. The fading sunlight hit him, and yellow eyes glowed back at me. Long, sharp teeth flashed as he tried to scream, but blood choked off the sound. I gasped, jumping to my feet. He fell to the ground, the light fading from his eyes. Trembling, I took a step closer to see if I could help. Was he dead? Behind him, a shadow loomed and light glinted off the steel edge of a sword.

Shrieking, I turned and grabbed my bike. Jumping on, I started pedaling as fast as I could down the hill. Was that guy just murdered? Was that shadow the murderer? Did he see me? Heart racing, I looked behind me to see if anyone was following. As I turned back to the street, headlights blinded me. I swerved, but too slow. I knew I was too slow.

Strong arms grabbed me around the waist and pulled me tight to a firm chest, hauling me out of the way of the car with super speed and strength. My legs tangled in the bike and it flew with me. We landed hard in the dirt at the side of the road, a jumble of arms, legs, and bike. The guy who'd grabbed me had cushioned my fall, but everything hurt. I lay there for a moment, staring at the hard pavement a few feet away. I wasn't dead. Groaning, I gingerly patted my body. A few scrapes and bruises, but everything worked.

Pushing me aside, my savior jumped to his feet, starting after the car. Whoever it was hadn't even slowed down. He yelled something at the fading taillights and then turned back to me.

My breath caught, dumbstruck. He was beautiful. Angelic. Was he a celestial? I'd never seen one before.

He was tall, with hair so dark it drank in the remaining light and glowing ice-blue eyes. What stood out though, were the red smoldering tattoos on his arms and crawling up the sides of his neck. They looked like pieces of ember from a dying fire.

A whimper escaped, and those light-blue eyes jerked, assessing me. "Are you injured?" His voice was rough, like he hadn't spoken in a while.

I shook my head. He held out a hand and pulled me from the ditch he'd thrown me into. When I was standing, his eyes ran over my arms and legs, checking for injuries. Gooseflesh dotted my arms as he assessed the damage. My body ached with bruises, but nothing like what I'd have felt if the car had actually hit me. "Thank you."

He nodded, saying nothing, and my eyes were drawn to a white scar curving around the base of his neck up to his ear, breaking up the perfection.

"I'm Zoey."

He picked up my bike from the ground. "Tristan." The bike looked a little worse for wear, the frame not quite right, but it seemed to work. Rolling it toward me, he asked, "Where are you headed? I'll walk with you, make sure you're okay."

"I don't know." Which was the truth. I wanted to go back to the cemetery, but there might be a dead body there. And the murderer might still be there too. I should call an ambulance. I patted my pocket for my phone, but it wasn't there. I searched more frantically. It must have fallen out when I ran away.

Tristan stopped and, long fingers gripping my chin, turned my head from side to side, looking into my eyes. Likely wondering if I'd hit my head too hard on the ground. "Your pupils look fine. Do you want me to take you to a hospital?"

"No, I'm fine. Just some bruising." Deciding where I wanted to go, I said, "Would you walk with me to the cemetery? I was headed there to visit my mother's grave and I don't really want to walk alone right now." He could walk with me back to the scene. I could look for my phone, and if there was a dead body, he would see it too. If needed, we could call an ambulance. And, if the attacker was there, we'd be safer together. Or at least, that was what I was telling myself.

He hesitated, but then shrugged and fell into step

beside me. As we started walking, I suddenly didn't know what to say. I was very aware of how close we were, of his body giving off waves of heat.

As we approached the graveyard, my pulse skyrocketed, and I grew lightheaded. From his nearness or the approaching murder scene, I wasn't sure.

Tristan stared strangely at me, and I wondered if he could hear the pounding of my heart. A lot of Others had enhanced senses. *Was it possible to have a heart attack at seventeen?*

"How long ago did your mom pass?"

I jerked at the quiet question. It was so unexpected after the silence. "A few months."

"I'm sorry. My mom died too. It probably won't help, but it gets easier."

"How'd your mom die?" I ducked my head, face getting hot. "I'm so sorry. That was rude. You don't have to answer that. Forget I said it. You go to school around here?" My nervous babbling seemed to put him at ease, and his shoulders relaxed.

He cocked his head. The wind brushed his hair to the side, showing off a silver earring. "It's okay. It was a car crash. It's why guys like that get to me." He gestured to where he'd saved me. "The driver didn't even notice he almost hit you."

"I'm sorry."

He took a deep breath and seemed to center himself. "It's okay. To answer your other question, I'm not in school right now. I graduated early and am helping with my dad's business."

"Here?" I couldn't help the blurted question.

He grinned, teeth perfect and white. "No, not here." He didn't elaborate.

The silence was awkward, so I said, "I help my dad too. At his store. Kind of a new age antique shop."

A soft growl sounded from a few feet away. I turned and Casper, his white fur fluffed to its highest height, stalked toward us. And there was my phone, at his feet. I ran and grabbed my phone, checking it for damage.

Casper growled again, the sound louder this time. I backed away, not used to this side of Casper. How had he gotten here? Had he followed me? Did he always follow me, and I never noticed? Looking at the fluffed fur, I wondered, not for the first time, if cats could See too.

"Yours?" Tristan sounded amused.

"Um, yes. Sorry, he's not used to strangers." Before I could pick him up, Tristan grabbed him by the scruff of his neck and stared at him. Casper hunched into himself and whined. Tristan patted his head and whispered something in his ear and then put him back on the ground. Casper scampered down the hill and didn't look back. I suddenly realized that it was dark. Full dark. I had been here a long time. No one was around, and my cat, who'd been brave enough to defend me, had left. I hugged myself, shivering. "Well, that was weird."

"Do you like weird?" His smile was flirtatious, eyes studying me, showing an interest he hadn't earlier.

I couldn't help but laugh at the situation, which eased some of the tension. "Maybe. I'll let you know."

He nodded, reached up, and tugged a strand of dark hair that had gotten free from my usual bun. As he tugged it, he looked at my neck and nodded to himself. He leaned toward me, his warm breath tickling my ear, and whispered, "It was nice meeting you. See you around, Zoey."

Bending down, he picked up a sword. It had been hidden in the grass. Wiping the bloody sword on his leather pants, he walked toward the woods.

Shit! He had a sword. A bloody sword. Was he the killer? Was it just a coincidence? I pulled my necklace out and, shoving it over my head, saw the sword turn into a hoodie. He didn't know I could See it.

I couldn't catch my breath as he walked away into the shadows. Looking up at the bright crescent moon, I took a deep breath and took the necklace off again. I had just spent ten minutes talking to a potential murderer. Being charmed by him. I didn't want to be surprised by anything else.

Looking at the grass, I realized the body was gone. I walked over and didn't See any blood on the ground. Where had it gone? Could a body be cleaned up that quickly? Resisting the urge to bend down and touch it, in case Tristan was still watching, I put on my backpack, adjusting the straps. *Had I imagined it? No, the sword was real. He'd wiped blood off it. That meant the body had been real too.* I shivered, suddenly very cold.

As I swung onto my bike, something pale floated toward the ground. Bending over, I picked up a playing card. A knight with a bloody sword was snarling at me, and then he changed and was a young man entwined with a young woman in a passionate embrace. My cheeks heated. "No." I dropped the card. A second later, it popped right back up and into my hand. "He is a monster," I whispered harshly to the card. "He killed someone. Not happening. And you don't belong to me. Stay here." I bent down, placed it on the ground, and found a large piece of rock to put on top of it, likely chipped from a headstone.

It wiggled fiercely and burst up. The rock banged me in the shins, and the card flew at my face. "Argh!" Grabbing the card, I shoved it into a pocket then rubbed my sore shin. "Bad card." It settled in, calm now. I briefly debated keeping the creepy card, it clearly had magic of some kind, but I worried the psychic would be able to track it and find me. "Now I have to go back and return you. Stupid, stubborn card." I pushed off down the hill and let the speed clear my mind and take away some of the crazy that kept happening.

The psychic had known I was an unregistered Mythic. I couldn't just walk up. She couldn't see me. The card wiggled in my pocket as if it realized where my thoughts were going. That unearthly wiggle decided for me. I would wait until she was busy, shove the card under her tent flap, and run. The card was small. There was no way it would be able to keep up with me, so it would go back to its old owner. I nodded to myself. I could go around the back. She wouldn't see me, and I would get rid of the disturbing card.

I coasted until I saw the rows of vendors up ahead. About half were gone or packing up with the late hour, but there were still a few that were fairly busy.

The tarot card reader was there, talking on her phone. I rolled my bike behind the stalls, stopping when I reached her tent. The space behind the booths was mostly filled with old boxes and crates. I shoved the card underneath the bright-orange tent flap and fled.

Once back in the street, I let out a shuddery breath and was about to mount my bike when someone gripped my arm, stopping me. Warm fingers pressed a small card into my hand. I tried to shove it back. "That's not mine."

The tarot lady pushed the card back toward me, her

beaded bracelets glinting in the streetlight. "The card has chosen a new owner. He will not return to me."

I pushed it back. "No, I don't want it."

She ignored me and, bowing her head, said, "May your Sight give you peace and help others to see their true paths."

I chilled at her words, whispering, "I don't have *the Sight*. I don't know what you're talking about." I tried to give the card back, but she was backing away.

"You have the Sight, or my cards would not have reacted as they did. That one was especially excited by you. I had to report you. Please understand." She looked upset and was glancing around as she talked. "If I'd have known, I never would have done your reading. They will come soon to get you registered. I am sorry. Good luck."

She couldn't mean what I thought she meant. It was a card. I took a stupid card. By accident. "What do you mean?" I glanced up, but she was gone. Everything was gone.

"Hello?" I turned in a slow circle. The tent, the sign, her entire booth, had vanished. It was like she was never there. A small flicker appeared out of the corner of my eye. Beating wings and a sparkle of green filled my vision, and then there was a prick on the side of my neck.

"Did you see that?" My words slurred, and the ground tilted, and then I fell, body slamming into the hard concrete.

Chapter 5

Opening my eyes, I groaned. My mouth was gritty and dry, my body ached, and pain radiated down both legs when I moved. I was lying on a cold, hard surface. Sitting up, I backed into a corner. I had scrapes along both palms and the knees of my jeans were scuffed from my close encounter with the road, but otherwise I seemed to be in one piece.

I was in a small gray room, on a smooth stone floor. It smelled a little musty, and there were cobwebs near the ceiling. One wall was made up of evenly spaced metal bars. The room was bare. No furniture. A young woman was leaning against the far wall, legs stretched out in front of her, ankles crossed. Was I in jail? It sure looked like a jail. How did I get here? Why?

I really wished Mom were here. My stomach clenched, and tears burned behind my eyes. That stray thought pounded at me and made it hard to catch my breath.

Now was not the time. I needed to focus. I bottled up the pain and buried it. I couldn't fall apart. Mom was dead, but I could do this. I took a deep breath and then another. I straightened against the wall and eyed the other person in the room.

The woman had multiple tattoos and piercings and pink hair so bright it looked like it could light up the room on its own. "You finally awake? They really knocked you out, huh? You dangerous?" Her voice had a lilting accent that made me think she wasn't from around here.

"Excuse me? D-Dangerous? Me? Where are we?"

She snorted. "Not dangerous, then." She spread her hands out and rolled her eyes. "We're in jail, duh."

I bumped her age down a decade. Her black suit jacket made me think she was late-twenties, but she couldn't be much older than me. "Yes, but why are we in jail? I haven't done anything. Were you drugged too? That can't be legal, right?" I had no idea who she was, so I decided to play dumb.

She scoffed. "Of course they drugged me. No way was I coming without a fight. Are you registered? I'm here for not being registered."

"To vote? No, I'm too young."

"No, lame brain. As a Mythic."

Mouth dry, I asked, "What's a Mythic?"

She rolled her eyes up toward the ceiling, as if begging for patience. "Are you registered as a magic user?"

"No. Mythics have to get registered? How do you know if you are one?"

She laughed, a loud honking in the silence. "Hoo boy, you are in for a fun day." She wiggled her fingers. "Welcome to the world of magic."

Mom had said that magic could be weak and only show as someone got older. That was the lie we had been planning to use if I registered, so that was what I was going with. I could almost pretend she was here, guiding me. I scooted closer and opened my eyes wide. "But I don't have magic. At least I don't think I do. How do you know?"

She leaned forward, her super-mascaraed eyes bright with curiosity. The mascara was layered on so thick I wondered if she could see through it. "Did you do something strange lately? In front of someone else?"

I remembered the psychic apologizing. She must have called the cops when her card followed me. "I got a reading with a psychic, and her card somehow ended up in my pocket. But I didn't steal it. I tried to give it back. They wouldn't jail me for accidentally taking a card, would they?" My act was so pathetic, I was sure she'd see right through it, but she seemed to buy it.

She leaned back and laughed. "Who was it?" I described the woman. "Ahh, bet she was pissed. It's hard to get a good lead card, and to have yours hop decks is not good."

"What are you talking about?"

"You must be a Diviner. Her card wouldn't have followed you if you didn't have the gift. Did you see anything in the cards?"

"Like a vision? No. You know, I don't want to talk about it." I reached up and didn't feel my necklace. It was gone. Patting my pockets, I found nothing.

"Whatever you're looking for, they took it."

The other girl was staring at me a bit too intently. I decided a change in subject was in order. "Are you a...a Diviner?"

"Me? No. I'm an Elemental. I work with air, see." She waved a hand, and a wisp of air ruffled my hair. As she moved, a pale-blue light trailed her fingers, marking the use of magic. "A bitch stole my boyfriend, so I may have flipped her skirt up in front of an entire football field of people. Someone noticed and reported it. I should never have been caught for something like that.

Just dumb rotten luck. But it'll be okay." Her voice held bravado, but her tapping fingers made me think she was not as unconcerned as she pretended.

"What do they do to unregistered people? Do we just have to register or something? Pay a fine?" I tried not to think about the unpaid bills on Dad's desk. If we had to pay a fee, I hoped it was a small one.

She licked bright-red lips. "For you, maybe. For me, I might end up sold in one of the Other realms. Unregistered Mythics don't have any rights. Worst case, I'll be killed, but I don't think they do that anymore." The tapping got faster.

I felt light-headed. Killed? For not registering? I'd always thought Mom was exaggerating, but maybe she'd been holding back. "If the penalties are that awful, why didn't you register?"

Her voice was whisper soft. "My power level is nothing."

I stared at her, not getting it. "So?"

"If you don't have power, you don't get a lot of choices. Pretending to be human, I got to do what I wanted to do. I got to be free."

The door clicked, sliding open. We both jumped.

"Anastasia."

"That's me. Good luck, new girl." She jumped to her feet and sauntered out of the room.

I waved. "You too." I didn't know her, but her leaving sent me into a slight panic. I didn't enjoy being stuck in this cell, alone, with no answers. It didn't help that the cold was seeping in through my jeans, and I was shivering.

They left me there for…An hour? Two? They had taken my phone with everything else, so I couldn't check. Small favor, they'd taken the card as well. It was enough time for me to think of every horrible thing they could do to me. Why hadn't I listened to my mom? I should have kept my necklace on and my head down. What had I been thinking? Although, in my defense, I'd never been told not to get my fortune read. I would let Dad know of this oversight. If I ever saw him again. Head in my hands, the thoughts whirled around and around.

Creak.

I opened my eyes to see the door had opened.

There was another person dressed in gray pants and a white shirt. They were holding a clipboard and called out, "Zoey?"

I looked around, wondering if anyone else had been added to the cell while I'd been panicking. Nope, still just me. I raised my hand, and the man nodded. "This way."

I stood and scrambled after him, body aching from having been on the floor for over an hour. "Can I have a phone to call my dad? He has to be worried sick."

The man ignored me and kept walking at a brisk enough pace that I had to jog to keep up. We passed more gray walls and dark-gray stone floors.

When we got to the end of the hall, we turned, passing an area with desks in cubicles to another hallway. From there, I was led into a small room with a table and chairs. Shoving me into a folding metal chair, the man left without another word. He seriously said nothing other than my name that entire time. After I'd been stuck in a cell. On the floor. I was a minor. Was that even legal? I focused on my anger, using it to help push away the fear.

An older woman in the same gray and white uniform came in and closed the door behind her. Putting small glasses on her slender nose, she squinted at the tablet in front of her. "You are Zoey Talbot, correct?"

"Yes. Should I be here without my dad? I'm only seventeen." Should I have said sixteen? Sixteen sounded a lot younger than seventeen. Although if she had my wallet, she had my ID and already knew how old I was.

"Mythics are old enough at age fifteen to be seen without a parent."

And there went that idea. "But I'm not a Mythic."

She stared at me over the top of her glasses. "Someone witnessed you using your divination on another Diviner's cards. You convinced one of her cards to align with you. Is that correct?"

What the hell? "What? I didn't use Diviner magic. I don't even know what you're talking about."

The woman looked at a small marble I hadn't noticed in her hand. It was an opaque green color. "You are telling the truth. What do you know about the Mythic community?"

"Nothing." The ball changed color and I quickly amended my answer. "When my mom was killed a few months ago, I saw something strange. Since then…" The swirling ball in her hand changed back to green. I had to tell the truth. "I sometimes See creatures, but I don't have any magic. I don't know what happened at the psychic's tent. Whatever it was, I didn't do it on purpose. Can I please go home? Whatever I did, I promise not to do it again."

She studied the glowing ball, the opaque color changing from dark to light green but staying green. "Interesting."

Interesting. What the hell did that mean?

She looked up and pushed her small glasses up her nose. "You are telling the truth. We rarely have a Mythic coming into their abilities so late. I wonder if your mother was spelling you and the spell died when she did. No matter."

My heart clenched at her callous mention of my dead mother.

"I will recommend you be given a warning and assigned a transition coach to help you learn the laws." She glared at me across the table. "See that you don't break them again. We are not usually lenient a second time." She stood and pushed in her chair, the scraping sound loud in the quiet room. "I will go file your paperwork and see if we can get you registered and on your way. Sit tight, and I'll send someone in to test your skills."

"My skills? A test? What kind of test?" I was clutching the simple metal table and tried to fight down the panic as yet another person came and went. At least I would not be killed. I wondered if Anastasia had just been trying to scare me. A newbie who knew nothing. *Let's let her think she'll be sold into slavery or killed.* Was I that gullible? But she had seemed scared. I hoped she was okay. I hoped *I'd* be okay. How bad could the test be?

****

The next person to come in was a thin, perky guy, maybe mid-twenties. He took me to another small gray room, this one with medical equipment, a bed, and two folding metal chairs.

I sat in one of the cold, hard chairs. My sore body was not pleased. They were not into comfort here.

"What's the test?" My voice may have been a little squeaky.

He chuckled. "Don't worry. It's a blood test. Mostly painless."

I tried to relax. He took a sample of my blood, surprisingly quick, and put it through a computer. Then he hit a few buttons, all while grooving to music. I heard a few lines even though he was wearing ear buds. It was a pop song I adored. I started singing along.

He grinned, turning up the volume, and the two of us sang along together while waiting for my results. When the results popped out, he whistled low and long. "Wow. Let me double check this." He left, talking to someone in the hall. He waited while someone else came and then showed them. After a whispered conversation, he came back inside, got a new syringe and a new sample, and ran it through a different machine. All those hush-hush conversations had me worried. What was the computer saying?

With a dramatic flourish, he announced, "You are a combined human and celestial. Your gifts are Seer and Diviner." He looked at me, and he looked...worried. That seemed odd.

"What's wrong?"

He turned and typed a few things into his computer. "Nothing." Looking up he said, "I just rarely see Seers."

"Why not?"

He looked around and then leaned in and whispered, "The rumor is that Master Gabriel killed or imprisoned all the Seers."

"Who? What?" My heart rate kicked up a notch.

He waved a hand. "The head of the Mythical Council. But don't worry about that. It is just a rumor.

It's more likely that Seers are just not as common anymore. Be proud to be different. I'm sure you'll be fine. Pull your hair aside, and we'll get your registration completed."

I pulled my hair away from my neck while he prepped a needle. His hands were shaking.

My stomach turned. "What is that for?"

He smiled, revealing bright white teeth. "Registered Mythics are tattooed with their class, gifts, and date of registration. Relax, this is an enhanced tattoo gun. It will take half the time."

"Does it hurt?"

He winced. "Truth? It hurts a little, but not nearly as much as with the barbaric stuff humans use. No offense."

"None taken." I stared at him. He looked human. So far, everyone had, but most of these people were also something else based on the bits of magic swirling around. "What are you? Are you a mix as well? A Mythic?"

After I said it, I wished I hadn't. The shocked look on his face told me this wasn't a topic that was brought up. "I'm sorry. You don't have to answer. Was that rude to ask?"

"As a newbie, it doesn't surprise me you're curious, but yes, asking is considered rude."

My face heated.

"Given your circumstances, I won't take offense. I'll even answer." He smoothed his hair. "I'm part fae and part human."

He leaned toward me with the needle. "Any other questions? Now is the time to ask. Once you leave here, be careful what you say."

The tattoo gun hummed as he started it. It wasn't

painful, but it was a bit uncomfortable, like someone running a sharp pencil across my skin. My fingernails dug into my palms. I tried to stay perfectly still. Everything was going to be fine. I just needed to distract myself. Staring at his very human looking face, I asked, "Why does everyone look normal?"

He stopped, the silence deafening. "Excuse me?"

I licked my lips. "You're part fae, but you look human. Why is that?"

He started up again. "Everyone looks human. For most of us it's just genetics, human traits tend to be dominant, but for the rest it's because of glamour. It's one of the first things kids learn how to do. If they can't do it, a parent does it for them."

"But not everyone looks normal."

He stopped what he was doing and turned my face so he could look me straight in the eye. His hand was rough where it gripped my jaw. His breath was hot by my ear as he turned my head and whispered, "Never say that again. Ever. We will both pretend I didn't hear you." He let my jaw go and pulled a few hairs away from my neck, grabbed a new needle, and started up his design again. "Now I believe you were about to tell me how magical my fingers are and that you don't feel a thing."

I nodded, my heart pounding in my chest, and his firm hand held my head still. He worked in silence for the next twenty minutes. I wanted to ask more, but his business-like manner made me think he was done with questions.

When he was done, he pulled out a mirror and held it up for me. "What do you think?"

I stared at the mirror. My wide blue-gray eyes stared back. Adjusting the mirror to see my neck, my pale skin looked smooth. "There's nothing there."

He grinned. "Look closer."

I stared hard and, moving my head back and forth, finally saw a faint glimmer. The ink was so close to my skin color that the swirling design was hardly visible unless I moved. I'd never thought I'd ever get a tattoo, and certainly not on my neck, but I found it oddly beautiful. He air-traced the design as he explained it. The middle lines were a bar code, unique to me, and the designs that bordered it showed my class and gifts. I could now be scanned. The lines were all interwoven together like a unique playing card. I liked it but did not like that I now wore a bar code.

"Thank you. It's beautiful."

"Be still my heart. A woman with manners."

I reached out a hand to touch it, and he slapped my hand away. "No touching for at least an hour. It heals much faster than human tattoos, but it still needs a little time."

"Of course. I'm sorry." I clasped my hands in front of me to keep myself from reaching for it again.

"You are so very welcome. Now comes the time when we must part. You will be introduced to your transition coach, but you will not like them better than me." He said it with a flippant attitude, but there was a warning in his eyes. The transition coach was someone I would need to watch my tongue around.

I nodded and watched as he left, my latest ally already gone.

Chapter 6

I leaned against a plain white wall in the interrogation room, not wanting to be sitting at the metal table like a criminal. I itched to run my fingers behind my ear, over the small, raised lines of the tattoo, but refrained. I wished I had a mirror so I could look at it again. I remembered Tristan looking at my neck. If I had been registered, would our interaction have been different? I shuddered, thinking of the bloody sword.

The door creaked open, and I blinked, momentarily blinded by the magic radiating off the woman in the doorway. Her golden blonde hair was tied back with a wide ribbon. She had a bow mouth and was the first person not dressed in a gray suit. Instead, she wore a bright-blue sundress. Hadn't anyone told her it was fall and she was going to freeze her ass off?

She smiled a toothpaste commercial smile, and as she got closer, a weird shiver ran through me. I didn't know why, but I had the urge to take a step back and keep some distance.

Keeping my feet rooted, I gave a small wave. "Hi, I'm Zoey. Are you going to teach me about magic?"

"Regina." She looked down her nose at me and held out her hand.

I grasped it and gasped as I Saw layers of magic peel away and reveal her true features. Sharp teeth poked out of thin, cracked lips. Her eyes were now a solid dark green with a black slit pupil, like a snake. She had no eyebrows. Instead, she had odd ridges in her leathery skin, which was now mottled green, brown, and black. She was taller, and her hair, still cascading in long waves, was a coarse green. I released her hand, perhaps too quickly for politeness, and sat down across from her, wanting the table between us.

I blinked. The reptilian features disappeared with the lack of physical contact. She must have a very strong glamour for me to need physical contact to See through it. She pulled out her own chair and took a seat, flipping open her tablet. "You're an interesting one. Both Seer and Diviner with no training." She steepled her hands over the bright screen. "What do you See when you look at me?"

"Nothing. Just you. I like your dress." I was babbling.

She raised a perfectly arched eyebrow. "You're lying." She trailed a finger along the edge of the table toward me. Goosebumps broke out along my arms. "Most of us with demon blood can tell. A rotten little lying Seer. Not worth my time." She touched my hand, and a surge of white-hot heat traveled from my hand to my heart, sending a jolt.

"Hey!" I tried to jerk my hand away, but she'd wrapped her fingers around my wrist and I couldn't break her hold. She had an abnormally powerful grip. Jolting me again, she held it even longer, and I screamed as my nerves burned, eyes watering at the pain. She threw her head back and laughed, the sound a deep cackle now that the glamour was lifted.

Pulling hard, I couldn't break free. "Let me go! Help!"

No one came running. I smelled ozone as the pain eased, and I caught my breath.

She inched her face closer, the alien features hard to read. I smelled a rancid scent under the ozone that reminded me of rotting cabbage. I struggled to remove my hand, twisting it left and right. She held so tight I would have bruises tomorrow. "I don't like liars."

My heart pounded, and my stomach turned. Was she going to kill me? Spots appeared in my vision, and I wondered if I was going to pass out.

She let go, making a disgusted noise. "Pathetic." She tossed an enormous book onto the table, and it landed with a loud thump. It looked like she'd pulled it from thin air.

I rubbed my wrist, red welts where her fingers had been clearly visible against my white skin. "What's that?" I hated the breathy quality of my voice, but my chest was too tight.

"Our laws." She raised a perfect blonde eyebrow, arms crossed. "You can read, can't you?"

I nodded, tongue tangled and unable to form words.

"Good. For the record, I don't like Seers. I don't think you should be allowed to exist after what your kind did."

"What did my kind do?"

She sneered, ignoring me. "You've already broken the law once. You'll get what's coming to you if you do it again, so please, for my sake, mess up."

"Are you a probation officer or something?"

She threw back her head and laughed. The sound was cold but musical now that her glamour was back in place. "What a quaint idea. Sure, think of me as your probation officer." Her voice slowed as she said the last two words, testing them. "I'm assigned to you for the next two years. I am to make sure you learn our laws. Then I get to watch and make sure you don't break them. If you are a good, law-abiding citizen for two years, you are taken off…probation." She said the word like it was foreign. "Learn the laws and follow them, and you'll see very little of me. Don't, and we'll get to know each other very well." Standing, she said, "Read and memorize that. You will be tested in three weeks. Fail my test, and I'll give you some extra incentive."

I picked up the heavy book. "I have to learn all this in a few weeks?"

She sighed. "These are things any idiot should know, and I don't feel like wasting my time. If you need me, my card is in the front. Don't need me, okay?" She turned to go, and I stood, the chair falling down in my haste.

Bending to pick it up, I asked, "But aren't you supposed to help me?" I hated the panicked whine in my voice, but I was *feeling* panicked. She may be horrible, but she was assigned to help me learn everything. I needed her.

She grinned, and even with her beauty still in place, it was a shark's smile. "I am supposed to make sure you learn. I find punishment is a better incentive than hugs."

She pointed at me, and another painful zap of fire coursed through my veins. I leaned against the chair until the wave of agony stopped. My body ached from whatever she was zapping me with. Not good that she could do it from across the room.

Her sweet voice sang out. "I'll see you soon. Zoey." She gave me one last zap and then turned and left.

When the pain had lessened to a bearable amount, I

sank back in the chair and opened the book. I flipped through the first few pages and then quickly flipped through the rest. It was complete gibberish. Was it in another language? "But how do I read….?" I ran to the door, opened it, and yelled, "Regina? Are you still here? Is this some kind of joke?" No one was there, and no one came when I yelled.

I went back into the room and closed the book. I picked it up and held it to my chest. Standing there, lost, I wasn't sure if I should stay or walk the halls looking for help, when a door appeared in the wall. It had been a wall, and now there was a glowing door. I walked toward it and only hesitated for a moment before opening it. Looking through, I saw my bedroom. My stuff that had been taken was arranged neatly on my bed. They'd even returned my necklace. I walked through and closed the door behind me and found myself in my bedroom.

I threw myself on my bed. "What the fuck?"

"Zoey." I jerked upright as I heard my name. "How'd I miss you coming home? You know what, never mind. It's busy down here. You going to join me?"

"Sure thing, Dad. Be down in a sec." I hid the unreadable book in the top drawer of my nightside table and placed the necklace around my neck. Thankfully, my phone looked fine. I wouldn't have put it past Regina to smash it. As I passed by my dresser, I glanced in the mirror at the amulet.

It was simple but powerful, sitting in its usual place, mid-collarbone, clawed prongs gripping the yellow stone. I'd always thought of it as my dragon necklace, my protector, but also a shield over the real world. A shield I'd never wanted but had worn out of love for my parents. But I was registered now. There was no more reason to wear it, right? I reached up and took it off. Opening the drawer, I placed it next to the book and went down to help Dad, feeling both lighter and more nervous than before.

Chapter 7

I threw the book across the room. Grim satisfaction coursed through me as it hit the far wall with a *thump*. I'd tried everything I could think of to read that stupid book. I'd sung to it, talked to it, tried silly phrases on it, put it in the freezer, put water on it, held it up to a light, held it over a flame. Nothing worked.

I was beyond frustrated and a little panicked that I was supposed to be learning this stuff and I couldn't even read it. Regina was trying to sabotage me. Probably wanted to zap me some more for incentive. Crazy lunatic. I'd called her number and left a message, but I wasn't expecting a call back. She'd done this on purpose.

Chewing on a cuticle, I debated my options. Unfortunately, I didn't have any contacts in the mythical world to help me. Even if there was something I could do about it, I didn't know where to start. I could try Gracie, but she'd been avoiding me, and I wasn't even sure she was a Mythic. The pixies were gone. I hadn't seen them in days. I had been expecting them to disappear for a bit after we'd moved, but this was terrible timing. Maybe Len?

Grabbing the heavy book, I went out back to find him, but he wasn't where I'd seen him last. I wandered around the yard, throat tight. Pushing aside branches, I worried he might be gone too.

A few minutes later, I let out a relieved breath when

I found him standing in the back corner, obscured by a shadow. I held up the book. "Hey Len, can you please tell me how to read this?"

Silence.

"Len?"

His black form was eerily still. Not even an ear twitch.

Did silence mean he didn't know? Did he know and not want to tell me? Was he sleeping and I should ask later? "Good chat. Thanks." I sighed.

Maybe Mom had something I could study in her secret compartment. I wanted to dig it up and see, but Len was right on top of it. Should I ask him to move? Why was he standing there, right on top of it, anyway? Would he hurt me if I picked him up and moved him just a little?

A lightbulb went off, and I slapped myself on the forehead at my stupidity. I couldn't believe I'd forgotten. Yesterday I had agreed to take care of the dog problem in exchange for the gargoyle's help and had done nothing. Len was on that spot for a reason. He was probably giving me the silent treatment for that same reason. I needed to uphold my end of the bargain. I turned back to Len and bowed, feeling foolish but wanting him to know how sorry I was. "I apologize for the delay with my end of the bargain. I'll get on that right away."

Running a hand through my hair, I looked around the yard. We had a fence, but it had so many loose boards that the term "fence" was generous. I debated talking with the neighbors, but Dad had tried that earlier in the year and it hadn't helped. They'd tried putting Reeses in an outdoor kennel when they were at work, but he kept escaping. The only way to ensure Reeses didn't make it over here was to repair the entire fence. Grabbing the hair band I usually kept around my wrist, I swept my hair up in a bun, ignoring the few dark strands that escaped my attempt, and headed toward the garden tools.

This was going to be a long day.

****

After digging a hammer and nails out of Dad's tool chest, I started swinging away. The hard labor made my arms ache but calmed my spastic mind.

Dad poked his head out after I had finished one side and whistled. "Nice work. What prompted the handyman routine?"

Wiping the sweat off my brow, I shrugged. "I wanted to help and felt like hammering a bit."

"If you finish the entire thing, I'll pay you for a day of work."

"Deal." I mentally cheered at being paid for something I was going to do anyway. Grinning, I got back to work with renewed energy.

A few hours later, my back ached, but it was a good ache. The fence was a little uneven, but all the boards were fixed, so there were no more gaps for Reeses to escape through. Dog problem solved. I headed toward the spot where I'd found Mom's hidden cache. As I'd hoped, now that the fence was fixed, Len was no longer blocking it.

Scraping the dirt away was easier the second time, the ground softer from my earlier digging. Exposing more of the latch this time, I realized it was protected with a spell. I could See the colored lines of the magical lock. It looked familiar.

After a minute, I realized the lines formed a pattern

Mom used to have me trace. Repeatedly. She had made it a game to see how fast I could do it. Had she been meaning to show me this someday? Swallowing past the lump in my throat, I looked away from the glowing lines of the spell, letting my eyes adjust and composing myself.

Turning back to the lock, I traced a finger over the familiar pattern and saw the magic disappear. I stopped, shocked. Did I just erase part of the spell? I tried it again, moving more slowly, and Saw the spell lighten as I moved my hand. My mouth dropped open in wonder as I stared at my hands. I was a magical locksmith. Could every Seer do this?

I started over again with the lock. I was pretty sure I had to erase the segments in the correct order. The pattern Mom had taught me.

"Oww!" Heat flared, burning the tips of my fingers. I sucked on the ends. I must have gotten something wrong. There was a little added incentive. If I remembered the pattern wrong, I got singed. Lovely. Nothing like getting burned for not remembering something you learned when you were ten. Shaking out my hands, I tried again. Tracing carefully, I erased some of the lines, exposing the lock. After about fifteen minutes, and numerous singes, there was a click and the latch opened.

Giggling with giddiness, I squatted and—smoothing my hands over the thick iron top—slowly opened the lid. The box was too wedged for me to pull the entire thing out without a lot more digging, but the lid opened easily.

On top was a picture of Mom, Dad, and me. Picking up the photo, I examined it. It was from the day we'd decided to go to the beach to see the puffins. I had been fifteen. It had been a little rainy, but we'd still had fun jumping in the waves and attempting to build a giant sand puffin. Blinking back tears, I ran a finger over Mom's beautiful face, then tucked the photo into a pocket. I didn't think I had any printed photos of her. Below the picture was a huge handbound book, filled with Mom's curly handwriting. It looked like a diary. Turning the worn pages carefully so as not to rip any, I skipped to the end, right before she died. The last page had two entries. I read: *"They are becoming more powerful every day. Should I give the resistance my daughter, hoping she might save us? Or protect her as I have done all my life? Today is another day I choose to keep her safe."*

A tear dropped onto the page, blurring the lines. Wiping the wetness from my cheeks, I wished with all my heart that she were here. Taking a deep breath, I reread the passage. What resistance was she talking about? I read on.

The last entry before she died made my blood run cold: *"I might have made a mistake. Working to find the artifacts has given me a great sense of purpose, but I swore I would never let it endanger my family. I was asked some questions today that worry me. I've only had it a few hours. What if they already know? I'm tempted to pack up and leave tonight, but I promised we would stay. I'm going to look into it first. I hope I'm wrong."*

Tears streamed down my face, and a vise squeezed my heart, making it hard to breathe. She had known something was wrong, but hadn't left. She had stayed because of me. I had gotten my mom killed. Because I was selfish and wanted to stop moving. Because I had made her promise we would stay until I graduated from high school. I was never going to see her again, and it was all my fault.

Tears came in a torrent and, chest heaving, unable to stop, I collapsed on the ground, sobbing. I let my tears flow, unchecked, watering the earth while my heart broke all over again.

When the tears finally ebbed, I noticed a small white cloth in my hand. I had no idea who had given it to me, but the simple act of kindness made me feel a touch lighter than I had a moment ago. The weight of a heavy rock still sat in my chest, but I sat up.

Looking through swollen eyes, I didn't See anyone but called out, "Thank you" in a scratchy voice. I wiped my face with the soft white fabric and looked back over the entry. Mom was gone, but maybe I could do something to make the pain a little better. Maybe I could find the demon that killed her.

The line, *"What if they know I have it?"* caught my attention. What was she referring to? She'd mentioned something to me the day she'd died too. What did she have? The demon hadn't stayed. Had he taken it?

Sniffing, I put the journal aside and opened a second book. It was filled with recipes and spells. Why would she have a book of spells? I tried hard to remember if she'd had a tattoo on her neck. I couldn't recall one. She'd always said she was a Mundane, someone without magic, from a magical family. Maybe the book was passed down to her. Or had she had some ability and been unregistered too?

There were a few more books and other oddities, and then, at the bottom, was an envelope filled with jewelry pieces. Shaking it, I sifted through them. Most were gaudy, but a flash of silver caught the light as a delicate ring fell out. It had three stones—white, gray, and black—with beautiful engravings encircling the band, giving the illusion of vines. My breath caught. It was gorgeous. Had Mom worn it at some point? Slipping it on my finger, I was surprised that it fit. I twisted the band to situate it. "Oww!"

A sharp pain pulsed, like a wasp stinging the same spot over and over again. A few drops of blood dripped and ran into the swirling pattern on the band, filling the grooves. I Saw magic activate and tried to pull the ring off, but it wouldn't budge. Instead, it dug in deeper, like a vicious animal claiming its prey.

I pulled as hard as I could, but nothing happened. The ring did not move. My hands were sticky with blood from my attempts, and my chest hurt from the pounding of my heart. This could not be good. Why hadn't she placed a warning on it?

The delicate vine pattern around the ring glowed red, then faded. The pain ceased. The blood had disappeared from the band, and now there were darkened swirls, black instead of red, encircling the band like a crown of black ivy. Was that blood magic? What awful thing did the ring do, that it was buried in the ground under lock and key? Why had I put it on? Because I thought Mom might have worn it at some point? I was such an idiot. I took a deep breath. Then another. Looking around with my Sight, I saw nothing out of the ordinary. Maybe it was just a ring with an anti-loss spell? A really scary one.

Before I could relax, the ring warmed. Getting warmer and warmer as the seconds ticked by.

Hot metal. Fingers slipping, I couldn't even turn it. Was it attached to my hand with magic? How hot was it going to get? I could smell a faint whiff of smoke, but there was no pain this time. My other fingers didn't burn when I touched it. Not yet. I looked around, hoping to see a friendly face.

"Len? Are you here?" Gazing around the yard, I yelled, "Anyone?" I hated asking for help, but desperate times and all that. "Len! Please!" Screw the fence. I would build the gargoyles their own house if they would help me get this ring off.

No one answered. The backyard was empty of gargoyles. Where had they all gone?

With shaking hands, I closed the chest. As soon as the lid clicked shut, the magic lock re-engaged. I shoved dirt back over the top to hide the soft glow. Then I dashed to the back door, tripping up the stairs in my haste and catching myself on my hands and knees. I sucked in a breath and glanced down at my raw palms and scuffed jeans. Closing my eyes, I took a deep breath. *Must. Not. Panic. Everything will be okay.*

Ignoring the pain, I limped inside and headed straight for the kitchen sink. I turned the faucet to cold and stood, hand in the icy water, foot tapping as the water sprayed. The ring sizzled, but then the heat subsided.

When my hand had grown numb, I tried to move the ring. The ring still didn't budge as I tried twisting it again. "This is normal. Don't panic. Just try something else."

Looking around the white and blue kitchen, I stumbled as something shoved into me. It was Casper butting his white head against my leg, big blue eyes staring up at me. I patted his head and let the motion calm my racing heart. "Thanks for being here, bud."

I pulled out a container of olive oil, dropping it twice

before slathering a bunch on my finger. I remembered a friend once telling me this was how they removed their rings when they got stuck. It should slip right off. My hands were gooey and slick, but no matter how hard I pulled, the ring wouldn't even twist.

"Get off, damn it!"

Casper jumped, startled, and trotted into the next room, leaving me by myself.

I yelled after him, "Sorry!"

I rinsed off some of the oil, got a toothpick, and tried to work it underneath to see how it was stuck, but the toothpick broke. Bringing my hand up to my face, there was no space between my skin and the ring. It was like it was fused in place, like it was a part of my hand. Thinking of the heated metal, my stomach rolled, and I fought back nausea. Dots filled the air, and it became hard to breathe. Leaning against the tile counter, I took a deep breath and counted to ten. Then I counted to ten again. There was nothing I could do. It was a ring. I would figure it out later. It was not fused to my hand. That was just my imagination, right? Panic flooded my senses, and I forced myself to focus on something else. There might be a spell in one of the books in the chest.

Heading outside, I paused on the threshold. The dangerous chest that had gotten me into this mess. Should I look for a solution there? I thought through my options and realized I had no one to ask for help. The pixies were gone for who knew how long, and the gargoyles were MIA as well. I could go see Carrion, but so far, we'd only managed a few polite words, and I'd maybe poisoned him with a brownie. I debated asking Regina about it, but gave up on that idea almost immediately. Regina would likely cut off my finger and call the problem solved. Bad idea.

I went back to the box outside and unburied it again, dirt sticking to my fingers where the olive oil hadn't washed off yet. With a shaky hand, I opened the chest and pulled out one of the books. This one had a red cover but no title.

Turning the pages, I didn't See anything magical. Flipping through the book, there were a few pages bookmarked, but the words made no sense, similar to the manual Regina gave me. It must be another language.

At the bottom of the trunk were jars of ingredients. I let myself get distracted by the odd items. Bat eyes. Sunflower pollen. Dragonfly wings. I was a Mythic. Could I do spells? Looking at the ring, I was sure that I could at least use magical items.

Trying to focus on anything other than the flash of silver on my finger, I flipped through another book, a spell book. There was nothing about removing enchanted items or rings. I stopped at a simple spell titled *Wind*. If I tried it and it worked, not much bad could happen, right? And wouldn't it be good if I could call wind? I could have tossed Regina on her butt and ruined her perfect outfit. I fought down a grin and focused on the page.

It was a series of gestures with an incantation. I looked at the pictures, but it was ridiculously hard to interpret hand gestures from a book. I needed a video. I felt a wave of hatred for Regina. She could have been helping me figure all this out, and instead, she was setting me up for failure. I could try the spell on my own, but knowing my luck lately, I'd create a tornado and bring down the store and get in trouble with the MEA again. No, I couldn't risk it.

Closing the book, I grabbed the envelope the ring had come in and saw a word inscribed on the outside flap. *Illustro.* Could that be how the ring was removed? Could it be that simple? Touching the ring, I whispered, "Illustro."

As soon as the words left my lips, I wished I could take them back. I should have researched it first. I squeezed my eyes tight. *Please don't kill me. Please, please, please.*

Nothing happened.

Cracking my eyes open, bright lines filled the surrounding air. I gasped. Different colors and textures pulsed with magic. What was it? When I took my finger off the ring, the lines disappeared. Pulling on the ring, it was still stuck tight. I closed my eyes and visualized the lines and shapes, realization coming quickly. Gazing at the glittering silver ring with dark black swirls, my throat felt dry. "It's a map."

Chapter 8

The light outside had faded, and the hedges cast deep shadows on the path below my window. I could see the outline of a gargoyle by the garden hose. Of course. Now Len showed up. Not when I was screaming out for help. *Creep.* Feeling his eyes on me, I pulled the curtains closed, almost tearing them down with the force I used. Itching to claw at the evil circle of silver still adhered to my finger, I pulled out my laptop. I was ready to spit fire. Time for some demon hunting.

I went online to the forums I'd been surfing and messaged a local guy I'd been chatting with, TheyAreOutThere12345. He said his name was Carter. We had been messaging for the last month about sightings and what the Others were up to. He believed they had hidden agendas and couldn't be trusted. He could be a psycho, but I needed information, and so far, he'd been my best source from the area. I couldn't put the questions I wanted to ask online. We needed to meet. I typed up the invite.

— *Can we meet?* — I hit Send.

Instantly regretting it, I wondered if there was a way to delete the message. Before I could do anything, I saw a response. My heart raced. He must have been online. Hand hovering over the message, I clicked on it.

— *I'd like that. I'm free later today. Would that work for you? If so, when and where?* —

I recommended a coffee shop down the road and hit Send before I could overthink it.

Dad would kill me if he knew I was meeting up with someone I met online. He'd spent days lecturing me about the horrors of meeting up with strangers. I'd have to tell him something else. I could tell Dad I had a project. That I was meeting up with a classmate to do homework. He'd buy that, and he'd let me go if it was for school.

This is such a bad idea.

****

Icy wind gusted in when I opened the door, blowing a pile of napkins onto the floor. The warm air stung my face, smelling faintly of coffee and cinnamon. The dark-crimson coat I'd told Carter I'd wear swirled around me as I bent to pick up the napkins. I was fifteen minutes early.

Purchasing a pumpkin spice chai tea latte, I sat in the back at an out-of-the-way table near a window. The room buzzed with quiet conversation. It was a small coffee shop with only eight tables. Despite the lack of people sitting at those tables, it seemed crowded due to the steady trickle in and out. The smell of pumpkin spice tickled my nose, and I took a deep sip, loving the warm pumpkin mixing with the hot chai tea. I watched as people came up to the counter. I was looking for a guy wearing a teal T-shirt and a black coat. Not very descriptive. He also said he'd bring a single flower with him. The flower was so cliche it made me wonder if I'd be meeting a twelve-year-old kid instead of a reliable informant.

It was five minutes past the time we said we'd meet. Since I had been early, I was getting antsy. I'd give it five more minutes. If he didn't show, I'd leave.

Five minutes later, I was scooting out from behind the small table when a young guy, maybe late teens or early twenties, came in wearing a ratty black leather jacket and teal T-shirt, carrying a single dandelion. Had he picked it on his way? When I lifted my head and our eyes met, his shoulders sagged with relief. He walked over. "Zoey?"

"Yes. Carter?"

"That's me. Sorry I'm late. There was a line at the flower shop, so I improvised." He held up the small yellow dandelion and blushed, the red color rising up his neck, making his auburn hair seem even redder. "Can I get you anything?"

I had just finished my latte and thrown the container out. I couldn't really afford to have another and wasn't sure if he wanted to be paid back or not, so I said, "Coffee, please."

"Coming right up." While he got the coffee, I had time to observe him. He didn't look familiar, so he likely didn't go to my school, but he had a boyishness about him that made him seem young. Maybe he went to one of the other high schools in the area. He chatted with the cute barista, and I noticed when he handed me my drink that she'd written her number on it. He gestured to the table with cream and sugar.

"Sugar, please." He grabbed a few packets and, after handing them to me, watched, wide-eyed, as I poured three in. I took a sip, eyes closing at the sweet, only slightly bitter taste. He sat down across from me, and I wrapped my hands around the warm paper cup. "Thanks." I turned the cup to face him. "Planning to call Stacy? If so, you should take a photo."

He ran a hand through his wavy hair, flustered. It stuck up on the left side, looking super cute. I took pity, grabbed his phone, and snapped a photo. "We're not on a date. It's okay to get another girl's number."

He leaned forward and said, "I'd rather get *your* number."

I blushed and nudged his leg lightly with mine. "Maybe. We'll see." It had been a while since I dated anyone. I thought back to the last guy I'd thought was cute, the one from the cemetery. At least Carter was hopefully not a murderer.

He blurted, "You're not what I expected."

I raised an eyebrow. "Better?"

"You bet."

Placing my chin on my hand, I said, "You expected a fat, white guy named Bob, didn't you?"

He laughed, playing with the rim of his cup. "Something like that."

We talked back and forth for a bit about menial topics, both feeling each other out. He was a high school student but went to a private school. A senior this year, he was looking for colleges that had majors in journalism. I steered the conversation back around to Others and asked about the different demon, fae, and celestial sightings. I mentioned the troll, and he took the bait.

His warm brown eyes lit up, giving them an amber hue. "Did you really see a troll? I read about the sighting but wasn't able to check it out. How big was it? Trolls are almost never seen. Do you think it was guarding a portal?"

Taking a long swallow of my overly sweetened coffee, I said, "It was huge. I almost didn't believe it was real. Not sure about the portal." I crossed my fingers under the table. I didn't trust him enough yet to give him anything important.

"Did you get a photo?"

I laughed, snorting coffee out of my nose. I wiped it away with a napkin. "No! I was terrified. I tripped, landed in mud, stepped in some troll turds, and had to crawl up to street level, wondering if it was going to grab me from below. Are they dangerous?"

He had been watching my coffee antics with amusement and sat upright at my words, hand banging down in triumph. "That's what that smell is! I couldn't quite place it, and it's been bugging me."

I sniffed toward my feet, catching a faint foul odor. "I still smell?! I've washed these boots a dozen times. I'm so sorry!" I leaned farther away, but there wasn't very far to go in the small corner table. "Do you know how to get the scent out?"

"No, but I can ask." He chuckled. "It's not that bad. I'm still here, right?"

My face got hot, and I wanted to disappear. I stank? How mortifying! I must have gotten used to it and stopped noticing. Although, how did you stop noticing you smelled? I sank a little deeper into my chair.

He gave me a reassuring smile and quickly got back on topic. "Nothing I've read about trolls is that informative. People are probably too afraid to get close enough to chat with one. Who knows? They might be super friendly, or they could bite your head off. Like this. *Rawr!*" He faked taking a bite out of my head, surprising a laugh out of me. Clearly liking my reaction, he tried again.

Giggling, I elbowed him away and took another sip

of coffee, the bitter warmth filling my belly. "That whole 'biting your head off' thing is likely why no one has tried."

He settled back in his seat, perhaps a little closer than before. "True. I wouldn't know. My focus is getting photos of Others without their glamour and posting about them, so I haven't talked with many. Catching a troll without their glamour is really rare. I'm bummed I missed it."

"Anything recent?"

"Sure, let me show you." He pulled out his phone and started scrolling through photos until he found one of a tiny brown man with twiglike arms. "Here's one, a brownie." He scooted his chair closer to show me and scrolled some more. My blood turned cold.

"What's that one? Go back one."

He flipped back. "This one? This one is even better. Have you heard about the Enforcer Demon? The photo is a bit fuzzy, but the celestials are super pissed. Supposedly, he didn't have permission to be here." He showed me a blurry picture of a tall, dark-haired guy with glowing runes. I knew immediately that he was the guy I had seen in the cemetery.

How did Carter know this stuff? How did he have a picture? He wasn't a Mythic, so he had to have an informant somewhere in the Mythic world. Cute and well-informed. I let my hand brush his as I looked at the photo. "A full-blooded demon? Here?"

Carter's intense gaze caught mine, and he said, "No, I think he was a half-blood. But it was right around here. Looks human, but they posted about him. See?" When he leaned in, his arm brushed mine, and I was acutely aware of each touch as he scrolled to the posting and showed me.

Goosebumps breaking out, I asked, "Why's he here?" Was he here to kill people? What was an Enforcer Demon? I shivered, glad for the warmth radiating off Carter.

"Not sure. Some people think he's trying to find his brother who went missing, but he might also be here on business."

"Why is it so weird that he's here? Aren't demons allowed here too?"

He leaned in, breath smelling of gingerbread latte. "Of course, but the other species are pretty heavily regulated. My sources said he didn't have approval. Unsanctioned visits are a big deal. How did he get here? Even if he's from a bigwig family, he can't just come whenever he feels like it. Everyone is buzzing about it."

I traced a star that had been scraped into the tabletop. "What if someone isn't human but doesn't find out until they're older? What happens then?"

He grinned and whispered in my ear, his breath warm. "You secretly wish you were a Mythic?"

"Maybe." I looked up. "Don't you?"

He nodded. "Sometimes, but since I'm not that lucky, I'm just going to report on what I know. Someone has to tell the world what's really going on. You should follow me."

I nodded. He grabbed my phone and typed in a link, and handed it to me. I shoved it in my pocket, making a mental note to look at it later. Knowing he reported everything made me doubly glad I hadn't told him anything of note. I could get into major trouble if I told him something important that humans weren't supposed to know and he posted about it.

"Hey, I read something earlier that made me wonder. Have you heard anything about a war?"

He smiled slyly, eyes sparkling. "Maybe."

"You going to tell me about it?"

He leaned forward, arms crossed on the table. "Say yes to lunch sometime. I'll tell you then."

I smiled back. "Yes."

Chapter 9

That evening, Dad was ready with his overnight bag. "You're late."

I closed the door behind me. "We were making good progress, and I lost track of time. I'm sorry." Guilt weighed heavily on my shoulders as I glanced at the old-fashioned grandfather clock in the back. I was almost a half-hour late. I'd completely forgotten that I was supposed to take over the shop so Dad could catch his flight. He was going to California to check out an estate sale in the morning. Even if I had actually been working on a project, I should have been able to keep track of time. I pulled my project out of my bag and shoved the pages I'd put together last night toward Dad. "Here. We got a ton done." The lie tasted bitter in my mouth.

He leafed through the work and made pleased sounds, but it didn't appease my guilt. "Are you going to miss your flight?"

He leaned over and kissed the top of my head. "No, pumpkin. It'll be fine, but I better get going. Close early tonight if you need to."

I gave him a tight squeeze. "You know, if you let me do online school, I could be home more often and would be able to help with the shop more."

"Absolutely not. You need to be social with your peers and not hang out all day in a dusty shop with your old man."

"I'm grounded. I'm not getting socialization, even *with* school." Pulling away, I said, "Think about it, okay? I can finish my junior year online and maybe even my senior year and graduate early? You'd like that, right?"

He sighed. I knew these conversations were starting to wear him down. He'd been dead set against it at first, but it was hard for him to run the shop without Mom and my reasons were good ones. If I could just get him to agree, I'd have more free time to help him *and* do what I wanted to do—search for Mom's killer.

"I'll forward you the information tonight, and you can look it over during your flight." His flight was a red eye, and I knew he couldn't sleep on planes.

He gave me another hug, squeezing me tight. "All right, I'll take a look. I'm off. Don't forget to check in with Delia, and text me if you need anything."

"Of course." Delia didn't watch me per se, but her husband, Joe, owned the coffee shop next door, and she was my check-in when Dad had to go out of town. Dad wasn't quite ready to leave me by myself yet, even though I pointed out that I'd be out of the house and leaving for college in another year and a half.

I stepped back, the clock ticking away in the background.

"There's some new inventory I priced in the back. Can you move it to the front? And I meant what I said; close early if you need to. It's been slow, and schoolwork is more important."

"Thanks. Have a good trip." Watching Dad walk away, there was a pit in my stomach. I needed to tell him about my registration, but I didn't want to. I knew he'd be upset. Before I could lose my nerve, I said, "Hey, Dad? Can we talk when you get back?"

His brow furrowed, and he put down his bag. "You never ask to talk. Is it important? We can talk now." He checked his watch. "Should I get a later flight?"

I blinked back tears. He was going to drop everything. For me. It was at times like this that I realized how much he loved me. I wished I knew how to show him I loved him that much, too.

I shooed him on with my hands. "Nothing like that. I just want us to catch up when you get back, that's all." And I needed time to think of what I would say.

His face relaxed, and he said, "Sure thing, pumpkin. I love you."

"I love you too." Closing the door behind him, I walked to the back and the boxes Dad had mentioned. Opening one, I examined a newly priced ceramic frog. I grabbed a rag from the pile on the table. It was part of my job to make sure items were clean and to move the products so new stuff was always in the front. After the frog, I grabbed an art deco lamp and gave it a good scrub. Then I walked it to the front and replaced a different lamp, which I moved to one of the side tables. Once I got into a rhythm, the time passed quickly.

****

The next morning, stomach rumbling, I wandered over to our stainless-steel fridge. I opened the door, letting the cool air wake me up. Dad had packed the shelves with eggs, carrots, celery, spinach, low-fat yogurt. It was all healthy. *Yuck.* I needed to go shopping. I also needed to figure out how to get the ring off my finger and tell my dad about my registration. Looking outside, I half-expected stormy rain clouds to match my mood, but it was sunny and cool.

Grabbing my computer, I went downstairs, flipped

the sign that said I'd be back in 15 minutes, and walked the block over to Joe's Coffee. I rarely saw Joe, but Delia was there as usual. We'd gotten to know each other pretty well from my daily coffee runs. She waved. I waved back. Check-in complete.

Staring at the display, my mouth watered at the pumpkin pound cake dripping with icing and the lemon muffin filled with raspberry jam. The place was busy, as always. While I was waiting in line, I listened to the middle-aged guy in front of me chat on the phone. Dressed in a suit and tie and carrying a briefcase, he kept tapping his foot impatiently. I could See magic around him. It wasn't a glamour. It was fainter than that and had an odd pattern to it. Maybe a charm? Now that I was keeping my necklace off, I could See all the nuances I'd been missing. I couldn't just See glamours. I could See spells. With practice, would I be able to tell what the spells were?

When he got to the counter, he demanded, "My usual drink! Last time the barista got it wrong."

The barista, a guy with spiky black hair and olive skin, said, "A half soy half nonfat mocha at 157 degrees with an extra squirt of chocolate, extra whipped cream but less milk so the lid still fits, and an added sprinkle of cinnamon."

My mouth dropped at the fact that he remembered this man's drink so specifically. He was a genius. I almost applauded. The guy in front of me didn't exactly fit the stereotype of the prima donna coffee drinker, but it took all types. Maybe his spell was to keep people from throttling him when he made annoying requests.

When he got his drink, he huffed and didn't even leave a tip. I rolled my eyes and gave my order, pumpkin spiced chai tea latte, exactly as it appeared on the menu. I looked at the pastries and had a moment where I couldn't decide, and then Delia handed me a warmed-up chocolate muffin with chocolate chips and pecans. "This is what you want, sweetie, I know it."

"And I'll have one of these too," I said to the barista, breathing in the warm chocolatey goodness.

The guy grinned back, and I was charmed by a small dimple at the corner of his mouth.

I reached into my bag, pulled out some spare change, and dropped it in his jar. "And hey, that was impressive earlier, remembering that guy's drink. You totally deserve this."

"Nah, you don't have to." He dipped his chin shyly.

"Too late, already did."

"Thanks." I got a full megawatt smile, complete with dimple.

I could feel my face turning red and wished it didn't do that. Why, every time I found a guy cute, did my face have to light up like a Christmas tree?

Delia winked at me and mouthed *He's cute* while handing me my drink. To which I blushed even brighter.

I returned to the store, flipped the sign back over, and then sat at the table out front, drinking my latte. The first bite of Delia's chocolate muffin almost had me moaning out loud. The decadent gooey chocolate with the crunch of the pecans was to die for. It was exactly what I'd needed to get out of my funk. After finishing the muffin—there was no way I was doing research first and letting it get cold—I settled in to look up what the creepy ring could be. I wasn't used to researching artifacts, but didn't think it would be that hard.

After almost an hour of clicking through different

sites and finding nothing, I wanted to pull my hair out. It was a ring for crying out loud. I should have found something, but it was like it didn't exist. Either the ring wasn't that special or I sucked at this.

I groaned, head falling to the computer. Who was I kidding? It had been locked in a buried chest, of course it was important. I just sucked at this. Sitting up, I tried taking the ring off again. Still stuck. Every time I did that, my chest hurt, and my heart raced. Thinking of it being attached to me forever freaked me out, so I tried not to think about it.

About ready to head back inside, I got a text from Carter.

—Hey. Look up. Want some company?—

I looked up and saw him on the other side of the street. He waved.

I waved back, and he jogged across the street, weaving between cars to join me. He looked great, red hair gleaming copper in the sun, and a tight shirt showing off lean muscles.

"Living dangerously, crossing the road there."

"What can I say? I'm a daredevil. I eat dessert first and occasionally jaywalk." He put his hands up. "And for the record, I am not stalking you. I live three blocks away."

I grinned, wondering how I'd not noticed him the last few months.

He sat down and leaned across me to get a look at my search engine.

I pulled the computer closed. "Hey."

He smirked, unrepentant. "You're looking for it too, huh? No need to hide it. Everyone is searching."

"Hmm?"

"The ring. The key that leads to the three daggers that meld together to create the Sword of Ages. The one all the psychic readings have been saying is close by. The town is crawling with Others today. It's been dormant for centuries. Wonder if someone found it or had it all along and only now decided to use it."

"Use it?" My voice was a little squeaky.

"The map. Exciting, right?"

The blood left my head, and I felt like I was going to pass out, dots swimming before my eyes. The Sword of Ages. I had no idea what that was, but the title made me think I was in deep shit. I surreptitiously put my shaking hands in my lap, under the ornate metal table. "How do you know so much?"

He gave a flippant wave. "I never reveal my sources." He leaned in closer, his breath minty and fresh. "Everyone is saying this could be life changing. If all three daggers are found and forged into the sword, the celestials can be overthrown. The prophecy isn't crazy specific, but this could be it. I can't believe this could happen during our lifetime."

I discreetly looked at his neck. He had smooth, pale skin with a few freckles. Still no tattoo. Unless he was using makeup, he wasn't a registered Mythic, although he sure knew enough to be one. "Where do you get your info? And why are the celestials bad? Do we want to overthrow them?"

He winked. "Can't reveal that first answer, but I can help with the second. From what I gather, the celestials, from a human perspective, are actually pretty great. They treat us fairly and are helpful. But there is an uneven split of power between them and the fae and demons. Basically, they have all of it and control what the fae and demons can and can't do. Think back to slavery days and imagine all other mythical beings as slaves. Even if the celestials aren't bad for us humans, they're enslaving the fae and demons by limiting their power."

"That sounds bad, but limiting their power isn't slavery."

"No, but I've heard that those that don't comply do become actual slaves."

"That's awful."

"I'm sure some need it. I mean demons, right? But who knows for sure. This is all theory anyway."

His flippant comment about demons gave me pause. There was at least one evil demon out there, the one that had killed my mom. And likely a second one, the guy who had killed someone in the cemetery, but were all demons bad?

Casper somehow snuck out and wove around my legs, his purr a soft rumble. I reached down and scratched his ears. Casper leaned his head into my hand, then turned and hissed. I saw a guy with green skin walk by. He hissed back at Casper, and I worked to keep my face blank.

Carter scooted his chair back a bit, away from the puffed-up kitten, but hadn't reacted to the green-skinned guy. "Friendly cat you have there."

"Casper?" I picked him up and rubbed my face in his velvety fur. "He's overprotective, that's all. He's such a sweetie, I haven't even gotten him to kill a spider for me yet."

"Of course not. Spiders are grand creatures that help keep bugs out of the house."

"Uh no, spiders are evil spawn that need to be killed at all costs. From a distance. With lethal fire power or bug spray." We chatted comfortably about nothing for a bit, and then someone stopped by the store, and I got up to go help. "See you around?"

"Definitely. Tomorrow?"

I could feel my face light up. "Sure."

"Great!" He glanced at my cup and the clear branding on the side. "Meet at Joe's Coffee at one?"

"Works for me."

"It's a date."

My heart pitter pattered at his use of the word date, and I grinned goofily. "See you then."

"Later." He saluted as he walked back down the street and disappeared around the corner.

****

It was closing time. I turned the sign and went to the till to count out. Sitting on a tall stool, I was halfway through the ones when the chime on the front door rang, a light cascade of sound. "We're closed, sorry."

Finishing, I looked up. There was a shadow moving near the back of the store among the cluttered knick-knacks. I stilled, gripping the desk tightly.

A moment later, my brain processed that I hadn't heard the bell ring again. I breathed out a sigh of relief. The customer must not have heard me when I said we were closed. It wasn't an intruder, just a late customer. Probably an old lady looking for a new teapot. Being alone at night did make me overreact sometimes.

I pasted on a smile and headed toward the back, wiping my hands on a rag. Getting closer, I saw a tall guy wearing a black shirt stretched tight over broad shoulders. Not a grandma. Clearing my throat, I said, "Excuse me? I'm sorry, but we're closed. You're going to have to come back tomorrow."

The customer turned, and I had to swallow a gasp. It was the guy from the cemetery. Up close, with his glamour gone, the red runes were bright against his dusky skin. His light-blue eyes seemed to glow. In this light, I could more clearly see the scar curling up the side of his neck. It wasn't straight, like from a sword, but curved. A whip, maybe? A claw? And there was his sword, hanging at his side. Remembering the cemetery, I wanted to step back and cower, but we'd flirted. He'd helped me. I couldn't be scared. I had to pull it together, or he'd know I'd Seen something I shouldn't have been able to See.

I swallowed hard. He was a customer. I could do this. I forced a chipper note into my voice. "Tristan, right? I hadn't expected to see you again so soon." *Or at all.* "Unfortunately, we're closed for the night. Can you please come back tomorrow?" Glancing my way, his eyes widened in surprise, but he recovered quickly. He smiled and took a step closer, an enticing hint of sandalwood and spice following, teasing my senses. His light-blue eyes caught mine, and my mouth went dry. I was not attracted to him. I couldn't be. Was he using magic? If so, I couldn't See it, but I was so new to using my abilities, that might not mean much.

"Zoey."

My name sounded like a masculine purr. I fought the urge to take a step back. I felt like I was being stalked.

"I'm surprised to see you as well. Pleasantly surprised. Could you help me find something? It is rather urgent and can't wait until morning. A special heirloom that was missing was found, and I think it is here, in your store."

"What kind of heirloom?" *Don't say it. Don't say it.*

Don't say it. But I knew he would. After everything that had happened over the last few days, he could only be here for one thing.

"A ring with three stones on it."

I furtively moved my hand to the pocket of my hoodie. "I'm so sorry, but we don't have anything like that."

A low growl came from him, rumbling and deep. I took a step back, bumping into a small table. I steadied the lamp that had started weaving back and forth.

"That's a lie."

I tried to take another step but was trapped, caged in by mismatched furniture. "What?"

"Demons can smell lies."

"You're a demon?" I couldn't stop the catch in my voice. A demon. A real live demon. Here. In front of me. It was one thing to guess. It was another to have it confirmed. My palms started to sweat, and I wiped them on my jeans.

He scoffed. "Half. Don't pretend you don't know. Why else would you stink of fear? You're unregistered, aren't you? Help me, and I promise I won't tell anyone. I can help you hide it better."

A hot surge of anger chased away the fear. I embraced it. He was trying to blackmail me? *The nerve.* I pushed my hair aside and showed him my slightly pink new mark. "Too late. Newly registered. You can take your overbearing demon ass and get the fuck out of my store."

He grabbed me and I flinched, but he was just pushing my hair aside to get a better look at my mark. He traced the thin lines with his finger. "You were free the other day. How did this happen?"

I was very aware of my chest pressed up tight against his, his hand fisted in my hair. Heart pounding, I tried to pull away but was held fast, his cool finger tracing the lines. "Why do you care? Weren't you just saying you'd turn me in?"

"I lied." He let me go, and I stumbled away, steadying myself on an antique dresser. My hand was out, and he was looking right at it. Would he see the ring? I shoved it back into my hoodie. His eyes bored into me as he continued. "I wouldn't have done it. I never would have turned you over to *them*." The venom in his voice at the word "them" made my veins go cold.

"The MEA? Why?" I hated that my voice sounded so shaky and weak.

He gave me a bitter grin. "Do you know why I can't wait until tomorrow? I have to get a pass to visit because I am part demon. I heard about the sighting at the same time as everyone else but only now got access to come here. If I don't find it soon, I'll be forced back to the Demon Realm. By the time I get another pass and come back, it will be gone. Being registered means you have to follow their rules. The oh-so-good rulers, those kind and gracious celestials, don't mind giving extreme punishments to those they call the lesser castes."

Hearing the resentment in his voice erased some of my anger. He had been wrong to blackmail me, but if I was in his position, would I have done the same? I licked dry lips. "In answer to how this happened, I had a bad tarot card reading. Someone knocked me unconscious, and here I am, newly registered. I'm supposed to be learning your laws, but I can't even read the book they gave me."

Tristan snatched my hand that was hiding in the

hoodie and yanked it out, turning it as he searched my fingers for the ring. My stomach was in knots. What would he do? Would he cut my finger off for the ring? Take me with him?

He stared right at the ring, the silver shining in the low store light. He turned my hand this way and that, and then let it drop.

"What are you doing?" My voice came out as a shaky squeak. He hadn't seen the ring. How had he missed it? Did it have some sort of protection on it? I struggled to keep the relief off my face.

"Nothing. I just wondered. You were being weird, and I thought…Never mind."

Tristan leaned casually against a bright turquoise desk. I loved the color and had secretly hoped Dad would give it to me for my next birthday. In his larger-than-life state, Tristan looked a little ridiculous in front of the dainty desk. He picked up a small bronze cup and studied it. "What if I could help you read the book and learn what you needed to know, stuff that won't be in the book? Stuff to keep you safe. Would you trade it for the ring?"

"I don't even know what the ring does. How can I trade it without knowing if I'm dooming everyone by doing so?" As soon as I said it, I realized I'd all but admitted I had it. Just because he couldn't See it didn't mean I needed to advertise I knew where it was.

He leaned forward, focused and intent. "What if I promise it will only be used for good?"

I rolled my eyes, annoyed. "You just admitted you lied to me. Why would I take your word?"

His eyes bored into mine. "What about an oath? A blood oath."

I thought about the ring, stuck on my hand. "What if

I can't give it to you?"

His light blue eyes were calculating. Thoughtful. "What do you mean?"

I swallowed, throat dry. "It's complicated, but I literally can't give it to you. You know I'm not lying. Is there anything else I could do? That you might want?" Nails digging into my palms, I said, "I do need help."

"With what?"

The words tumbled from my lips. "Help reading the book of laws and finding the demon who killed my mother." As soon as the words were out, I wished I could take them back. I was asking for help. From a demon. Why?

His interest in me sharpened, and he stared. I tried not to focus on the glowing red runes on his skin. Were they some sort of weird tattoo?

His low voice pulled me back. "A demon murdered your mother? How do you know?"

I waved an arm expressively. "Dark horns. Spikes. There was a gray mist around him. Looked like a demon to me."

"You saw him like that?" Before I could blink, Tristan was right in front of me, eyes fixed on mine. How had he moved so fast? "What do I look like?"

"I'm sorry?" My voice was breathy.

He grabbed my chin and forced my head up. I hadn't realized I'd started looking at the ground. "When you look at me, what do you see?"

His sword swung next to him, barely avoiding a collision with the desk. Must ignore the sword. Normal people wouldn't see what I see. I thought back to the boy in the cemetery. "Dark hair, blue eyes, black hoodie."

"You're lying." His voice held wonder. "You know

my glamour, but you aren't seeing it now. Do you choose when you see through them?"

Stupid, lie-detecting demon powers. I twisted my head, pulling away from his grasp. "I don't want to talk about it."

He let me go. "Fair enough." His head jerked to the right, listening. He drew his sword.

I squawked in alarm, backing up.

The blade was dark-gray steel and thankfully had no blood on it. Glancing back at me, he asked, "Can you fight? Do you have a weapon?"

I stared dumbly, stunned. "No? Why?"

"We have company."

Chapter 10

Tristan said something under his breath, and his sword glowed with a soft red light.

Glancing around the cluttered store, I whispered, "I don't See anyone."

Ignoring me, he strode forward, pushing me behind him. I still didn't See anything, so I was stunned when I heard the clang of steel on steel and the quiet whoosh as Tristan parried an unseen assailant. Turning, he shoved me out of the way. Without warning, multiple attackers appeared, wearing long flowing cloaks and smelling of rot. He grabbed me and threw me across the room. I slammed into a table, a stack of ceramic orange and blue dishes sliding off the top and onto the floor with a crash.

"BC, attack!" A huge dog-like shape exploded into existence, crushing everything in its path and blocking my view.

"What the hell?" I was momentarily mesmerized by the shining black scales in front of me, blocking the sight of the dark circle of slender forms converging on Tristan. The black dog-beast grabbed one of the tall, spindly creatures and bit it in half, steam pushing out of its nostrils as it tipped a triangular head back and swallowed.

The shrieking cries from the intruders paralyzed me. I couldn't move.

I snapped out of it when I heard, "BC, no. Bad. No

eat."

The giant beast bit into another, snarling as he shook the corpse, sending gobs of dark goo flying. Tristan dispatched a different attacker, muttering under his breath.

The bad guys kept coming, dark and slithering. The attackers were spectral, but not. They faded in and out but were always solid when Tristan hit them. How he knew when they were turning solid, I did not know. When they were solid, they smelled like rotting dead things and had gray, leathery skin stretched tight over long bones. Tristan moved faster than I thought possible, dodging and slicing, but there were so many. They were surrounding him. He needed help. The smart thing to do would be run out the back door before they noticed me, but…

"Shit. Shit, shit, shit." I searched around for a weapon, hands fumbling until they landed on an iron sculpture of some scantily clad woman. I gripped it tightly and crept closer, sweat making my hands slick. I should be running out the back. What the hell was I doing?

A clawed hand reached toward Tristan's back. I didn't hesitate. I swung the sculpture at the thing's head, knocking him to the side. The hollow thud echoed across the room. The statuette slipped from my grip with the impact, and I dashed after it.

The one I'd hit had seemed like it was going down, but it twisted mid-fall and seconds later had me by the throat. Stars filled my vision as it squeezed. It chortled in joy as it pressed its bony fingers harder, claws digging into my skin. Its eyes were solid pits of black and its pointy teeth were yellow, breath like boiled onions. I gasped for air, clawing at the skeletal hand that gripped my throat. It squeezed tighter, lifting me off the ground. I gagged, unable to make a sound, feet thrashing and kicking. Fragile merchandise shattered as I struggled to get free.

Casper jumped out of nowhere, fur fluffed, teeth and claws slashing. Distracted, the creature loosened his grip enough that I grabbed a breath. Casper yowled as he was knocked aside. The grip around my neck tightened.

A deep hissing voice bellowed from across the room. "Stop. We might need her if we can't find it."

Psycho killer frowned and focused on my face as he continued to squeeze.

"I said stop."

The creature hissed, his face a tight mask of anger. Everything was going fuzzy, and then he threw me across the room. I crashed into the wall at an odd angle. There was a sickening snap, and I fell to the ground.

Someone swore. Swords clanged. I was yanked from the floor, tossed over a shoulder glowing with red runes, and then a door slammed. We were outside. Unceremoniously dropped to the ground, patches of dirt and weeds passed before my eyes. A warm hand lifted my chin and examined my neck. Ice-blue eyes met mine, dark with concern. "Are you okay?"

I tried to say something, but no sound came out. I couldn't even croak. Couldn't breathe.

I couldn't breathe.

I tried to reach up to touch my throat, but my arms wouldn't move. Panic set in as I tried desperately to shift, to do something. I needed air. My chest was tight, lungs burning.

The creature had broken my neck. I was going to

die.

Tristan looked back and forth between me and the shop, growls coming from inside, and then turned back to me.

"Damn it." Eyes closed, he touched my face and whispered soft words in an odd, guttural language.

Power seeped into my skin, at first tingling. Then my neck was on fire. I couldn't move, couldn't make a sound. Burning. I was being flayed alive, pain exploding everywhere. I wanted to scream, to writhe away, but I was trapped, screaming inside my own head.

Abruptly, the pain ceased. Tristan lifted his hands, staggered a bit, and then fell onto his butt on the ground. His voice was weak when he asked, "Can you breathe?"

The cool air on my tongue tasted sweeter than anything I'd ever tasted before. That first breath was not smooth, but I could breathe again. I nodded, not sure I was up for words, but thrilled when my head moved. I could move again. I wiggled my fingers to be sure and started crying, unable to stop the tears of relief from dripping down my face.

Tristan nodded. He took a deep breath, pushed himself to his feet and, with a grim set to his jaw, headed back inside. *Was he going back to fight the monsters on his own? Was he crazy?*

"Wait." The croak made my throat ache.

He ignored me, and the wooden door swung closed behind him.

From the shop came the faint sounds of skirmishing, sword hitting sword. He couldn't do this alone. He needed help. I pushed myself up and then fell back to my knees, leaning against the steps. I couldn't stand. I was too dizzy. Guilt weighed heavily on me. He'd just saved my life. He needed me, but I was useless right now.

A few minutes later, the back door slammed open, and Tristan stormed back out. His runes glowed, creating a red aura around him. Behind him, the large dog barred the door, his barbed tail swinging as he snarled at whatever was left inside.

"Damn it." Tristan ran his fingers through his ebony hair and then leaned against the trellis next to me. Pulling out a phone, sword propped up against his side, he typed in a text.

My voice a scratchy whisper, I asked, "Who are you texting? The police? Do they take texts?"

"Don't be daft. We don't call the human police for Mythic business. I am calling a brownie to come and clean up the shop before your father gets home. She owes me a favor. She will get rid of the bodies as well."

"Bodies?" I squeaked. I'd known the place was trashed, but I hadn't thought there'd be dead bodies. For some reason, my mind assumed Tristan was injuring them and they got away, despite literally seeing some ripped in half.

He sneered at me as he put his phone away. "Are you feeling bad for the people who almost killed you? Your neck was broken. You couldn't move. You couldn't breathe. If I hadn't been here, you would be dead. Your mother should have prepared you better."

A white-hot anger filled my body, and I surged to my feet with it, poking him in the chest. "Don't you ever talk bad about my mother. Ever." The words came out as a rasp. I had to stop and gasp for air before continuing, but I was too angry to stop. "Whatever she did, she did because she loved me."

Only about half of the words were intelligible, the

rest too raspy, but he nodded, grasping my hand and stopping me. "I understand. Stop talking. You're hurting yourself. I can't heal you again, not until I recharge."

I leaned heavily next to him, the dizziness and exhaustion threatening to put me back on the ground. "Thank you. For saving me." I hadn't even known demons could heal, and he'd done it without asking anything in return.

He nodded curtly.

I reached a hand up and touched my throat. I remembered him looking between me and the shop and asked, "Are they gone?"

"BC is double checking, but yes, they left. And since they left, they likely got the key. Scavengers like that rarely leave until they have what they came for."

I nodded, knowing full well the key was safely on my hand. I wondered what they'd taken instead.

He turned to face me, his expression unreadable. "I have a new deal for you. I need an ingredient from the Celestial Realm. You are half celestial and can go there, but I am banned. Get it for me, and I will help you read the book of laws and find the demon who killed your mother."

I hesitated.

"You said you needed help, right? That was what you requested?"

I struggled to make sense of what he was saying. It seemed too good to be true. There had to be a catch. "Is the ingredient hard to get?"

Tristan's face was in shadow, barely visible in the soft glow of the moon. "For you, no."

"But how do I get to the Celestial Realm? What do you need?"

"Just some water from a lake. You can get there from one of the portals. I'll show you how."

He made it sound so simple. "Are their lakes in the middle of nowhere?" I shivered as I imagined traipsing through huge deserts or dangerous woods to get to a hidden lake.

He laughed. "No. It's a short walk from the main portal. It's not a hard task. I just can't do it since I'm part demon. Do we have a deal?"

I hesitated and then held out my hand. When his warm hand enveloped mine, I felt tiny and weak, but this was my first real chance of finding the demon who'd killed Mom. And he'd healed me when he might have gotten the key. That made him a decent half demon. I hoped. "Deal." When I let go, the warm imprint of his hand on mine remained. "Now what?"

"Now you go inside and take a shower and get some rest. I gave you a partial healing, but I have restrictions here. You need to take it easy for a bit."

"What happens when your time here is up?" My throat burned as I forced the words past my lips.

"I return to the Demon Realm, or I'll be tracked down and punished, and I won't be allowed back for a few months. I wasn't lying when I said we were restricted. Although, I may have exaggerated how little time I had left on this particular trip. I have Realm Tokens for the next few days. I'm going to see if I can track the ones that got away. I'll come back in the morning, and we can start working on our deal."

"Thank you."

He nodded curtly. "You're welcome."

Then he was gone. I didn't see him move, he just vanished.

I shuddered, remembering how quickly he had moved during the fight. I had made a deal with him. With a half demon. What had I been thinking? I was so dumb. Mom would have grounded me for life if she were still alive. I could only blame the adrenaline of the moment, but what's done was done. And Tristan had saved my life, so maybe he only chopped up demons?

I pushed off the trellis, standing in the cool breeze. Who was I kidding? He was dangerous. He wasn't a friend. He was helping me because it helped him. I needed to remember that.

Dizziness no longer overwhelmed me, but I felt off. My limbs were weak and uncoordinated. I used the railing to help me to the back door and then went inside. My glance around the place showed a monumental mess that no one could hope to salvage. One of my favorite vases was in pieces on the ground. So many shattered blue fragments. There would be no way to repair it. A quilted pillow was ripped with three long marks across the front, probably used as a shield against claws. The stuffing was fluttering in the breeze of the open door. Scratches in the wall, light fixtures torn out, smoking holes burned into the wood floor, books with holes in them, likely from the sword. I saw a few dark shapes on the ground and chose to focus elsewhere. Dad would kill me. There was so much damage. Was our insurance bill even paid for this month?

There was nothing I could do about it tonight. I needed a long bath and sleep. Ignoring the mess, I inched my way to my room.

By the time I'd washed and soaked, it was at least an hour later. I stood up and saw myself in the mirror. My pale complexion looked ghostly, and my dark-blue eyes were still wide with shock. I had bright-purple bruises around my neck and arms and even some on my back and legs, likely from the toss across the room. What had I looked like before Tristan had healed me?

A wave of exhaustion hit me, bright dots stealing my vision, and I had to lie down on the floor or risk passing out. When the wave passed, I crawled across the room and into bed, pulling the soft covers up. Mom had always insisted on nice sheets, and mine were a pale blue to match the checkered blue and green comforter. Pulling the sheets up to my chin, I stared at the white stucco ceiling.

I'd almost died tonight. That realization hit me hard, and I missed Mom worse than I'd ever missed her before, a deep ache in my gut. I wanted her to wrap me in her arms and tell me it would be okay. But it wouldn't be okay. Mom was gone, and tomorrow I would be working on a deal with a demon.

A deep purr sounded next to me. Casper snuggled in under my chin, letting my tears wet his fur. I pulled him close, burying my face in his side as I mourned and worried what tomorrow would bring.

Chapter 11

My alarm beeped. I knocked it off my nightside table while trying to get to the off switch, and it slid across the floor. I buried my head in my pillow. The persistent beeping from the floor hammered away, not stopping. Pulling the covers over my head, I could almost ignore it and keep the blissful cloud of sleep. Almost, but not quite. I turned to roll out of bed and storm across the room and decimate my alarm, but my body protested. That one roll shot aching pains down my back and legs. I groaned.

Stupid alarm just kept beeping. Crawling out of bed, I felt like death warmed over. I grabbed the small red alarm clock and switched it off. Leaving it on the ground, I stumbled to the bathroom, each step sending sharp pains across my body. Grabbing some pain medicine, I popped a few pills and almost choked on them when my usual dry swallow didn't work. Spitting them out, I grabbed a glass of water and tried again. In the mirror, the ring of bruises looked even worse than they had last night. Tracing the purple and brown marks, I could make out long, thin fingers. Shaking my head, I tried to clear the terrifying memory of the skeletal creature squeezing my throat. Strangling me. In a moment of panic, I yanked the curtain from the shower, half expecting to see his grotesque form hiding there. The shower was empty. Shaking, I started to get ready for the day.

Feeling a little more myself after a hot shower, I went to the kitchen for a cup of coffee, wondering when Tristan would show up. My phone buzzed, and I looked down at a text from Dad checking in.

I started a quick text back and then stopped. I was attacked. At our home. What should I tell him? Thinking of the disaster that was waiting for me downstairs, I decided to wait. This conversation would be better in person. The pit in my stomach got bigger as I wrote my typical, — *All good* — and hit send. He was going to kill me for lying when he got back, but I couldn't make myself admit what had happened. Not yet, anyway.

Dad had made me see a therapist after Mom died. The therapist had stressed focusing on the positive and the things you were grateful for, and I now completed a gratitude list every morning. Sipping my coffee, I thought, *I am grateful for coffee. I am grateful I'm alive. I am grateful that people think the key was stolen from the shop, so no one will be trying to kill me.* Not my usual three things. Well, except for the coffee.

Finished with my coffee, I headed downstairs and steeled myself for the mess that I'd have to clean up. How on earth would I explain this to Dad? My better mood vanished as I tried to imagine how the conversation would go. *"Yes, you can trust me. I let a bunch of demons fight in the store and break everything. So, did you ever pay that insurance bill we're behind on?"* Trudging down the stairs, I clung to the handrail, my body sending sharp stabs of pain with every step. Who knew a body covered in bruises would be so stiff?

I paused on the last two steps and gawked. If there were flies there, they could have set up camp in my mouth and built a quaint little treehouse in the time it took my jaw to find its way closed. The place was pristine. It was actually cleaner than it had been yesterday. Not a single broken piece, everything gleamed like someone had spent the night scrubbing every nook and cranny. Walking farther into the room, I traced the edge of an ivory vase that I knew shattered. I couldn't see a single crack or line. Had Tristan's brownie replaced everything? Or fixed it with magic? Could magic do that? I didn't know whether to laugh or cry, I was so relieved.

Smiling, I went to open the store and found Tristan leaning against the wall outside. I was getting used to the slight red glow his runes gave off. It made me think of the northern lights, beautiful and mysterious.

He's dangerous, I reminded myself. He killed the intruders last night. He cut someone's throat the night before. I thought about him fighting; his power to move at lightning speed and the way he used his sword so effortlessly. It gave me chills. Right now, I was useful, but that could change. I had to be careful.

I opened the door. "Hey." My voice came out in a guttural croak, likely due to the bruising and swelling. *Great.*

He pushed off the wall. "Come on. We have to talk to a few contacts."

I hesitated. When we talked last night about getting together this morning, I had assumed, wrongly, that the store would be unable to open due to the "burglars." I had not expected to have to close the shop when it was fine. We needed the income. Dad would kill me if I didn't open. It made the shop look bad to be closed randomly.

Tristan turned back to me, eyebrow raised. "Unless

you don't want to come?"

I did not trust him. I didn't even know what we were doing. Were we searching for Mom's killer, or was he planning to show me how to access the Celestial Realm? Both? Regardless, I had made a deal. I needed to uphold my end.

I grabbed my favorite red coat and locked the door behind me, leaving the closed sign in place. Saying a quick prayer that none of Dad's friends would stop by, I took off after Tristan. And by taking off, I mean I was practically running to keep up. While being up and moving about had loosened my muscles some, my aching body still protested. "Tristan, do you have to run?" I croaked. "Short-legged person back here. One who's injured, remember?" I had worn a turtleneck to hide the bruising, but he should have remembered from last night.

He halted, and I slammed into his back.

"Oof. A little warning next time."

He pulled my collar down and looked with impassive eyes at the purple and brown mix of color shading my throat. When he pushed me into an alley, I stumbled past a broken bottle and had the insane thought that I shouldn't have complained and that he was going to off me. And then started laughing at my thought of the phrase "off me."

"Why are you laughing?"

I stifled the hysterical giggle. "I'm fine. I…" I trailed off as his rough fingers touched my neck and he whispered an incantation. A warm fire caressed my skin, and my voice failed me as pain surged and then vanished. I reached up and touched my neck. It didn't hurt. I could swallow again. "Wow. Thanks."

"Humph. I couldn't keep dragging you around injured. You'd slow me down."

"Yeah, and people might think you beat me."

He grinned, baring sharp canines. "Zoey, that wouldn't hurt my reputation."

I swallowed hard, glad I could swallow again, but a bit terrified of what his reputation actually was. Before I could stop myself, my stupid mouth, I asked, "You mean like when you cut that guy's throat in the cemetery?" He turned ice-cold eyes to me, and I started babbling. "I'm sorry. It's none of my business. It might not even have been you. It could have just been a coincidence that you had a bloody sword and…maybe he tripped and fell."

He stalked toward me, and I backed up until I hit the wall of the building next to us. We were in a dark alley, and I had just told a demon I knew he'd killed someone. I was going to die. And I deserved it. I was that stupid. I closed my eyes and leaned away, waiting for the blow.

"I cut his throat because he was stealing from my father. I am my father's sword, and I deal out whatever justice he deems necessary, regardless of what I think of it." His breath was warm on my face. "Does that scare you, Zoey? Do I scare you?"

"Yes." My heart was pounding. I was backed up against a wall with nowhere to go.

I could feel his nod, we were that close.

"Good. It should." He backed away and started walking back toward the street. "First rule of Mythics: We are not governed by democracy like humans." He said "humans" with a touch of scorn. "Our fates are often controlled by the whims of a single individual, and it is not something we can challenge. Never trust a Mythic. All Mythics, no matter how good, need to report to someone else. That someone else isn't always right in the head."

I jogged a little to catch up, jumping over a puddle. Could have been pee, but I was going with a rain puddle. "Okay. Don't trust Mythics. Can I trust you?"

"No." He turned to me, an exasperated look on his face. "Please try to listen, Zoey, or this will take forever." We waited for some people to pass us, and then he said, "Second rule of Mythics: Don't depend on the registry to be accurate about what a person can do."

"What do you mean? Why wouldn't it be accurate?"

He pointed to my neck and my new tattoo. "Some are correct, but people can fix their results. And sometimes the tester is just bad at their job and makes a mistake. If they really wanted it to be accurate, they would re-do tests every few years since abilities can evolve, but they don't. Lazy bureaucrats, but I guess it's good for the rest of us."

We had gotten to a busy street and were silent as we waited for the crosswalk.

I traced my tattoo with a finger, feeling the raised skin. I leaned in close so the couple waiting at the light with us wouldn't hear. "I don't even know what the symbols stand for. Hard to trust something you can't even read."

He chuckled, but the sound held no mirth. His breath was warm as he leaned down and whispered in my ear. "We'll get to that. But we're almost there, so not today." After crossing the street, he stopped in front of a two-story brick building and opened an ornate door with a sign that read, *Bubble Tea*. Inside were a bunch of tables with different-colored tops and a long counter at the far end with shelves of tea behind it. A perky young woman with a ponytail and a green apron asked, "What can I get for you?"

Noticing Tristan, her face went pale, and she said, "Oh. It's you." Her bright voice had an even brighter note when she asked, "Bubble tea?" The two other people in the shop left, giving us a wide berth. *Who was this guy?*

Ordering two bubble teas, Tristan handed me one. I was surprised at the flavor he'd ordered for me. Did he know I loved raspberry, or had he guessed? The little bubbles in the tea had an odd chewy texture, but it was sort of good. He led me to a table, and we sat on the tall chairs. *Were we going to sit here and drink? In silence?* Nervous, I noticed he'd already finished his drink. I chugged away, the liquid cool and tangy. Waiting until I'd finished mine, he took the empty glasses, put them in the tray to be cleaned, and then guided me toward the back. With a hand on my back, he escorted me through a nondescript door.

"If we were headed back here, why did we get the drinks?"

"Mythic hospitality requires that you support the place you visit by buying something. The shop might be a front, but it needs business to stay open. Being part demon, I need to follow all the rules, or I will be kicked out on a technicality."

"Oh." I couldn't think of what else to say. I tried not to notice his proximity, but his hand was still on my back, covering most of it and flooding my body with warmth. He was an evil guy who had killed someone. My stomach was *not* fluttering.

I stepped away, putting some space between us.

He had a small smile on his face, and I wondered

how much of my physical reaction he had picked up. *Stupid demon senses.*

Behind the door was a short staircase leading down, and then another door. A laminated sign on the second door read, "Demon Dog" with a picture of a furry, black animal that resembled a massive wolf with horns, howling at the moon.

"Demon Dog? Isn't that a bit obvious?"

"It was recently renamed, and there was a vote. I'd keep your opinion to yourself."

I stared at him, unsure if he was serious or joking, but he gave no hint as to either.

Tristan was about to open the door and then stopped, turning back to face me. "Try to stay close. This place is a haven for Mythics and Others, but they're mostly demon and fae, not celestial. They might not appreciate your presence."

I huffed. "If no one here has celestial blood, how would they See what I am?"

"You don't have to be part celestial to See auras or smell the difference between Aerellians. Seers are the only ones who can See through glamours to exactly what is beneath, but others can still tell what you are. Don't underestimate the other races."

My mind raced with questions. If others could find ways around glamours, then why were Seers so special? Was being able to See the details beneath a glamour that important? And could I See auras? What was an aura? Tristan wasn't a big talker, so I focused on the most important. "Why is my kind hated so much?"

Tristan was quiet long enough that I thought he wasn't going to answer. Then he said, "Seers, being able to See the truth of everything, were absolutely trusted.

One betrayed everyone. That betrayal started a war. By the time the dust settled, that Seer and most like her had been killed and the celestials ruled Aerellia. Seers have been mistrusted ever since."

Aerellia must be what they called the Other realm. Interesting that I'd never heard its name before. Before I could ask any more questions, Tristan said, "That's all I'm going to say on that." He hesitated, then asked, "Would you rather stay out here?"

Would I rather sit in an empty bubble tea shop cooling my heels like a naughty schoolgirl, or go into my first Mythic pub and try to get answers about my mother's killer? That was a no brainer. Of course, I wanted to go in. Was I nervous? Yes. Was I still going to go? Absolutely. I gestured for him to open the door. "Lead the way."

Chapter 12

"Welcome to a Mythic pub."

As we stepped through the door, I stopped and gawked. The noise assaulted me, loud and boisterous. It had been so quiet outside. The pub was basically a large room set up with tables, booths, and a long bar across the back. People were talking loudly over the music in the background, but the noise wasn't what had my mouth hanging open. Not all the patrons were…normal. One had blue skin, and another used a long green tongue to lick a plate clean. Next to them, a feathered man used his claws to spear a piece of chicken. His companion had rough bark for skin and was no taller than my knees. I had known there were many species outside of pixies, but seeing the diversity of everyone all at once was jarring. I had a childish urge to grab my necklace, put it on, and erase the strange sights. Assuming they were even using glamour and that would work. But I didn't. I, as Mom would have said, pulled on my big-girl pants and continued in. I was a Mythic. *They were like me. They just looked different. Different did not mean bad.* I kept telling myself that as I watched a large guy use his raptor-like claws to scrape the edge of his table. I forced myself to smile at him.

"*Grrr.*" The low rumble vibrated along the floor, and I swallowed hard.

Tristan grabbed my arm and pulled me forward

through the tight corridor between tables.

"Come on, shark bait. Stop antagonizing the locals."

I pulled my arm out of his grip. "What? I was being friendly."

He looked pointedly at the still-grumbling man with sharp teeth.

I shrugged at him. "What?" He shook his head and started pushing his way through the crowd. People were packed in tighter than a horde of fans during Sunday night football.

Everyone stepped aside for Tristan. But because of my gawking, and because he was a few steps ahead, people closed ranks before I could pass. I was pushing through bodies, trying to catch up but falling farther and farther behind, when I got stopped by a tall man with a broad chest.

He had long, protruding fangs that reminded me of a saber-toothed tiger. He sniffed me and stepped close. "You're new. Aren't you a pretty celestial bitch?" His voice was a deep purr, and before I could sidestep him, his hand was tracing the small of my back and pulling me close.

I let out a small shriek. "Tristan!"

I pushed hard against the man's chest, but he didn't budge an inch. His hot breath stank of stale beer, and I shuddered as he licked my ear. I could hear some of his friends egging him on, yelling "Bite the bitch," and cheering.

My small fists beat at him but did nothing but make him more eager. I fought down my panic as he scraped my neck with his fangs, his body pressed up tight against mine. I shoved my knee up between his legs, but he blocked me, tutting at my failed attempt.

"You'll pay for that."

Before I could contemplate what he meant by that, he was shoved away with enough force that it knocked over a few chairs. I was pulled into a warm side and was surprised by the growl that left Tristan's mouth. His red runes lit up like fireworks, smoke crawling over his skin.

The man backed away, hands in the air, face ashen. "Sorry, man. I didn't realize."

I blinked, and he was gone. I was sure he just moved fast, but it was like he poofed away with magic.

Tristan looked around at everyone nearby, growling a deep warning rumble. Everyone backed away, looking down, almost bowing in submission. There was a faint sour smell in the air. Fear.

Tristan grabbed my hand and dragged me behind him. I walked quickly, trying to keep up with his long stride. People stepped aside when they hadn't before. They looked at me with surprise, anger, jealousy, and curiosity. Blue eyes, green, black.

I stuck close to Tristan.

He looked back at me and, pulling me into his side, whispered in my ear, voice barely a breath so only I could hear. "I can protect you, but you must stay close. I didn't think they'd be so hostile. Maybe I should take you back outside." That last was muttered more to himself.

There was no way I wanted to miss whatever information he was trying to get here. I pressed closer to him, feeling very small. "I will stay close."

His hand tightened on mine, but otherwise he didn't respond.

When we got to the back counter, Tristan ordered. "My usual."

Still twitchy from the encounter, I couldn't believe he'd get something for himself in this hot, crowded place and not for me. Talk about inconsiderate. He could have at least asked. I elbowed him. "Plan to order me something?"

He gave a feral grin that made me wonder if I'd made a mistake pushing the issue, then waved at the bartender. "One for her too." A tall skinny guy with curly hair started grabbing bottles. As the guy was making our drinks, his hands were shaking. He swallowed and asked in a low voice, "Who are you here for?"

Tristan raised an eyebrow.

The guy licked his lips and pushed two bloodred drinks toward Tristan. "Look, could you at least take it out back? We have a good group of regulars right now, and I don't want to spook them."

Tristan reached for his wallet, and the guy rushed to say, "It's on the house."

Tristan nodded. Putting his wallet away, he picked up the two square glasses, handing one to me and taking a sip of his own. "Is Milo in?"

The barista nodded and said, "In the back."

I couldn't help but notice that Tristan's runes still glowed extra bright. I wanted to touch one and see if it was as hot as it looked. I clutched the glass, ignoring the impulse.

Tristan chugged the rest of his drink and, slamming the glass on the counter, walked toward a door in the back. He turned back to me and asked, "Coming?"

I stared at my drink. The thick red liquid clung to the sides of the glass. "Is this blood?"

Tristan stared at me, eyes challenging. "Maybe."

I sniffed it and caught a slight whiff of cinnamon. If

this was blood, I was going to throw it on him. And then vomit. Taking a deep breath, I took the smallest sip possible, just barely wetting my tongue. An explosion of flavor hit me. Definitely some cinnamon and spices and something sweeter as well. Following Tristan's example, I chugged the rest and put the glass on the counter, licking the thick liquid off my lips, sure it looked like I'd just downed my enemy's blood. What a visual.

Looking up, I caught Tristan's small nod of approval. Then he opened the back door, and I followed him into darkness. On the other side of the door, it was like we were transported to a completely different place. The walls were paneled in dark wood to match the warm tone of the floorboards. Paintings of trees in every season adorned the walls, and fresh flowers in tall vases let off a light floral scent. The place was lit with balls of light in glass casings, and the music was now a calm nature track.

A burly guy standing guard at the door nodded to Tristan. Tristan nodded back and walked past him. I hurried on his heels, careful to not let more than a step separate us. It was odd staying so close to someone everyone else was avoiding. What did they know that I didn't? Who was Tristan, and how badly had I messed up making a deal with him?

We walked down a long hallway lit with the round lights, past closed doors, toward a dark room at the end. About halfway down, Tristan opened one of the closed doors, and we walked into a spacious office littered with papers and books.

A tall man with Einstein-like salt-and-pepper hair and pointed ears sat behind a large, cluttered desk. He pushed small glasses up his nose and wrinkled his brow at Tristan. "What are you doing here, boy?"

"I need to know who is in the Human Realm right now. Someone got the key, and I need to get it back before they figure out how to use it."

I swallowed hard as I realized he was talking about the ring I was wearing.

The man sighed, taking his glasses off and rubbing his face. "Your father has forbidden me from giving the list to anyone, including you."

Tristan nodded. "I see."

I tugged on Tristan's sleeve. "What list?"

Tristan glared at me.

"Who's this lovely creature?" The man stood with surprising grace and was standing in front of me before I could so much as blink. "I'm Milo."

I worked at keeping my face blank. How had he moved so quickly and without knocking even one paper out of place? His attention was riveting and disconcerting. I would not let him know he startled me. I held out my hand. "Zoey. What list?"

He took my hand in both of his and kissed it. His lips were cool and dry, and the sharp touch of his fangs made me want to pull my hand back, but I didn't. Was he a vampire? "It is a pleasure to meet you…Zoey." His gaze was intense, and I felt myself drawn in.

His attention turned back to Tristan, and I could breathe again. Had he put me in some sort of trance? "It's a list of all demons who enter the Human Realm. The celestials have a copy, but we keep our own copy as well." What I heard from that was that sometimes demons entered outside the regular channels.

He released my hand. I hadn't even realized he'd still held it. I stepped closer to Tristan, stumbling as I tripped over a pile of books. Tristan reached a hand out and steadied me. Milo watched the action and, with a small smile, said to Tristan, "I cannot help you, sorry. But watch your back. You were specifically named, which does not bode well for you."

"My thanks. What about the list from a few months ago? Zoey, what was the date?"

I stuttered out the date my mother died.

Milo brought a hand up to his chin, thoughtful. "I might be able to get you that list. I'll see what I can do."

"Appreciated. And in return?"

"I'll let you know."

Tristan nodded. "We'll be on our way."

Milo waved us out. "Take care, Tristan. It was a pleasure to meet you, Zoey."

****

Exiting the shop, I felt like I could breathe for the first time in over an hour. I may have been one of them, but I also wasn't. Not really. Outside, I rested against a red brick building and took in a deep breath of cool, crisp air.

"Milo was kind of…intense. Is he usually like that?"

"Yes."

Tristan walked a few feet away and then paused, head cocked to the side, listening. That was the only warning I had before a fist buried itself in my side and threw me down the street. Slammed into the ground, five shapes converged on Tristan. The attackers varied in height but all had long arms and legs. Short gray fur and black clothes covered their bodies. Dark eyes glimmered with malice, but black cloth concealed the rest of their faces.

"No!" Picking myself up off the ground, ignoring

the stabbing pain in my side, I ran back and shoved an assailant away from Tristan. Or at least, I tried to. He didn't budge. I shoved harder, his pelt coarse and prickly under my hands. Another attacked, and Tristan easily evaded. I stepped aside and managed to dodge, but then there was another.

Tristan shoved me out of the way and turned to face them again.

"Zoey, run!"

There were too many. There was no way I was leaving him. Ignoring him, I searched the rocky ground. The pavement over here was broken up a bit, but most pieces were too small to use. I needed a weapon. A discarded liquor bottle was half hidden in a grassy spot a few feet away. I grabbed it, broke it against the side of the building, and stabbed the pointy end toward another attacker. It stuck in with an awful squelch as I pierced him in the side. I stumbled back, feeling sick. He grunted in pain, still fighting Tristan with the bottle shard hanging from his side. He swung back at me, and I sidestepped, avoiding the blow but getting in the way of someone else's swing.

A knife slashed, and the pain was immediate and intense. I pulled my arm in tight, looking down at the wound, preparing myself to see that my arm might be cut off, but it didn't look deep. The cut itself was shallow but long. They'd barely gotten me, but it stung something fierce. I let out a shaky breath. They'd likely been aiming for Tristan and I got in the way.

Arm throbbing, I grabbed one of the larger rocks from the ground and came back and slugged one of them with all my weight behind it. "Ahh!"

They didn't budge, just bled a little from the impact

of the rock.

I shook my hand, dancing around in pain, the rock now in my other hand. Tristan was a blur of movement, knives slashing left and right and keeping everyone at bay. He kept picking at them, and they couldn't get close, always just out of reach. He got one, and they fell to the concrete, not moving. They were all using knives, which seemed odd. Wouldn't a sword work better? Then, as suddenly as they had appeared, they disappeared into a mysterious mist. The same dark mist that appeared the night Mom was attacked, although these men had looked nothing like the demon responsible for her death.

Walking up to Tristan, I asked, "Where did they go? Are you okay?" I searched him up and down, and despite a rather impressive black eye, he seemed fine.

Tristan glanced over at me and seemed to hone in on the rip in my shirt. He grabbed me and looked at my arm, which was lightly bleeding. He prodded the wound gently and then put my arm down, apparently deciding I would live. "They were likely here illegally and noted someone tracking them and had to leave before they were tagged. I'm fine. You're not. Why didn't you run? You can't fight five trained fighters."

He searched the rest of my body and touched my face—which, now that he touched it, felt a little raw. Likely courtesy of smashing into the street after that first punch. I turned my head away. "No? Well, neither can you. I was trying to help. *Asshole.*" I whispered the last part, but he heard.

He grabbed my chin, forcing me to look at him. "It was stupid. You're not a fighter. Besides, they weren't trying to kill me, just rough me up a bit."

"How do you know?"

"They were trained fighters. We were outnumbered, but they carried knives and none of them were going for a killing blow. I have a lot of enemies. There was no need for you to get hurt as well."

I ignored him. He and I clearly had a difference of opinion here. There was no way I was leaving someone I knew to get beaten up. It didn't matter how badly I fought or how outnumbered we were. It wasn't happening. I changed the subject. "Was that about the key?"

"No, Milo warned us. That was my father telling me to mind my own business."

"Your dad? He sent trained killers to beat you up? Nice family. Should we worry about those guys you stabbed?"

Tristan was wiping his blades against his shirt. "No. Everyone is fair game in this realm. My father shouldn't have sent them."

Dropping the rock I still held, I brushed off my pants. There was something wet near the hem. Wine from the bottle, maybe? If it was demon blood, I might vomit. Therefore, it was definitely wine. "Any other murderous family members?"

He gave a half smile. "A sister, but she's not quite as bad. She's kind of sweet and usually just sends venomous snakes and such." His smile faded. "My brother is…indisposed."

I checked my arm. It bled a little, but wasn't that bad. "Oh, is that all? They sound lovely."

He walked over to me. "Come on. Let me walk you home."

We kept a nice, companionable silence as we walked through the tree-lined streets. The leaves were starting to change color, and the rainbow of reds and oranges both lifted my spirits and reminded me of the blood and death behind us.

Tristan was being weirdly nice. He even walked at a semi-normal pace for once, which I knew had to be for my benefit. Did he feel bad about the attack? His body was giving off a lot of heat, and I leaned closer, letting it warm me. I was shaky and cold. Adrenaline, maybe?

It took three tries for me to get the shop door unlocked. Thankfully, I didn't get any snide comments from Tristan.

"Eat something, clean and bandage your arm, and get some rest. I'm going to ward your place, just in case. Stay inside, and you should be fine. If the cut gets worse, let me know. Here's the number for the bubble tea shop. They can send a message to me." He wrote the number on my palm with a black pen from the front desk. Capping it and tossing it back on the desk, he said, "See you tomorrow."

"Wait." I touched his arm, and he looked at me in surprise. I realized I'd never initiated contact with him before. I pulled my hand back. "Before you do that, could you show me how to read my manual? Please."

He sighed, running a hand through his hair and making it stick up on one side. He looked tired, and I instantly felt bad for asking, but when else would I ask? "Where is it?"

I led him into the shop and locked the door behind him. Walking through the store to the stairs in the back, I realized I was walking a guy up to my bedroom. I thought of my room and realized the place was trashed. I hadn't made my bed, there were clothes everywhere, and a large stuffed bear was on the bed. My bra was on the floor! I took a deep breath. Nothing to worry about. I wished my racing heart would believe that. He was a demon. A cute demon, but he was still a demon. Who cared what he thought of my room? I wasn't trying to impress him.

I paused in front of my room and turned to him. "Give me thirty seconds to clean up first." Without giving him time to respond, I opened the door, went in, and closed it behind me. My bra was still on the floor with my panties. At least they were lacy and cute. I threw my dirty clothes into the hamper and put the red alarm clock back on my nightside table. I tossed the covers over the bed, and hid the stuffed animal under the bed, and then the door opened.

"It has been thirty seconds."

I blushed. We stood there in silence for a moment. And then I remembered what he was here for. I rushed over to the mahogany nightstand, pulled the top drawer open, grabbed the manual, and shoved the drawer closed again. Thankfully, there was nothing too embarrassing inside. I handed him the brown leather–covered book. "Every time I open it, there's gibberish." Hands clasped behind my back, I rocked on my heels while he flipped through it.

He closed the book. "It was coded for a demon, not a celestial." He walked closer and brushed my hair away from my neck and the registration mark, and then looked back at the book again. "I don't know why they would have coded it this way. It doesn't make any sense. Who's your transition coach?"

"She said her name was Regina."

He stopped looking at the book and let it fall by his side, his eyes wide with surprise. "They gave you

Regina? Part demon, Regina?"

I sank onto the edge of my bed, the fluffy blue and green comforter giving slightly under my weight. "Oh, so you've met her? Is she as bad as she seems?"

"She's worse. You need a celestial to code the book for you. There aren't many coaches, so it's not too odd to get assigned someone outside your species, but the coaches know better than to give you a book that's been coded wrong. She probably did it on purpose. Did you do anything to piss her off?"

I toyed with the soft blue fabric, not wanting to meet his gaze. "You mean besides see past her glamour?"

He gave a loud sigh. "That'd do it."

The door banged softly against the wall, and I looked up.

Tristan was paused in the doorway, on his way out. "Celestials don't really hang out with demons, but I'll try to find someone to bring the book to. Get some rest. You look beat."

"Okay, thanks." I was not going to get some rest, but there was no point in arguing with him about it. I studied him. He had dark-blue bruising on his face and had been walking a little funny earlier. I stood and walked toward him, hand raised to touch his bruised cheek. "Are you okay?"

He stepped away, putting space between us, and I dropped my hand. "Nothing I can't fix."

I nodded and then walked him to the front, closing and locking the door behind him. After saving the bubble tea number in my phone, I took a quick shower, bandaged my arm, ate a light lunch, and got ready for my date. A nice human date. With a cute human boy. I wasn't stupid; I was resilient. A little nice and normal was what I needed right now. I had a tiny pang of guilt that Tristan was warding the shop for me and I was sneaking out. But he'd said that the attack was meant for him, not me. I wasn't in danger anymore. Right?

Chapter 13

Walking toward the coffee shop, my gaze darted around, every little sound grabbing my attention. A shape moved between the buildings, casting an enormous shadow. I froze, heart racing, hand reaching for the screwdriver I'd grabbed from Dad's tool chest. A shaggy creature burst out between cars, tail wagging, and rushed down the street.

I let out a shaky breath. A dog. It was just a dog. Not even a big dog. It was one of the cute shih tzu ones, all fluffy fur. What was wrong with me? I hadn't been this jumpy earlier.

As I stood still in the middle of the sidewalk, people were staring. I forced my legs to move and continued on my way. This was stupid. I came here at least once a day. It was Joe's coffee shop. Why was I so skittish? It was one block away.

Opening the door, a burst of heat rushed over me, paired with the sweet aroma of pumpkin spice and coffee. I loved this time of year—the colorful leaves, the spicy scents, and the soon-to-be creepy decorations. I focused on the positive and tried to forget the last few days.

Carter was at the counter, chatting with Joe, the owner, who was here for one of his rare visits. I waved, and Carter fist bumped Joe and headed over. He gave me a tentative hug, his arms strong and comforting. "Glad you could make it."

I squeezed him back and breathed in his coffee and fresh soap scent, glad we were now on hugging terms. I could use more hugs, especially from someone as cute as him. "Me too."

"What can I get you? Pumpkin spiced chai tea latte? I noticed that's what you had the other day." It was my usual order lately. I nodded, pleased he'd noticed, and he winked and said, "Be right back."

Looking around the familiar shop, my nerves disappeared. It was midafternoon. I was in a coffee shop. With humans. I'd found I could See auras if I focused and human auras were definitely white. The first time I'd seen one was at home. I'd been glaring at Dad, and a faint shimmer of white had appeared around him. It had been soft and out of focus, just a halo of light. I hadn't figured the other colors out yet, but plain white auras glowed comfortingly around me. The only Mythic was a stooped woman in the corner with four arms instead of two. She had a light green aura and was working on a crossword. Crosswords were not the stuff of evil villains. Everything would be okay.

Handing me my drink, Carter reached a hand down and said, "Let's go for a walk."

Fear came rushing back, making my stomach drop. "Are you sure? There are tons of empty seats." I gestured around at the mostly empty tables.

"It's kind of crowded in a different way." He looked across at Joe and his wife, Delia, who were watching us. They smiled and waved.

I smiled and waved back, and then took Carter's hand and followed him out the door. It was cold outside, but the sun warmed my back as we strolled down the street. Normally I'd love a walk this time of year, especially with the sun shining. Unfortunately, by the time we were a few blocks away, the dread I'd been working to suppress had returned, making my heart race and my palms sweat.

I took a deep breath and focused on Carter so I wouldn't be tempted to keep jumping at shadows. The attackers hadn't even been after me. I was being ridiculous. "The other day, you said you were originally from the coast. Do you miss it?"

Carter shook his head, auburn hair shifting with the movement. "Nah, I love it here, but I do miss surfing. We're a bit too far from the ocean for me to go much anymore. You ever been surfing?"

I shook my head, casually dropping my sweaty palm and sipping on the creamy chai tea latte. I let the vanilla and spices warm my insides while he talked on about surfing. The technicalities flew over my head, but I loved that he loved it and enjoyed listening to the passion in his voice.

A shadow passed overhead, the darkening path making me catch my breath. I looked up, muscles tense, ready to run.

A plane.

My shoulders relaxed. I really was jumping at shadows today. Shaking myself, I attempted to focus on the story Carter was telling about surfing with his family, but my mind kept drifting. I couldn't help but notice that the streets were deserted. That didn't seem normal. There were usually more people around this time of day.

Red and orange leaves fell to the ground, blanketing everything in the warm colors of fall. Their movement accentuated how silent it had become. Where were all the people? I interrupted Carter, grabbing his arm. "Let's head back."

"Huh? Shoot. I'm sorry, I've been blathering on, and I haven't asked you anything about you. I love surfing so much I forget sometimes others find it a bit boring." His ears and cheeks turned a faint shade of pink. "What's your favorite thing to do?"

He thinks I'm bored? Shit! I was ruining my date, jumping at nothing. It had been a dog and a plane earlier. This was probably just a stalled car or something blocking a road. I took a deep breath, clenching my fingers to keep the trembling down. I needed to fix this. I smiled, trying to work some enthusiasm into my voice. "It's okay. I enjoy listening to you. It makes me want to try surfing. You'll have to take me sometime and give me a lesson."

He seemed to relax at that.

Another shadow passed overhead. I jumped. "Did you see that?" Looking up, there was no plane. Was it some sort of flying creature, or was I imagining things? Either way, it was time to go.

"See what?"

"Never mind." I pulled on Carter's arm, looping mine through his, and steered him back the way we'd come. "Come on, let me show you one of my favorite cupcake shops." It was always packed. Perfect. Just a few more blocks.

Up ahead was a bench, and Carter steered me toward it. It had a placard on it that said, *In Loving Memory*. "We're still working on our coffee. Why don't we sit here first and chat? Unless I did bore you and you're trying to get rid of me?"

"Of course not."

He pulled me down beside him, warm brown eyes crinkling as he smiled. "Then sit with me. What's your favorite cupcake flavor?"

"Chocolate Caramel Lava Cake." I didn't even have to think about that one, thankfully. I didn't want to stop in this isolated corner, but couldn't think of a reason not to. I looked around. The dark shadow had passed. Maybe it was a large bird and I'd just missed it? I was being super jumpy. I took a deep breath and settled onto the bench next to him. "What's yours?"

"Chocolate S'mores. It has the chocolate, but it also has the graham cracker crust on the bottom and marshmallowy goodness in the middle. It is beyond perfect. Have you tried it?"

I thought back and fondly remembered the gooey morsel. He had good taste. "It is one of my favorites heated. It has to be microwaved, but I like some others better cold."

"You know, I've never thought of microwaving it. I guess that's because I would never be able to wait that long to eat it."

I laughed, letting my worry slip away and my shoulders ease. "Yeah, but I used to live a few blocks away from one of their stores, so not that long a wait."

"We'll have to get two to go so we can eat them later." He leaned down and swept up a handful of leaves and presented them to me. "For you, milady."

I took the colorful bouquet. "Why, thank you. To what do I owe for this oh-so-great honor?"

He leaned in and kissed me. His lips were warm and tasted chocolatey, like the mocha he'd been drinking earlier. It was just a quick kiss. A sweet kiss. One that was firm but tentative at the same time. He brushed a strand of hair behind my ear, fingers caressing the dark locks. "I'm glad you asked me to meet up the other day. I honestly was half expecting a crazy old lady."

I leaned into him, smelling his clean, fresh scent. "What? Not a crazy old man?" Grinning, I said, "I'm glad I did too."

I initiated the kiss this time, leaning in and wrapping my arms loosely around his neck. It was sweet and gentle. Not earth shattering like everyone wrote about, but it was nice. He was nice. I needed that in my life right now. Nice and normal.

A gust of wind slammed us into the bench, and my coffee cup was flung across the path, landing in the gutter. We both laughed, surprised, working to regain our balance. I looked up at the clear blue sky, and my stomach dropped, laughter dying on my tongue. "Where did that wind come from?"

He chuckled, leaning in to kiss me quickly. "I don't know, but let's get going before it blows us away." He took my hand and helped me off the bench. Once I was standing, another gust of wind hit, this time blowing us in opposite directions.

Something wind shouldn't be able to do.

My heart raced, and I grabbed onto the bench with both hands and held on tight. The air chilled and my breath came out in misty puffs. Carter got yanked away and was slammed into a nearby wall so hard he fell unconscious to the ground.

"Carter!" Reflexively reaching for him, I released the bench and was whipped away. The strong wind picked me up, dragging me across the grass toward the hard wall Carter had crashed into. I stretched my arms out, pulling up fistfuls of grass to stop myself. Before my head could slam into the wall, strong arms reached around my middle and pulled me to a hard chest. My insides lurched as I was tossed over a shoulder in a fireman carry, and each powerful step jostled me as we sped away.

"Help!" I screamed, struggling to get free.

My abductor squeezed me tighter. "Stop squirming, you heathen. I *am* helping."

I knew that annoyed tone and relaxed. From my vantage point, I couldn't see his face, just his butt. He did have a good butt. "Tristan?"

"Who else, you daft woman? Now shush. I'm trying to get them off our trail."

"Who? Who attacked us? Is Carter okay?"

"Qui-et." He dragged the word out. "I can't hear them with all your yammering."

I swallowed my protest as Tristan moved more quickly than I thought possible. He dodged through alleys and backyards, staying in the shadows, away from the crowded streets. Likely a good thing, or someone would call the cops on him for abducting me, seeing as I was hanging over his shoulder like baggage.

After a while, he stopped, dumping me onto squishy, water-logged grass. It was cold and smelled faintly of manure.

"We lost them."

My fingers dug into soft mud. I looked around and noticed the river. He'd brought us to the waterfront. Wet and muddy, I asked, "Did you have to throw me in the mud?"

He shot me an annoyed scowl. "Did you have to leave the bloody house? I spent over an hour warding that damn place, just for you to leave and lead the assassins right to you."

"Assassins?" I jumped to my feet, wiping my palms against my jeans. "What assassins? You said the attackers were after you." I stepped forward, finger pointed accusingly. "*You.* Not me. If they were after me, don't you think that's something you should have mentioned? Maybe so I didn't do something stupid, like leave the house and hang out with a human and let him get knocked out?" I thought of Carter lying still on the ground. "Is Carter okay? How badly was he hurt?"

Tristan ran both hands through his thick hair, making it stick up in all directions. "Who knows? And I didn't know they were after you until recently. That's why I was looking for you. Somehow, word got out that you know something about the key. Who did you talk to about it besides me? Your boyfriend?" Tristan's words were accusatory, and his runes brightened, creating a menacing glow.

My stomach churned. "No one. Not even my dad." How could people know? He must be wrong. "We need to go check on Carter and make sure he's okay." I glanced toward the river, trying to orient myself so I could go find him. And to avoid looking at the scary demon. "You're glowing."

He glanced down at himself, and the runes immediately stopped their fiery dance. He took a deep breath and said, "Stop trying to get yourself killed. We have to get back to your place. I didn't want to drag you there over my shoulder—there are too many people in that area. I'll check on the boy after I get you home and behind my wards."

He had a point. One I most definitely did not want to admit. At least not out loud. I took a step and slipped and almost fell, but he caught me. I shrugged him off. "I'm fine. Let's go." I didn't know why I was so angry with him. He had come to help me, and he had saved me from the assassins, but what I really wanted to do right then was punch him in the face. I took a few deep breaths and tried to ground myself.

We walked in silence. Him speeding along as usual at an inhuman pace. Falling behind, I focused on a trail of colored mist following him. Was he casting a spell? The longer I went without the necklace, the better I found I was able to control my Sight. I focused my attention and tried not to See it. At first, nothing happened. I tried to follow the connection I had with the mist to myself and see where it led. Then I pinched it like a wire. The color slowly faded. It was like turning a light switch off in my brain, and it gave me a burst of energy. I wondered if using my gift all the time was part of why I was so tired sometimes.

Letting the switch go, I focused on the reddish mist, but staring at it just made my head hurt. I had no idea what it did or how to find out. Finally, I gave up and asked Tristan, "What are you doing?"

"Walking." His voice was curt and angry. Okay, I deserved that. Thinking more on it, leaving for a date had been a bad idea. But it was partly his fault for not sharing that people might be after me, too. If he hadn't said the last attack was just his dad sending people after him, I might have been more cautious.

"What's the red mist?"

He looked up. "The what now?"

I pointed. "The red mist that's following you. What is it?"

"You can See it? It's the cloaking spell. Once I get

you home, I'll double check that no one followed us and then go check on your *boyfriend*."

"He's not my boyfriend. At least not yet. That was our first date. I have a feeling it might also have been our last. I just deserted him, unconscious, in the middle of town with no explanation." I put my head in my hands. "Carter must think I'm a horrible person."

We walked the rest of the way in silence, and rather than focus on my quickly deteriorating love life, I spent the time studying the red mist and the faint symbols that seemed to float within. Was that the spell? If I focused enough, would I be able to see how he cast it? I tried focusing, but only succeeded in giving myself a headache.

When we got back to the shop, Tristan said, "Stay. I don't care how cute the boy is."

I blushed. "That wasn't why I left."

"Both a truth and a lie." He shook his head. "It doesn't matter. Stay here while I search the area. I'll be back. Promise you'll stay."

"Fine." I glanced around at the overflowing shelves. Should I open the store? I didn't really feel up to customers, but I'd be there. I looked around, debating.

"Don't open the store. And you didn't promise. I want to hear your promise."

Him telling me not to open the store made me want to change my mind, but instead I said, "I promise," in an exaggerated way. He wasn't bringing out the best in me.

He slammed the door shut behind him, making the sign bounce against the window. He might have been mad, but I was mad too. And worried. I sent a quick text to Carter.

— *You okay?* — Pacing back and forth, I went out

back and sat in the small garden. The wards, glowing faintly red, looked like they extended to the fountain. I grabbed a handful of gravel and started tossing the stones one by one at an old birdhouse.

Miss. Score. Miss.

Len hobbled up, dark form stiff. "Why are. You out here? You're never. Out here."

I picked up another small piece of gravel and threw it. Score. "I'm waiting."

"Waiting. For what?" His head was tilted at a quizzical angle, and even though his expression hadn't changed, I could sense the curiosity.

"To see if the guy I was on a date with is okay and if he'll ever speak to me again. And to see if the goons who attacked us followed me home." I checked my phone. No response yet. Wait, were those three dots? They disappeared. Then reappeared. Then disappeared.

Just freaking send already!

I wondered what he thought had happened. Did he think a random tornado came and pushed him into a wall, or did he think we were attacked? Either way, there was no way around the fact that he had been wounded and unconscious and I left him there. Alone. It's not like I could tell him I was abducted by a demon to keep me safe from assassins. Even if he believed me, it would put him in danger.

Finally, there was the ding telling me I got a text back.

— I'm embarrassed that I fell and bumped my head so hard I had to go home. Try again sometime? —

I was dumbfounded but wrote out, *— Sure —* And then hesitated, finger over the send button. Had Tristan changed his memory? He must have, but that didn't

141

change the danger I was to be around. I erased my answer and typed, —*I'm not sure, but I'm glad you're okay* — I hit Send before I could change my mind. I sat there, foot tapping, staring at the three dots, waiting for his reply.

— *Still friends?* —

I breathed out a sigh of relief. — *Of course* —

He sent a smiley emoji.

I put my phone back in my pocket. "Damn." I'd really liked him.

"The little. Box. Isn't saying. What you. Would like?" Len's gravelly voice interrupted my thoughts, and I jumped.

"Sorry, I forgot you were there." I blushed. "That was an awful thing to say. I'm sorry. I had to break up with a guy I like because, well, it's not safe to be around me right now."

"Sounds like. A hard. But wise. Decision. Much like. What your. Mother did. For you."

I turned, curiosity bright in my mind. "What did she do?"

"Hiding you. Moving every. Year. Making a new. Home. Each. Time." His black wing moved more smoothly than I would have thought the stone could move as he gestured to the small garden. "But it was. Hard."

"You knew her well, then? What can you tell me about her?" I turned, eager to learn more, but Len was gone. "Len?" Of course he was gone. No one ever wanted to tell me anything about Mom. I kicked a rock, which just made my toe throb.

My arm ached too, and I realized I should probably inspect the cut on my arm. I pulled my sleeve up and took off the bandage. Small red lines ran from the thin scrape.

Was it getting infected? I pulled the sleeve back and stood to go inside and put some antibiotic ointment on it, when there was a rustling off to my left. The bushes moved aside, and I saw Tristan's now familiar scowl as he trudged in.

"Your boyfriend is fine."

I put my hands in my pockets, scuffing my shoe on the ground. "Thank you. You adjusted his memory? That was kind of you."

"It is standard protocol. I am not kind."

"Okay." I dragged the word out. "Is everything good?"

He nodded, standing there. Not moving. Not leaving.

"If so, go do whatever you were going to do." I waved him away. I wanted to fix up my arm and then sit and have a good cry for my lost love life, thank you very much. A brooding bodyguard kind of ruined it.

His scowl deepened, but he didn't leave.

I looked around the yard to see if there was some hidden danger I was missing, but it was the same long grass and dirt that was there before. No bad guys that I could See. Why wasn't he leaving? "What?"

"I was going to ask if you wanted to come to a Mythic hangout with me tonight. There is a type of demon that goes to this place that matches the description you gave for the guy who killed your mother. I wasn't sure if tonight was a good night or not."

I squealed, barely resisting the urge to hug him. "Yes, thank you! Are we leaving now?"

"No, I'll be back in a few hours. Wear something a bit more…" He hesitated.

I rolled my eyes. "Spit it out."

He sighed. "Revealing." His hands moved to point at my body without really looking at me. "Girls don't wear so many clothes to this club, and we want to blend in."

I nodded. "Dress like a slut. Got it. Charming place we're going to."

He laughed, and the rough sound warmed me. I didn't think he laughed much. "We are hunting a demon, aren't we?" His blue eyes sparkled and almost made me want to like him. Almost.

"Yeah, yeah." I waved him away, excitement coursing through me. I was going to get answers tonight, I just knew it. "Go away. I promise I'll be ready. What time?"

"Eight. See you then."

I looked up to say goodbye, but he was gone, only the slight movement of the bushes betrayed his passage. What was it with everyone disappearing, and how could I learn how to do it?

Chapter 14

After taking another shower, I got dressed. Or I tried to. Twenty minutes of flipping through the neatly hung clothes in my closet, and I was still in my towel. I needed to borrow something. My mind immediately went to Ava, a friend from my last school. She'd have something, but we hadn't talked in weeks. She'd tried to keep in touch after I'd moved, but I'd blown her off so many times she'd stopped inviting me places. Ava had been a good friend, and I should have tried harder to stay in touch. She was great at this kind of stuff. Pulling out my phone, the glittery case catching the light, I quickly texted her before I could change my mind. I got an immediate ding in response.

— You're going to a club?! I'll be right over! I have a dozen things that will look great on you. And when I get over there, we'll discuss why I'm not invited. —

Laughing, I texted her back. *— I'm going with a guy.—* I pulled on a long red robe and underwear and started combing through my clothes again. A wave of dizziness washed over me, and I leaned against the wall for a minute until it passed. I needed to eat something.

Grabbing a granola bar from the kitchen, I chowed down and then went back to flipping through clothes. Still nothing. I was probably the lamest teenage girl for miles. The best I could come up with was a pair of super-tight dark jeans with holes in them. My legs looked great.

I paired them with strappy sandals that had a slight heel. Not quite clubbing material, but I could walk in them, which was a plus. I was still shirtless when the doorbell rang. It was broken so only made a halfhearted ding noise. One of the many repairs on the to-do list.

I ran to the back door to let Ava in. We used the back door for personal guests and the front for the shop. Her curly black head poked over the top of a humongous pile of clothes. How many people did she think she was dressing?

"Okay, so who is this guy? Is he why I haven't seen you in a while? I know some girls go AWOL over a guy, but I hadn't pictured you as the type. You guys in looove?"

I blushed and grabbed half the pile of clothes, then led Ava upstairs to my room. "No, we're just friends."

"He's taking you to a club. I think we need to assume he's ready to take the next step. Are you ready? I know you've dated a few guys, but none of them were for more than a few weeks."

"Ugh, they were all so awful. Jeremy couldn't keep his hands to himself and was always trolling other girls. Derek failed Geometry twice because he kept skipping class to go get high." I shoved my door open and tossed the clothes on the bed.

"What about Andrew? He seemed nice." She dumped her pile next to mine and then dug through and started putting her top choices in a separate pile. I grabbed a short black dress and put it back in the maybe pile. She raised an eyebrow and then tossed it back in the yes pile.

"He believed women shouldn't work and should sit at home all day serving men and having babies."

"Definitely not your type."

"Nope."

She tapped a long, manicured nail on her chin. "Although I might not mind that…A cute guy working, and I get to stay home all day with our two point five children." She grabbed the first of her top picks and threw it at me. "Note to self—spend more time around Andrew."

I laughed and pulled on the tight gold top. I looked in the mirror. It was backless and was a bit much for me. I pulled it off, and she tossed me another. Ava saw my arm and gasped.

"What is that? Go wash it out and put on antibiotic ointment. Now!"

I didn't even try to tell her I'd already done that. She was pushy that way. I treated it again with her supervising and clucking over me. When I was done, she drew some lines around the redness. "If it gets any worse, you are skipping your date and going straight to urgent care. Understood?"

I nodded, not wanting to argue, but she was totally over-reacting. It was just a little red and didn't even hurt. Besides, this was my first real lead. I didn't want to miss it. After a few more tops, she tossed me a deep-red shirt that was made of a soft, suede-like fabric. It was corset like and had laces up the sides, showing small bits of skin. Best of all, it was long-sleeved.

I was wearing my push-up bra, and it pressed my small breasts up against the edge of the corset, making me look moderately well endowed. I looked great. Ava and I curled my hair and let the dark waves run wildly down my back.

I was looking for jewelry when I heard a deep voice

say, "You look stunning."

I jumped, heart in my throat. "Thanks. So do you." Tristan was leaning in the doorway, wearing leather pants and a leather vest with nothing else for a shirt. His runes covered his arms and swirled toward the middle of his chest in a sweeping pattern. He had his sword on his hip and some knives strapped to his legs. Dangerous and sexy. I tried to keep myself from staring at his perfect abs. Demons should not be allowed to have six packs. It was completely unfair.

Dragging my eyes away, I said, "Tristan, this is Ava. Ava, Tristan."

He smiled a charming smile and said, "Nice to meet you."

I vaguely wondered what Ava saw when she looked at him. And what she thought about him just appearing in my bedroom without even knocking at the back door. I'd have to have a word with him about that.

"You too. You guys have fun. Talk to you later, Zoey." Behind Tristan's back, she fanned herself, mouthing *So hot,* and *You'd better text me later.*

I gave her a slight nod.

Tristan turned to look, but she was already headed down the stairs.

He quietly asked, "Do you have a large purse? If we can take the book to the club, I know someone who might be able to change the spell."

"Sure." I rummaged through my closet and pulled out a large black purse, a staple for me. It kind of ruined the outfit, but I transferred everything from my small purse, added the book, and was ready to go.

When we got outside, Tristan directed me to a red motorcycle parked out front. He put on a helmet and tossed me a second one. I fumbled, but caught it. So much for all that work on my hair. Sighing, I strapped it on and gingerly got on the bike behind Tristan. "How does this work?"

He grabbed my hands and wrapped them around his bare waist. His skin was smooth and warm, rippling muscles flexed as he started the bike. He said something, but I completely blanked. "Excuse me?"

He turned and said, "Hang on tight. You'll be fine." With that, he revved the engine and took off down the street. I clung to him, trying not to think of his bare chest under my hands or my legs pressed tight against his.

My face was so hot, I knew I was beet red. I tried to put some space between us without letting go, but we were going too fast, and I didn't want to die. Burying my face against his leather-clad back, taking shelter from the wind, I was glad he couldn't see me.

He liked to go fast. Thankfully, the speed helped cool down the blazing blush. He took a curve sharply, and I squealed, clinging to him tighter. Good thing Dad hadn't seen me climb onto this bike. He would have had a conniption fit.

When we hit the east side, he slowed down, stopping in front of a nondescript beige building. It was two stories and had windows, but they had that reflective stuff on them you couldn't see in through. I'd always wondered who would want windows like that. *Were there Others that couldn't be in sunlight?* "Do vampires exist?"

"What?" Tristan turned off the bike, staring at me with a bewildered expression.

We took our helmets off, and I handed him mine, trying to finger comb my hair to its pre-helmet state.

"Vampires. You know, they have fangs and drink your blood." I gestured to the building, untangling a few strands of dark hair that had gotten knotted. "I saw the tinted windows and was wondering if the protective coat helped with sunlight too, and then I wondered if there really were vampires and…"

He was staring back at me, smirking.

"You know what? Ignore the question. It was stupid." I got off the bike and then stumbled on my mini heels in the gravel. I should have avoided heels altogether. Tristan, off the bike without me even seeing, steadied me, his warm hands on my waist. His quickness was both welcome and alarming.

"Vampires are real. Sort of. They are rare. They drink blood and live a long time and can use magic, but they are not affected by sunlight, garlic, or any of those myths."

"No pointy sticks?"

He chuckled. "No, no pointy sticks. That'll just make them mad. Can you walk?" He looked questioningly at my heels.

I shrugged him off and grabbed my purse. "Yes." He let me go and walked ahead. I shivered and immediately missed his body heat. Now that I wasn't right next to him, it was chilly out.

"Come on. The entrance is around the back."

Guess they didn't want random people showing up. I followed him toward the back and saw a group of girls I used to be friends with at my old school hanging around the front of the club next door. They were passing a bottle around and chatting.

"Hey, Zoey," Amber said.

I waved. "Hey." I stopped by them, not sure what

else to say.

Princess—her mom named her after *all* the princesses—stepped up, giving me a once-over. She tossed her long blonde hair over her shoulder. Her short, tight dress accentuated her long, slender legs. "What are you doing here? Please don't tell me you're seriously trying to hit up some company in that trashy outfit. Where'd you get it? A thrift shop? No one is going to let you in, even if you brought a fake ID. You look twelve."

My stomach dropped. I hadn't thought the outfit was that bad. And did I need a fake ID? I didn't even think to ask. I stood there, dumfounded, unsure how to respond. I looked to Jules and Amber for help, but they looked away, careful not to make eye contact.

I blinked back tears. I'd half expected something like this from Princess, she often went out of her way to be cruel, but Jules and Amber not sticking up for me hit a little harder. They could have ignored her, said something nice, told her to be quiet. Anything. We hadn't talked in a while, but I'd thought we were friends.

I was trying to think of a response when a muscled arm crept around my middle and pulled me back against a hard chest. Tristan bent down and kissed the side of my neck, his soft lips sending shivers down my spine. "She doesn't need to pick up any company. She already has some. And I think she looks great. Perhaps you could take some tips?"

My chest warmed. Tristan was sticking up for me. Princess stood there with her mouth hanging open, for once unable to come up with something to say. Tristan squeezed me again and then led me away.

I leaned into him, surprised and bolstered by the support.

When we'd gotten out of hearing range, I whispered, "Thank you."

He said, "Don't thank me yet. If anyone saw they'll think we're together. Most don't like demon caste. Especially an Enforcer like me. They fear us. They wouldn't date us. They won't say anything to your face, but they might be cruel behind your back."

"They'd have done it anyway. It is easier to face ridicule if there is someone to stand next to." As I said it, I realized it was true. "Let's stand together and get through tonight."

Tristan reached down and grabbed my hand, long fingers entwining with mine. "Let's." When he led me toward the entrance, the world started spinning, and I stumbled. He caught me before I could fall to the ground.

"I'm sorry. I keep having these dizzy spells. It's so weird."

Tristan immediately shoved my shirt off my forearm. The red was already creeping past the bandages. He swept me up, into his arms. "Damn it. I told you to let me know if it was getting worse."

I wanted to tell him to put me down, but everything started sounding kind of funny, like an out-of-tune radio station, and then there was nothing.

Chapter 15

When I came to, I was lying on a hard bed in a room I'd never seen before. There was medical equipment on a nearby table, next to a small kitchenette with cheery yellow cabinets. My borrowed shirt and bandages were gone, the cut on full display. I was still in my bra and was covered by a blanket, but red heated my face. *Who took off my shirt?*

I held the blanket tight to my chest and focused on what I could see of the wound. I had to admit, it looked awful. When it had been a scratch, I had let myself ignore it, but the creeping red marks were taking over my arm, well past the lines Ava had drawn earlier, and the cut itself seemed deeper than before.

A bent old woman poked at the wound. "Ah, that got her up. How you feeling, honey? Does this hurt?" She poked me again.

"Oww!" *Sadistic bitch.* "Yes, it hurts. Where's my shirt?"

Tristan's deep voice came from behind me. "Unfortunately, it didn't make it."

"What?" I twisted, trying to see him.

"She cut it off. I tried to tell her it was just your arm, but she was in a hurry."

Damn. Ava was going to kill me. I owed her a new shirt. The old lady poked me again, and I tried to pull my arm away, but it was clamped down in some sort of contraption. "What's this for?" I rattled the cuffs, trying to shake them open.

"I'm going to draw out the poison, but it will sting and I don't want you moving."

"Poison? What poison?"

"The poison on the knife. Which I would have known about sooner if you'd mentioned the wound getting worse." Tristan's voice was clipped. "Like I'd asked." I couldn't see his face since he was behind me, but he definitely sounded annoyed.

The old woman walked with small, dainty steps to a stove, a mouse-like tail twitching behind her. I lowered my voice. "I might have paid closer attention if you'd mentioned I was on the lookout for poison." The woman used big mitts to pull a boiling pan of liquid off the burner, the bubbles visible from the elevated bed.

I craned my neck, trying to get a better look. "What's that?"

"Your cure."

"My…You think you're going to pour boiling liquid on me?" I searched for a latch around the cuffs holding my wrist and elbow in place, pulling at them with my fingers. "No, absolutely not. Let me out of this thing." I tried to slide off the bed, arm still trapped, but Tristan grabbed me. He sat on the bed behind me and pulled me into his arms, holding me tight and keeping my hands away from the restraints.

"I've got her. Do it."

I struggled, but he'd gripped me in just the right way that I couldn't budge. "Let me go!"

His fingers dug in, holding me firm. She poured the liquid, and it scorched over my skin before running into grooves off to the side of my arm.

I screamed. My skin was on fire, pain shooting up and down my arm in a never-ending wave of agony. Spots dotted my vision as I thrashed and yelled, but Tristan held me still. My skin turned red, and blisters formed. I could smell the acrid scent of my flesh burning, and I twisted violently, trying to get away.

After a minute, the burning agony eased, numbing. I stopped thrashing. Stopped screaming, throat sore. Trembling, I looked down at my arm and whimpered. It looked like a hunk of meat, raw with large open blisters that had popped and oozed.

As I stared, one of the blisters started to shrink. Then another. The burns and blisters were healing before my eyes.

The old lady took her mitts off and smoothed her curly gray hair. "It has a healing potion brewed in as well. Give it a few minutes." Then she wandered into a back room, tail swishing behind her.

Tristan loosened his grip, rubbing small circles over my back. "It's okay. It's over now."

My voice was hoarse. "You're a monster. I can't believe you did that to me." I stared at my reddened skin as the blisters disappeared. The pain had dulled, so I no longer wanted to cut my arm off, but it was still throbbing.

Tristan's low voice murmured softly in my ear. "You let it get bad. It had to be done."

I pulled away from him, and this time he let me, arms dropping to his sides.

The doctor—I was assuming that was what she was—came back after a few minutes to prod at my skin. I could see a faint line where the cut had been. "The poison isn't gone, just receded. It's too strong for my skills. There is nothing I can do."

"Wait, what? What does that mean? Am I dying?" My voice was high and tight, and I couldn't seem to breathe right.

Tristan tsked at her. "I know you better than that. What will it take to heal her, and what do you want for it? Maybe some harpy feathers from the Barrens?"

The old woman smiled, patting her gray curls. "I do love a man who knows how to bargain. I have a stronger antidote that might work, but I never use it. The ingredients are too hard to get."

Tristan's voice was calm and even. "What are they?"

She gave an evil grin, displaying deceptively small teeth. In that moment, I was pretty sure she wasn't an old granny. She was a predator that ate her prey for breakfast and then spat them back out. "I do need a feather from the Barrens. From the phoenix, not the harpy. I need water from the celestial pools. Not a lot, a few drops. I need the bone of a loved one, and pink algae from the bottom of the Endless River. Get me those ingredients, and I can make the potion to cure her. You will also owe me a favor, son of the Dark Lord. That is the price."

"I can pay the favor," I said. I was the one poisoned. The favor should be from me.

"No," Tristan said, his voice firm. "The dagger that poisoned you was meant for me. I will pay the debt, but it can't be a debt that goes against any of my oaths."

She nodded, completely ignoring me. "Understood. Are we agreed?"

"If you can save her, we are agreed. If she dies, our agreement dies as well."

"That is fair."

She pulled out some white paper and a quill and ink pot. What century was she from? She wrote out their terms twice. Tristan looked them over and then pricked his finger with a knife and signed both. The woman did the same. They each kept one copy.

"You better hurry. She has a few days, at best."

She grabbed a few small bottles from a drawer. "These will help give her strength when hers flags. And it will. Use them sparingly. While they give strength, they can also speed the poison."

Tristan took them and tucked them in his belt.

She gave me one of the small bottles and nodded at me encouragingly.

I took the top off and stared at the dark interior. The potion gave off a faint rotten orange smell. I put the top back on. "I can wait. I don't feel that bad yet, but thank you."

She shrugged. "Don't thank me. He's paying for it."

I looked at Tristan's brooding face. "Thank you," I said stiffly, still mad at the boiling cure.

He nodded, but said nothing.

We left the healer's place a few minutes later, me in a borrowed T-shirt that said, "Kiss My Ass" and had a picture of a donkey on it. She'd refused to give me the ruins of the old shirt to try to repair and it made me wonder if she had a treasure trove of torn clothes hidden somewhere.

Tristan, who'd been silent for a while, asked, "How are you feeling?"

I was tired, and my body ached, sending pulses of dull pain through me with each step. "Not great. Why?" I'd learned he wasn't one for idle chitchat. If he'd asked, there was a reason.

157

"We should split up."

I protested, and he held up a hand. "Hear me out. The phoenix feather is in the Barrens, which is in the Demon Realm, and that is not a great place for a half celestial to go. The water from the celestial pools is from the Celestial Realm. That's a place I can't step foot in without an alarm going off, but you, as part celestial, can walk freely there. That's the water I needed you to get me to fulfill our bargain anyway. We should do those two tasks separately and then meet up at the cemetery. Are you okay if we use one of your mother's bones?"

I nodded, swallowing the lump in my throat. I knew she wouldn't mind giving me a bone to save my life, but I couldn't imagine digging her up and taking it.

"I can give you a transport charm to send the water straight to the healer."

I took a deep breath, staring at the gray concrete beneath my feet. Something normal and safe. Looking up at Tristan, his arms giving off a faint red glow, I whispered, "Okay."

"Okay?"

"You gave that woman a favor to help make sure I don't die. If you think this is the best way, I believe you. And as you said, I need to get that water for you anyway to fulfill our bargain. Now, how do I get to the Celestial Realm?"

****

We went back to my place so I could change, have a quick bite to eat, and grab a few supplies. When I'd asked Tristan what I'd need, he'd scoffed and said, "Pack as if you're going for a hike." I currently lived in a city. How often did he think I went hiking? Not helpful.

Sighing, I stuffed some snacks, water, and a few

other supplies in a sporty red and black backpack. I also grabbed another vial of the healing potion and shoved it in my pocket, just in case. Tristan wasted no time driving us out to the bridge where I'd seen the troll. Getting off his bike, I asked, "Isn't there a troll here?"

"Harry? Yeah, he guards the gateway."

"The troll's name is Harry?"

"Well, no, but he refuses to give me his name, so that's what I call him. Grumpy old fart. Here." Tristan swung his leg over the motorcycle and handed me a small tube. "For the water. Fill it to the top, and that will be enough both for the healer and for your payment to me."

He handed me a folded map and a small white sticker. "When the water is in the tube, adhere the sticker to the tube, read the incantation, and it'll go straight to the healer."

"What's the incantation?"

"*Itinerantur esse unum*. It's written on the sticker." He helpfully pointed it out on the sticker.

Of course, it's not in English. I repeated it to myself a few times and then stuck everything in the pocket of my hoodie, which could thankfully zip closed so I wouldn't lose anything.

"You'll do great. Just ask the troll if you can pass. He'll be a dick, but hand him this Realm Token, and you will be allowed passage for a day." He handed me a gold coin. It was about the size of a quarter but thicker and had a dragon patterned on the back.

"I need to get that book translated."

"Yeah, you do. One step at a time."

I wished I knew how dangerous the phoenix feather would be. I was terrified of my task, but worried about him too. His task seemed riskier. I was collecting water from a lake. And barely any water at that. I could see how it could be difficult to get for castes not allowed in the Celestial Realm, but for me, this should be a cakewalk. You know, once I got up the nerve to approach the troll and ask for passage.

Tristan started walking away.

"Wait, aren't you going to introduce me to the troll?" My stomach churned even more. I'd thought for sure he'd at least be there in case the troll ate me.

"No, it wouldn't do for him to associate us." He shoved his hands into his pockets and looked up through his dark hair sheepishly. "He doesn't like me much."

"What'd you do?"

"I played a prank and turned his fur green for a few hours."

I laughed, having a hard time picturing serious Tristan playing pranks. "You?"

He held a finger to his lips and shushed me. "I was ten. It was funny, but trolls are particular about their fur and have long memories. He hasn't forgiven me. He's under the bridge on the right-hand side. He looks big and mean, but he follows the rules and has strict guidelines not to hurt anyone unless they break them. You'll do fine."

That didn't make me feel any better, but I gave him a jerky nod and started walking toward the bridge. Carefully. I didn't want to step in troll dung again. One step after the other. *Deep, slow breaths. You can do this, Zoey.* The grass was damp, but it wasn't too slick and there were no mysterious brown patches. The air smelled sweet from some nearby violets. Maybe it would be the same troll as before? He liked me, right? Unless I'd accidentally poisoned him last time. I should have asked Tristan if trolls could eat brownies.

Walking down the hill, I saw nothing under the bridge, just the gently flowing water, grass, and near the bottom, lots of mud. At least I had a reason for going slow. I didn't want to slip in the mud and slide down the hill. It wasn't because I was terrified. Nope.

I stepped closer and closer to the bridge. There he was. Big potato nose and all. The same troll as before. Relief made my shoulders droop. I waved and said, "Hi, Carrion. How are you?"

The troll grunted, the sound both terrifying and reminding me of an annoyed older brother.

He seemed unchanged outside of a nasty cut across his face. I tried to imagine doing this job day in and day out, people being mean. That must be terrible for him. "Did you like the brownie? I have a granola bar. Do you want it?"

He looked at me in surprise, and I pulled the bar from my bag. "Here." I took the wrapper off and handed it to him.

He put it in his mouth and swallowed. He didn't yell or scream, so it couldn't have been that bad.

When he was done, I asked, "Can I have passage?" He stood there, tall and imposing, not moving. "Please?"

His voice came out as a low rumble, nutty breath from the granola bar wafting my way. "I cannot give passage for food."

"What? Oh no, that was for you." I fumbled in my pocket for the coin Tristan had given me. "I have the fee." I dropped it in my haste to show it to him and picked it up, having to wipe it against my jeans to get the mud off. I held it up. "See?"

"What do you want for the food?"

"Nothing. That was a gift. Is that okay?"

He made a grunting sound I couldn't interpret. Then he held out a hand bigger than my entire head. I dropped the small coin into his palm and tried to ignore the musty old cabin scent he carried. Despite thinking he was moderately friendly, my heart still raced. He picked up the coin and placed it in a bag at his waist and then held up a small device. He waved it near my head, and it beeped. Was it reading my tattoo?

"What realm?"

"Celestial."

The troll walked to the wall of the bridge and drew out some symbols with a fat stick of chalk. The symbols shimmered, then they and the rock wall they were sketched upon vanished and a golden gate appeared. A shining scroll of words ran along the outer edge in a language I didn't recognize. He swung the heavy door open, just enough to let me through.

"Be back by this time tomorrow, or you will be penalized." His voice was so low and gravelly I could barely understand him, but I understood well enough. Tristan had already warned me the Realm Token was for one day, that we were under a time crunch, and to take only a few hours if I could. I debated asking what the penalty was, but realized I didn't really want to know. I nodded and walked up to the gate. I touched the edge of the door and tried to open it a little more. It was cool and hard and didn't budge. Letting go, I slipped through and into another world.

Chapter 16

In front of me was a path of clouds. I froze, afraid to move. What if the clouds didn't hold me up? There was a huge gaping void, and I was supposed to just step into it and hope the thick mist supported me?

A gate stood behind me, bigger than the one on the other side and framed by an indigo sky. The color differed from what I was used to. It was darker, like the deep ocean. The gate was made from both silver and gold, the two twined together to form vines stretching up and down the open doorway, a similar scroll of words along the outer edge. There was another troll on this side too, and like the gate, it was larger than its counterpart. More grandiose. This one's hide was more of a dark gray, and he had an enormous gold ring stuck through his nose. I hoped he took it out if he got sick.

A young "man" stepped in front of me, wings flapping impatiently. "You done?" His words sounded strange, but I somehow understood.

He was okay on the clouds, but he had wings. I looked back at the troll. He wasn't sinking either. Taking a deep breath, I took a tentative step forward. Then another. My stomach dropped, but I wasn't falling. The man shoved past me as he walked toward the portal. I continued to walk forward, away from the gate, steps small and measured. The shifting ground made me dizzy, and it was a little like walking through sand, but I didn't fall. Thankfully, the cloudy area was only around the gate, encircling it like a halo. Farther out, the paths were made of a smooth gray and white marble.

Reaching solid ground, I turned in a slow circle. I appeared to be in a main square. The buildings surrounding the square glittered in the sunlight, constructed with a light-colored stone that looked like granite but with more sparkle. Doorways and windows were decorated with carved scenes of hunts and battles. They were beautifully wrought, each line bringing a story to life.

Everywhere I looked in the square was the soft blue of what I was pretty sure was celestial magic. Most celestials appeared to be tall and slender, with pointed ears, and hair that sparkled in the sunlight in a variety of jewel tones. Their eyes were too big and their nails were a little too long. Those with squat forms, horns, and other oddities were glamoured to blend in. Shading my eyes, I found my attention drawn to a woman on a corner, dancing. She had an ornate silver bowl out in front of her with some coins in it. She moved in ways I knew my body couldn't move, limbs fluid and graceful. Her thin gossamer wings helped her hover and float above the ground. Some of the surrounding magic looked jagged and sharp. I stared, but couldn't figure out what it was for. Was it helping her dance?

Walking on, people manned little stalls along the sides of the square. They were hollering out their wares like at any other market. The difference was what they were selling. Beautiful jewelry with stones in colors I'd never seen before. I ran my hand over scarves and shirts made from material so soft it seemed like the finest silk, yet much sturdier. A vendor demonstrated by stabbing the cloth and showing how the fabric held up. I instantly wanted to buy it, but I didn't know what currency to use. They probably didn't take credit cards. I glanced at my phone and sighed. I would have loved to stop and browse for a few hours, but I was under a time crunch. I needed to get the water and get out of here. I could come back another day when I wasn't literally dying.

I pulled out Tristan's hand-drawn map and oriented myself. The big spires in the distance between tall mountain peaks must be the palace. The "do not, under any circumstances, head this direction" direction. I noticed a large skull-and-crossbones drawn on one of the spires on the map and chuckled.

Turning in the opposite direction, I started walking. The path in this direction switched to gray stone after a few blocks. After another few minutes, tufts of yellow grass started poking through in spots. The path was still smooth and multi-faceted, but it wasn't quite as awe-inspiring, and the crowds got a little thinner.

As I moved farther from the gate, there were still stalls around, but I noticed some workers wore collars around their necks. The ones with collars glowed with more of that sharp, jagged magic. I got a bad vibe from it and had to stop myself from turning back. The one nearest me with a collar had a bruise on her face. Although she smiled and acted cheerful, her thin, twitching hands spoke of hunger and abuse. She dropped something, and a large man yelled at her. Small, rodent-like animals scurried into dark corners, afraid of the booming sound. I stayed mid-path and quickened my pace.

This section of town immediately dampened my awe over the main square. I had been thinking that the celestials weren't so bad, but seeing these people changed my mind. These streets spoke of a group of desperate, uncared-for people. The main square was just a showpiece.

After a while, the towering buildings faded. Simpler, smaller stone structures popped up instead. No more engraved scenes. Plant life started taking over, and I soon passed through trees and fields. A strange yellow fruit grew on white, willowy branches, the trees planted in neat, even rows. I was hungry, but I didn't dare touch them. After seeing the people in the collars, I didn't want to risk breaking a law and getting myself in trouble. The day was warm with a cool breeze that was refreshing. I took off my red hoodie and tied it around my waist, basking in the nice weather.

After what seemed like a few hours of walking—*it'll only take you a few hours total*, my ass—I spotted a deep purply blue up ahead. My feet hurt, and my bones ached with a deep throbbing. The poison was spreading. I needed to get the water and get out of here.

The healer's potion sat heavy in my pocket. A promised way to take away the pain and exhaustion, but it would speed along my death. My hands twitched with the urge to grab it, but I clenched them and moved on. I needed to hold out as long as I could.

As I got closer, I could see glimpses of water through the scrub on my left. It was so much closer than the water straight ahead. My body hurt so much. Did I need to follow the path? The water was literally right there.

After a moment of indecision, I stepped off the path and walked through the bushes and rocks. Some strange creatures skittered away. A green spider as big as my hand crept past a plant that snapped closed on a dragonfly.

Climbing up some rocks, I glanced around. From my higher vantage point, I could see the water more clearly. There were no gates or signs saying you had to stay on the path, and nothing looked alarming or dangerous. "I'll get the water and go home. I am being resourceful, not stupid." *Maybe if I keep telling myself this, I'll believe it.* I jumped down to the other side, knees buckling as I landed. I tried to stand, but my gut clenched so tight I stayed down, doubled over with pain. When the wave passed, I climbed to my feet. I was running out of time. Fingering the bottle in my pocket, I forged ahead. One foot in front of the other. I could do this.

A few minutes later, I came to a little cove. Brief panic halted me as I wondered if this was the correct water. I hadn't followed Tristan's directions exactly. What if I got it wrong? I pulled out my map. It looked like there was just the one large body of water in this area. They must connect.

I looked around. Bright sandy beaches surrounded the cove with white sand. Crystal-clear violet water lapped at the shore. A dark cave off to the side provided shelter for an eggplant colored dragon with black eyes.

Wait, what?! My heart stopped. *A dragon?!*

Peeking out of the cave was what looked like a dragon, but it was smaller than I expected a dragon would be. It was more the size of an elephant. Deep purple and blue scales transitioned to more of a lavender on the soft underbelly and neck. Its eyes were solid pools of black. There was a thick metal collar holding its head down, dark goo oozing around it. Blood? I had a powerful urge to move closer. But it was a dragon. What if it ate me? It was definitely big enough to eat me, and it looked skinny and hungry.

I was one hundred percent a dragon nerd. I loved dragons. I had always said if I ever saw one, I wouldn't be scared, but here I was, frozen with terror and indecision.

The dragon's scales were dusty with sand but still glittered more brightly than anything I'd ever seen. Its chest rose and fell slowly, and its triangular head tilted my way.

I was turning toward the water, away from the dragon, when a strong surge of sadness enveloped me. The dragon let out a low moaning sound that was so pitiful it made my heart ache. Could I leave it there? Serve myself and do nothing to help when the dragon was chained up and in distress? What if this beautiful, majestic creature was dying? I gritted my teeth, torn.

"Damn it." I dropped my bag and headed toward the dragon. "This is so stupid. I can't believe I'm doing this."

I approached cautiously. The dragon was bound with heavy chains connected to the cave so tightly it could barely move. I didn't think the dragon would hurt me. Although, I supposed it could probably breathe fire. *Stay away from the head. Check.*

One step and then another. It didn't make any sudden moves. It lay there watching me, dark eyes following my approach. That was almost worse.

This was beyond stupid. I should be focused on my task and leave the despondent dragon alone. But I couldn't. It was a *dragon*.

I approached from the side, reached my hand out slowly, and touched the skin on its back leg, as far away from its face and its many strong teeth as I could. The hide was cool and smooth. The minute I touched the dragon, a presence solidified in my mind.

The sadness surged, and the dragon's fear and anguish overwhelmed me. An image appeared in my mind of the water. It was warm and deep. Close to shore were large, shining eggs. The dragon had buried her eggs. A scene whipped through my mind. Men had chained her, laughing and talking about her eggs being priceless. The men left, saying they'd be back when the eggs were closer to hatching. My body swayed, struggling to control emotions so strong I fell to my knees.

A feminine voice demanded, '*Save them*!' The sound echoed in my head with the force of the words. The dragon let out a low keen of anguish. She showed me another place, and I got a feeling of warmth and safety. She showed me how she would gather her eggs and get there by flying.

"What can I do to help?" I couldn't help myself. The words tumbled out before I could think them through.

She showed me taking her eggs and walking them to the place they'd be safe. Her safe space wouldn't take long to get to by air, but walking…

"That's too far away." The adrenaline of seeing a dragon had made me momentarily ignore my state, but I was going to have to take a potion soon, or I would never make it back to the gate.

Her despair made me want to fall down onto the ground and bury myself, so deep was my grief. "Stop!" I crawled away, and the desolation lessened to a bearable amount.

Turning back to her, I asked, "What if I freed you and *you* saved your eggs?"

Despite the lack of physical contact, she showed me her attempts. The pictures flew by. The men always came the minute her collar came off. She showed me darts, making her sleep, and waking to burns on her body, to punish her. Again and again, she tried and failed.

Damn. "What if I got the eggs and put them in my bag, and you were completely ready to go before we took the collar off? You could carry the bag with the eggs. They should all fit." I hoped. How big was a dragon egg?

I could feel her hesitation, but her worry was stronger. Her mind was alien and strange, thoughts not going together the way I would think them. The pictures were jumbled, colors unfamiliar and different, but it still made sense. From what I could tell, her eggs were near to hatching and they would be collected and sold soon. She felt it was better to try to save them and fail than to not try. All this information without one word spoken. She seemed to have a grasp of the human language but struggled to form words.

I kicked off my shoes and took off my pants and shirt as well. I hesitated and ended up keeping my underwear on. We were in the middle of nowhere, but I couldn't get myself to strip naked. What if the people who had chained up the dragon came back? If I was going to get caught by slavers, I needed clothes. The dragon huffed at me impatiently, but I ignored her.

When I was ready, the dragon showed me exactly where I could dive to get the eggs. Based on her impressions, they weren't deep, but they weren't near shore either. I waded out into the water. It was warm and clear. Swimming to the spot she indicated, right on the edge of the cove, I dove, kicking hard as I plunged below the surface. I didn't make it to the bottom. Not on my first try, my second try, or my third. Clearly "not deep" to a dragon meant "really deep." What was it with these super-powered beings claiming things were easy?

Gasping for breath, I looked around, searching for some way to get more momentum. I climbed out and up onto a nearby rocky ledge. Sharp edges scraped my naked skin as I climbed, but the ledge I was aiming for was about ten feet above the water and right next to where the dragon's eggs were. Looking out over the clear water, I dove in, using the momentum to take me down faster. At the bottom, I dug in the sand where she had shown me, fingers scraping until I hit a hard object. My lungs burned. I pulled hard and wiggled one of the eggs free. The egg was about the size of two fists on top of each other. The shell was firm and swirled with many colors. Holding it tight, I kicked to the surface and swam side stroke until I reached the shore. I staggered out of the water. The egg was heavy. I brought the egg to its mother, and she buried it in the soft sand and covered it with her body, keeping it warm.

My arms ached. I walked back to my rock, ready to dive again…but I couldn't. Spaghetti-like, my arms wouldn't hold my weight as I tried to climb. Grip failing, I fell to the ground. My body was too weak. Everything hurt. Just lying there breathing sent spikes of agony through my chest. I crawled across the hot sand back to my clothes and pulled out one of the bottles. My hands were shaking so badly I almost dropped the potion as I tipped it to my mouth.

The brew was bitter with a slight orange aftertaste. It warmed my stomach, chasing away the painful cramps. The burst of energy coursing through my limbs was instantaneous, and my head cleared for the first time all day, making me momentarily second-guess what the hell I was doing. Looking at the dragon curled protectively around her egg, I realized I couldn't stop now. It may not have been the wisest decision, but there was no way I could leave without finishing.

Taking a deep breath, I went back to the rock and dove for eggs two more times. It was ten times easier than the first time, and it worried me. What would be the cost for the added strength?

Finishing, I put my clothes on over my wet underwear. Turning to look out over the cove, I asked the dragon, "Are these celestial waters?"

She gave a regal nod and somehow managed to convey both superiority and disdain with that simple movement. Her know-it-all attitude was annoying, but I reminded myself that she was chained up and worried about her kids. Manners were not really on her mind.

Smiling, I said, "Thanks." I took out my tube and walked to the water's edge, filling it with the purple-tinted water. I peeled the label off and put it on the tube, staring at Tristan's neat blocky handwriting. "Stupid incantation." I started sounding out the words and the dragon's fear surged.

I heard her panicked voice. *'Wait!'*

I stopped. Thinking it through, I could see why she would worry. Magic could be what summoned her captors. I would wait until I was away from the cove before saying the incantation. I put the tube in my pocket and the eggs in my backpack, stuffing the remaining space with warm sand. We were ready.

I grabbed the chain around her neck. I wasn't sure how to break it. The dragon started coughing and hacking, eventually coughing up a huge black blob that sizzled when it landed, eating through a patch of rocky ground. I backed away. She showed me an image of the black blob smoking and burning through the chains. I looked and could see that they chained her in a way that she'd never be able to reach them herself. She wanted me to move it.

I hesitantly agreed, not sure if I wanted to be that close to her acidic spit, but not ready to give up. I wandered off to look for some sticks. Long sticks. I happened to like all of my fingers and toes.

It took a few minutes, but I finally found two that looked thick enough to withstand the acid and headed back.

When I got near, I could tell she was trying to tell me something. There was a soft murmur in the back of my mind. Touching her smooth hide, the murmur solidified into a word. *'Scales.'* She sent an image of her scratching at old scales and them falling out.

I found two loose scales and tentatively tugged at them. Encouragement and warmth flooded me, and I pulled more firmly until they fell out. I held the palm sized scales up to the dragon. "Now what?"

She glanced pointedly at the scales and then at the smoking black blob. *'Move.'*

This would be so much easier if she could communicate with more than two-word phrases. I poked at the blob with a scale, and nothing happened. Using both scales, praying I didn't burn my hand off, I grabbed the huge smoking lump and carried it to the chain. It slowly worked on the chain, bubbling and smoking. While the acid worked, I rinsed off the scales in the lake. I tried to hand them back to her, but she said, *'Yours.'*

I looked at the iridescent purple, and my heart leapt. "Thank you." I put them in my hoodie pocket and zipped it closed.

When the acid blob was getting close to eating through her collar, I began to worry that it might burn her. Her scales had seemed to do okay, but where the chain was, she had a softer hide. "Should I wash it off?"

She ignored my question and said, *'Back up.'*

I backed up.

When the chain was loose enough, she took a deep breath and then bellowed. The sound echoed around the cove; a challenging, deep roar that made the hair stand up on my arms. Her neck swelled, and the crack of the chain breaking and falling to the ground added a final note to her rage. The dragon grabbed the backpack in one paw and me in the other and leapt into the air. My body went cold. She had grabbed me! Her sharp talons were digging into my side. That was not part of the plan!

Wings beating, she was leaving the cove when figures appeared below. Roaring, she sprayed acid toward them, and then she shot off faster than I could have ever imagined, the speed making my stomach drop and my head spin. She circled and sped away. A minute or two later, she dropped me in a place about halfway back to the city center, landing beside me. I imagine she thought she gently placed me, but it was a bit more forceful than I would have liked. Standing, I rubbed my bruised backside.

We were near the strange fruit trees again. I was pretty sure I knew which way to go. I pointed. "That way to the gate?"

'Yes. Thank you.' Glowing with blue magic, she brushed her soft snout against my waist. A hot, fiery

sensation burned above my hip, leaving behind a thin black line.

Lifting my shirt up, I wondered what the dark mark meant. I rubbed a finger over it, and it didn't smudge or fade. At all.

'Gift.'

I wasn't sure that I agreed that the dark line was a gift, but I didn't want to insult her. "Thank you."

She sent a feeling of warmth, happiness, and gratitude toward me and then leaped up with her dragon eggs in my backpack and was gone. There was a faint purple sparkle in the distance, then nothing.

That was going to be hard to explain to Dad. "Yes, I gave a dragon my backpack. Can I please have another one? Oh, and by the way, the dragon gave me a tattoo." Shaking my head, I took the water out and, turning the tube so I could read the words, said, "*Itinerantur esse unum.*" Runes glowed on the tube, and then the tube disappeared with a snap. I really hoped I'd done that right and the water made it to the healer.

A guard in a silver uniform appeared in front of me. Had I summoned him by accident? Before I could say anything, handcuffs were clapped on my wrists.

"What the hell?"

"You are under arrest for stealing the sacred waters."

What?! If Tristan had known this would happen, I was going to…A burning pulse ran through my body. My eyes rolled back, and I knew nothing else.

Chapter 17

When I came to, I had an eerie sense of déjà vu. I was lying on a hard stone floor, the cold seeping into my limbs. I could feel my wet underwear rub uncomfortably and was self-conscious over the fact that my outside clothes were wet in two obvious places. I should have taken my underwear off to dive into the pool. Too late now. Not like I'd known I would be arrested. Again. The walls in this cell matched the one I'd been in before. Was I back on earth, or did Mythics have a standardized cell they all used?

This time, there was no one else with me and my hands were cuffed in front of my body. Scooting up against the wall, I sat up. I could feel that my phone was gone, but the hard edge of a dragon scale dug into my side so no one had taken the scales. They must not have patted me down that thoroughly. Assuming, based on the timing and what the guard had said, that I was in trouble for taking the water, the cuffs seemed a bit much. I took a small tube of water. *Oh no. I must be super dangerous.* It wasn't like they didn't have an entire lake of the stuff.

Being cold, wet, and scared was making me grouchy.

I didn't have long to wait before a guard came, this time in a silver uniform but of a similar style to the last prison. I started giggling. I'd been a Mythic for only a few days, and I was already comparing prison uniforms.

I wasn't that great at being a Mythic.

The guard ignored my hysterical giggles and snorts. He led me to a large room filled with a half dozen other people wearing handcuffs, chained to various sections on a long gray wall. My cuffs were attached to a manacle on the wall slightly above my head. All the prisoners were evenly spaced apart. My arms ached. I hoped we didn't have to wait too long.

A little while later, a door opened. A small girl with dirty blonde hair went from person to person with scoopfuls of water. She was looking down, so I couldn't see her face, but she seemed familiar. When she got to me, I gasped. "Gracie?"

"Zoey?" She closed her mouth and offered me a sip of water.

My throat was dry. Head bent to the ladle, I greedily gulped the warm liquid down.

"He's in a good mood, and you guys are next." She smiled encouragingly at me, but I could see genuine worry in her hazel eyes.

"What are you doing here?" I couldn't help the blurted question.

"What are *you* doing here?" Her voice had the vicious snap I was used to, which oddly calmed me. Then she bowed her head and said softly, "Never mind. Now is not a good time to talk. Good luck."

I watched as she passed. Were those black wings on her back? How had I never noticed before? And why was she here? Did she work at the Mythic prison? It seemed so out of left field that it made little sense to me.

Gracie didn't return. Time passed slowly, the ache in my arms punctuated by an annoying drip from somewhere nearby. Eventually, we were unchained from the wall and led into a large, opulent room. My hands tingled. I rubbed the feeling back into them as we walked, preferring the pins and needles to the numbness.

The ceilings were high and covered with large sections of stained glass. Actual columns, like from the Greek era, lined the entryway. Across the room was a raised dais with a large, ornately decorated throne. The colors, gold and white, matched the gold-streaked marble floors. A young man leaned back in the large throne, one leg hanging over the armrest in a nonchalant position. There were two other people on the dais, standing off to the side, large forms hidden in shadow. On the left was a seating area with a host of people watching and chatting, dressed in ridiculously lavish garb. They wore colorful silks, ornate lace, and some even had long trains held high by attendants. Slim women in gray uniforms edged with silver fetched beverages for them. Out of the corner of my eye, I saw hot-pink hair. Was that Anastasia, the girl from the prison cell? She was gone too quickly for me to be sure, but how many Mythics had hot-pink hair that exact color? My shoulders relaxed a touch. Maybe she hadn't died.

There were roses everywhere. All different colors, their scent permeating the air with a thick sweetness. The man on the throne shone with power. Some others in the room were aglow with magic as well, but everything seemed dim next to him. I swallowed hard, mouth dry. I had a feeling I was about to meet the very bad, awful person I was supposed to avoid at all costs. The person both my mother and then Tristan, with his skull and cross bones on the map, had worked hard to keep me away from.

A tall, nervous man with a clipboard stepped out and introduced the young man on the throne as Lord Gabriel, the head of the Mythical Council. Not just someone from the Council, but the head of it. Stunned, I blanked out for a minute, but forced myself to focus as a short man with a round belly hanging out over his belt was brought in front of the dais. He had to be pushed forward and fell to his knees before standing awkwardly in front of Lord Gabriel.

After listening attentively to the charges read out by the nervous skinny guy, Lord Gabriel's warm tenor voice said, "I charge you with two days in the stocks. Naked. That should cure you of your need to show yourself." There were nervous titters from the crowd. He waved a long-fingered hand. "Next."

That seemed downright stupid to me. Why was having someone who liked to expose himself be naked a punishment? What was it teaching him? The next was a man caught stealing. He had pointed ears and a slight greenish cast to his skin. He was shuffling his feet as he waited for his verdict.

"You will lose your hand."

I thought he was joking. Then, in front of everyone there, Lord Gabriel waved his hand, and a burst of pure golden light traveled across the prisoner's wrist. His scream ripped through the air, and I could smell scorched flesh as his hand fell to the ground, the stump now cauterized.

Shit! I broke out into a cold sweat, hands shaking. That man had stolen something. *I* had stolen something. Were they going to take my hand? I had a sudden urge to scream at the top of my lungs, but I didn't. If I made it out of here intact, I was going to kill Tristan. *Why hadn't he warned me?*

No one said anything. Everyone waited while people in the gray and silver uniforms cleaned up the few drops of blood, and then the next prisoner came forward.

This was a petite woman. Beautiful, with perfectly symmetrical features and large hazel eyes. "You also stole. But instead of stealing money, you stole food. I have some sympathy. You will work off your debt and will belong to the owner for three moons." A guard stepped forward and wrapped a collar around her neck, and she was led off with terrified eyes. Then I was motioned forward. Lord Gabriel's dark-blue eyes lingered on the wet parts of my clothes. His gaze had a weight to it. He looked young, but I got the impression he was hundreds of years old.

"Crime?" he asked in a hard, cold voice.

The skinny scribe flipped through a small notebook. "She stole a vial of the sacred waters and sent it to the Human Realm."

Silence. My throat was dry, the metallic scent of blood still heavy in the air.

Gabriel idly played with a ring on his hand. "Who did you send it to, and why?"

My mouth opened, and words fell out without my intending to say anything. "I don't know her name, but she needed it for a potion and asked me to get it for her. I registered a few days ago. I didn't know it was a crime. I'm sorry. It's a lake. There was a ton of water. How was I supposed to know?"

He stopped playing with the ring and leaned forward, elbows on his knees, as I got his full attention. "It's in your handbook. Haven't you read it yet?"

"No. I tried. I really did! I can't read it. The letters

don't make any sense." I couldn't get the words to stop coming out of my mouth. It was like word vomit that I couldn't stop.

"Who is your transition coach?"

I tried not to say her name, but it spilled out anyway. "Regina."

"Ahh, yes. Regina. Let's call her, shall we?"

My eyes widened in alarm, but I couldn't say or do anything to stop him.

He snapped his fingers, and Regina showed up in front of him, eyes wide, but otherwise keeping her cool at being transported. She was wearing sweats and had obviously been going for a run or something similar. She glowed with a bright light, glamour still firmly in place.

She blinked and then bowed low. "Your Highness. What an unexpected surprise. To what do I owe the pleasure?"

"Is this your charge?"

She finally noticed me, and her expression grew dark. I was in so much trouble.

"Yes. Has she gotten into trouble so soon? What a pity. I can punish her for you." She cast an evil grin my way, and I winced, waiting to hear my judgement.

"I need the book you assigned her."

I blinked in surprise. Not the request I was expecting.

She swallowed hard. "Of course." Snapping her fingers, a book appeared before the man in the throne. He grabbed it and flipped it open. He turned a few pages and looked up, his eyes alight with interest.

"This is coded to a demon. She is part celestial, not demon."

"Oh, is it? My mistake. I will fix that right away."

She waved a hand, and a new book appeared.

The man flipped through it and then tossed it to me. I awkwardly tried to catch it with my manacled hands. I failed and then bent to the ground and picked it up off the marble floor. Hugging the book to my chest, fingers white, I awaited my verdict. The soft floral scent of the roses mixing with the lingering scent of blood was making me sick.

"Regina, while an easy mistake to make, your lapse has put some sacred water in the Human Realm. You will be docked three weeks' pay and will work with the constable on your off time until your charge has passed the test. You will check every book produced to make sure it was done correctly."

Her lips tightened, but she said, "Of course."

"Zoey…" He said my name like a caress. He leaned forward, arms resting on his knees, glowing blue eyes entrancing me. "You will get…" The silence stretched out and made me cringe, my heart about to beat out of my chest. "A warning."

I looked up, eyes wide, unsure how I had escaped punishment. "While stealing sacred waters is a horrific crime, I have been to the Human Realm and can see why you would have thought it harmless. You are but a baby. You will not travel to any of the Other realms until you have read the entire book and passed your exams. Is that understood?"

I found myself stuttering but able to talk. "Y-Y-Yes."

"Good. I will let the gatekeepers know. Once you have passed your exams showing you know our laws, I will remove the restriction. Regina, I will leave her in your capable hands." He waved a hand in my direction, and the manacles dropped off my wrists, cut in half by his magic.

I glanced down to the floor and the broken halves of the manacles, still smoking from the white heat that cut them, and then quickly looked away. "Thank you."

He nodded and waved for the next person.

I hurried toward the exit, legs trembling, but the look Regina shot me told me I was far from out of trouble.

Chapter 18

The minute we cleared the door, Regina grabbed my elbow and dragged me to an empty room, small sparks flying off her fingers. With a wave, the lights on the cameras blinked off, smoke rising from them. "How could you embarrass me like that? Are you trying to get me killed? You will pay for that!"

I jerked away, backing up but saying with bravado, "I'm not the one who gave me the wrong book. I called and left a message. You never called me back. And I had no choice but to say something. He compelled me. This is your fault, not mine." My voice was brave, but my knees were shaking. Even though I had done nothing wrong, I knew she was going to punish me. I just didn't know how. *Would she shock me again?*

She turned on me, hair blowing out behind her like writhing snakes. "You can fight compulsion if you have a strong enough will. I am saddled with a stupid charge who can't even figure out how to read a book or fight a compulsion. Pathetic." There was a tickling sensation on my arm, and I brushed my other arm against it. A small bug fell to the ground. Then more little feet crept along my skin. A faint rustling accompanied a wave of darkness as it moved across my body.

"Do you like my gift? Think of it as your incentive." Regina's voice was cold. I looked down. Thousands of little legs. Spiders. I was covered in tiny spiders. I screamed, trying to brush them off. They climbed inside my shirt, and I yanked it off, throwing it across the room. They were still there, little mouths biting, crawling under my clothes and in my ear. Scrambling to get them off, I tore at my clothes and my skin, falling to my knees and eventually rolling around on the ground in a panic, tiny little pinpricks of pain everywhere.

Regina threw her head back and laughed, the sound echoing in the small room.

Looking down, there were no bugs on the floor. It was an illusion. I closed my eyes and tried to imagine they weren't there. *They don't exist.* But their little legs kept moving. Crawling all over my body, mouths biting and leaving painful welts behind.

"You're weak. Useless."

I could see through glamours. I should be able to break through this illusion, but no matter what I told myself, they kept crawling and biting. I was sobbing now, tears and snot wetting my face, my voice hoarse from screaming. Finally, Regina snapped her fingers, and the illusion disappeared, but the welts stayed. Hundreds of little bites all over my body.

She bent next to me on the ground and whispered, "You are weak. Get your pathetic ass up and learn that book fast. I will be by in two weeks to test you. Do not disappoint me."

She grabbed my shirt from the floor and threw it at me. "Cover up. You don't want to give anyone the wrong idea, do you?"

I was so terrified I could barely get my limbs to move, but somehow, I managed to get the shirt on. She snapped her fingers, and a door appeared. "Take the book and go. Get out of my sight before I do worse than a little illusion."

I grabbed the book that had fallen to the ground during my struggle and walked through the door.

On the other side was the troll. Carrion appeared impassive as I walked through the gate, shaking with hundreds of bite marks covering my body. He glanced at his device. "Right on time." He nodded.

Everything ached. I nodded back, tears in my eyes, unable to form words. I started stumbling away from the portal, worried I would trip and roll down the hill and end up in the frigid water.

The troll's deep voice stopped me. "Pick the flowers at the river's edge and steep them into a tea. Drink it, and it will help heal the bites."

I looked up at the troll in surprise. "Thank you." My voice was rough and tear-filled.

He grunted and returned to whittling the stick he was working on.

I wiped my face, embarrassed over how I must look. "What are you making?" I stepped closer, and he grunted louder and turned away. I patted his back, and he stiffened, growling. "I'm sorry. I just…Thank you." I hurried down to the bottom of the hill, not sure what had prompted me to touch him. Maybe I needed physical contact, so I thought he might too.

Stumbling along the water's edge, I pushed the soft grass aside, revealing small blue flowers I hadn't noticed before. I knelt, my pants getting wet from the water-logged bank, and picked a few handfuls.

I sat up and then stood before hearing a low growl. "More."

I sank back down and crawled along the riverbank, picking more. When I had three times the amount tucked into my hoodie's pocket, I stood and looked questioningly at the troll. He grunted and nodded. I nodded back and slowly made my way to the street, wondering if there was something he might like that I could bring him for his generosity. Had he liked the brownie or the granola bar? I wasn't the greatest cook, but I was pretty sure I could make something from a box. I made a mental note to buy a mix of some kind, maybe chocolate chip cookies, so I could bring him a treat.

Getting home took a long time. After I got there, I put some water on for tea and ran to my room to change. My phone and other belongings were laid out neatly on my bed, like last time. I tossed the book down next to them. My phone had a bunch of messages from Ava begging for details about my date with Tristan. I smiled, started typing an answer, and then stopped. Like Carter, she couldn't protect herself. With everything happening, could I stay friends with her?

I sent a quick message saying that Dad had seen Tristan's motorcycle and I was grounded, but I'd try to get in touch when I was allowed my phone again. There. That gave me time to think about what I should do.

New clothes helped make me feel more human. Seeing the bites on my arms, I looked away, grabbing another, cleaner hoodie to cover them up. I should shower, but I didn't want to look that closely at them yet, and they'd be unavoidable if I washed up. Instead, I washed the tiny blue flowers and put them in a tea strainer. Then I poured the hot water into a travel mug, tossed the tea strainer in, and grabbed my bike for a quick ride to the cemetery.

When I stopped at a stoplight, I took a tentative swig of the tea. It tasted earthy and strange, but I felt better.

The pain wasn't so sharp. At the cemetery, I locked up my bike, grabbed my mug, and trudged up to my mother's grave. It was the first time I had visited without bringing flowers, and for a moment, I had an overwhelming urge to leave. I couldn't visit without gifting her with something. But then I calmed myself down. Visiting was a gift. And she was dead and wouldn't know anyway. The sadness that filled me at that thought almost took me to my knees. Taking a deep breath, I walked on. Finding a small daisy as I walked, I picked it. She would love it.

Chapter 19

Around the bend up ahead, I heard two voices arguing.

"It is too dangerous. You have to wait. She will be here soon." I didn't recognize the voice and slowed down, approaching more cautiously.

I heard a scuffle.

"What if she's not?" The second voice was strangled, but the smooth baritone sounded like Tristan. There was more scuffling. "What if he's torturing her for taking the water? You know how he can get. I never should have asked her to go."

"She's fine. Trust me."

A surge of white-hot anger coursed through me. I rounded the bend, feet pounding the dirt. "So, you knew it was illegal, huh? You knew I'd get arrested, and you sent me to get it anyway."

Tristan and another man, with almost black skin and spikes sticking out from his arms and head, were wrestling on the ground. Tristan's head popped up. Staring at me, he let his shoulders relax. "You're okay." He rolled to his feet and took a step away from the other man, reaching for me.

I stepped toward him and let fly with a punch to his chin, my fist connecting with a loud *crack*. I knew my anger was irrational. We'd needed the ingredient, but he should have told me.

He stood there, letting me hit him. I had no doubt he could have dodged the blow. My fingers throbbed. Shaking my hand in pain, I watched as Tristan backed away, hands up. He didn't even bother to rub his face. I likely didn't even cause a bruise. *Asshole.*

"I took a calculated risk. You needed the ingredient. New Mythics are given a lot of leeway until they've taken their exams. You haven't even cracked your book yet." He waved my direction. "And see, here you are, good as new."

"Yeah, I was given leeway by the head honcho, but Regina wasn't too pleased with being blamed for failing in her duties."

His face blanked, no expression, and his body stilled. It was eerie. "What did she do?" His eyes roamed over my body, and I was sure he could see some bites.

Pulling my sleeves over my hands, I took a step back, remembering the golden-haired leader cutting off that man's hand. Remembering the fear that had stopped me cold. "It doesn't matter. What does matter is I need to trust you. And I don't anymore."

"If I'd have told you, the truth spell would have detected it. You had to go in blind."

My anger and fear warred with each other. I wanted to hit him and scream at him and run down the hill and away from him forever. But I needed him. I would die without him. Instead, I said, "Whatever. You have a shovel?"

He shook his head, black hair flopping with the motion. "I already dug up the grave and took a finger bone. It's been almost a full day since you left. I was worried about time. And I didn't think you'd want to do it."

I nodded. Now that he'd mentioned it, the ground did look disturbed. I must have been really tired to not notice earlier. I was too mad at him to say thank you, but appreciated that I didn't have to dig up my mother's grave. "That leaves one more item, right?" The cold pit in my stomach flared, reminding me I didn't have much time left.

He nodded. There was a shuffle off to the side.

"Who's your friend?" The guy he'd been arguing with had ducked into a shadow and I couldn't see him well, but I saw enough to know he was still there.

"This is Barley. Promise to keep an open mind with him. He's a good guy. He can help find who killed your mother." That was when I registered how similar in appearance he was to the demon that had killed Mom. *Wow, I was out of it tonight.* He was smaller, and he had fewer spikes, only lining up his arms halfway, but the resemblance was uncanny.

"You."

"It wasn't me." His voice had an odd, sibilant accent, very different from the other guy, but they were definitely the same species.

"What are you?"

He huffed. "'*What are you?*' That's a vulgar question, River Girl."

"'River Girl'?"

Tristan cleared his throat. "That is what they are calling you for stealing the river water. River Girl. Sometimes you get a nickname in the Mythic world, and it can supersede your actual name. I am known as Hammer."

"Why?"

Tristan looked away and didn't answer. Barley

stepped in and, arm slung across Tristan's shoulders, said, "Because the first person he punished for his dad, he used a hammer to pulverize their hands."

I blanched, getting light-headed. Leaning against a headstone, I asked, "What did they do?" If they had stolen something, I was walking. I didn't know if I could do this without him, and I was feeling sicker by the minute, but I couldn't work with him if he could do something like that. Something so barbaric and inhumane. I just couldn't.

Tristan shrugged away from his friend, crossing his arms. "Does it matter?"

I forced my head up and looked him right in the eyes, letting his pale-blue irises hold mine. "Yes, it matters."

Tristan didn't say anything.

Barley scoffed. "It is well known; you might as well tell her. The man had been abusing little girls. He had been showing an interest in Tristan's little sister. Tristan protects his own."

Cool air filled my lungs as I breathed. Tristan wasn't a monster like Regina. He was a protector. "Thank you for explaining." I focused on the dark head, hidden in shadow. "You have avoided my first question, though. What are you? You look like the…" I stopped myself. I almost said "thing," but the being in front of me was a thinking, reasoning man, not a thing. "Man. You look like the man who killed my mother."

He bowed his shaved head and said, "We are of the Black Salamanders. Human and demon half breed. There are few of us around here, but most of us do contract work. I can introduce you to the most likely suspects. Tell you who was working around the time your mother died, but you would need to promise not to harm the contractor unless he did something outside our laws. If it was a sanctioned kill, then he is protected."

I gritted my teeth. "Excuse me? What is a sanctioned kill?" The words were clipped and forced.

Tristan rubbed a hand over his face. He looked tired. Or maybe dark circles were a demon thing. "We need to get that book of yours fixed."

I sighed, my bites hurting again. I took another sip of the earthy tea. "Regina already did it. She was not thrilled about it."

Tristan came forward and pulled my shirt sleeve up roughly. I was not prepared so couldn't stop him. "Hey!"

His nose wrinkled in disgust. "She put bugs on you, didn't she? She always had an affinity for them." He ran his fingers over the red welts.

"But wasn't it an illusion? Why do I have bites?"

"If you believe in the illusion enough, she can make it real. Were they poisonous?"

"I don't think so, but hey, I'm already poisoned, so what's a little more, right?" I wished my voice didn't sound so weak and small. That little hitch made it sound like I was about to cry. I would *not* cry. "I took one of the potions the healer gave me earlier. That helped. And the tea the troll told me how to make is helping too."

Barley spoke this time. "The what, now? The bridge troll told you how to make a restorative tea? Are you sure he wasn't giving you something to get you to go away?"

"I don't think so. It has been helping." I took a quick sniff of my travel mug.

Barley immediately grabbed it and opened the lid. He took a deep whiff and then closed it again. "Well, I'll be. You must have either made a positive impression or he felt you were too unfairly dealt with. The trolls are usually neutral to the extreme. It is very rare for them to help someone, even if they were dying by the gate door."

"Oh." That was all I could think of to say and then I blurted, "Do trolls like cookies?"

Tristan snorted. "You're going to make the troll cookies?"

I folded my arms across my chest. "Yeah, why not? They eat, right?"

Barley chuckled but said, "I don't think it could hurt, and I'm sure he'd be pleased. I don't think anyone has ever thought to bring them something before. You are very human. Most of us have been in the other world our entire lives and think a bit differently than you do." He nodded at me, seeming to have come to some decision. "I have to go. I will look into which of my brothers might have killed your mom, but I will not give you my information until I have your promise not to break our laws. Read the book and then let me know your answer. Tristan will know how to reach me." He reached out a hand and clasped arms with Tristan. "Go swiftly, my friend."

"Go swiftly."

The night swallowed Barley until he was just a memory, dark trees swaying gently as he passed.

"Come on. We need to get to the Endless River and get the algae and then get you back to the healer. How are you feeling?"

"Okay." I was surprised to find this was true. After leaving the Celestial Realm, I had felt like hell warmed over. Tiny pinpricks of pain all over my body and a painful ache starting deep within, likely from the poison eating away at me. But now I was okay. The ache was there, but distant. The pinpricks minor annoyances versus debilitating my ability to move.

He looked at me dubiously.

"I mean it. There must be something in this tea besides flowers."

Tristan's jaw dropped. "The troll gave you some of his flowers?!" The incredulity was unmistakable. I had shocked him.

"Yes. Is that bad?" I had a sudden image of falling dead at the end of the night because I was so stupid and trusting and ate flowers from a stranger. I was such a gullible idiot. Tristan took the mug from me again and held it reverently. He sniffed it and closed his eyes, his brow creasing in concentration. Opening them, he pulled out the tea strainer and gave it a closer look, opening it to expose the small, dark flowers. Putting everything back together, he handed it back. I'd half expected him to take a sip, but he'd sniffed and looked but left the liquid alone.

"What is it? Am I going to die?" I was getting light-headed and wondered if that was from the tea I was drinking or from fear of what was *in* the tea.

He shook his head. "No, of course not. Trolls are very trustworthy. If he said it will help, it will help. That is why they are the gatekeepers. However, they rarely give away their flowers. They are said to hold great healing properties, but no one can take one without a troll offering it, or it would have the opposite effect. The tea is a rare and special gift and shows the troll's favor for you. I am simply surprised."

My mouth dropped open in shock, and I looked at the tea with new eyes. Holding it tighter to my chest, I sipped the tea, taking time to appreciate the subtle earthy flavor. I definitely had to find time to make the troll cookies. Maybe with walnuts and extra chocolate chips.

"Come on. My bike is over there." He waved down the hill.

"My bike is there too. How far are we going?"

He snorted. "We are taking my bike. We need a motor, or it'll take us all night. Come on." He waved me along, and I practically ran to keep up with his longer stride. Not that he was running. He just walked so purposefully and had such long legs that it was almost impossible for me to keep up.

I gave up trying after a few running steps and continued my shamble after him. The tea was helping, but I was still tired and in pain. I did not need to run down a steep hill and trip and crack my head open. By the time I reached the parking lot he was already sitting astride his red monstrosity, the engine running. He tossed me a helmet and motioned for me to get on behind him. He looked quite perturbed at being kept waiting for the whole extra thirty seconds, and it made me want to smile.

I chugged the rest of my tea, and then secured the mug in the cup holder on my bike. Ready, I shoved the helmet on my head and swung up behind him. The minute I was situated, he took off, and I lurched forward, clinging to him, lest I fall off. "Ass," I whispered under my breath.

He chuckled and said, "I never said I wasn't." Hitting the gas, he swerved out of the parking lot and away from the cemetery to…I had no idea where. He seemed to know, so I buried my face in his back and tried to forget the last few hours of my life as we sped toward the Endless River.

Chapter 20

An hour into the drive, I was having trouble staying awake, so we stopped to grab coffee at a rest stop. The poison was really sapping my strength. The place was empty except for a few large trucks. The shadowy canopy of trees and the still silence gave me creepy horror movie vibes. Squat, square bathroom structures bordered a small vending machine alcove. Taking a steaming cup from the vending machine, I took a sip and almost spat it back out. A few granules were stuck in my mouth, and the taste made me question if someone had accidentally tossed in motor oil. I was likely spoiled by my daily coffee runs at Joe's, but realizing that didn't make the vile liquid taste any better.

Exhaustion making my limbs feel heavy, I took another small sip. I needed the caffeine—or another energy potion, and I was saving that for an emergency. Maybe if I drank it faster, it wouldn't be so bad? I took a few large gulps, the bitter liquid warming my belly but destroying my taste buds. I grimaced. *Nope, just as bad.* It was hot and cheap and I had no other options, so I forced it down. Between sips, I asked, "Where exactly are we going?"

Tristan turned wary eyes to me. "I'm no longer sure if you should go."

"First off, that didn't answer my question. And second, if I shouldn't go, why am I here?" I took one last chug and threw my coffee cup at the garbage. I missed. Stomping off, I picked it up and threw it in the can.

"The Endless River is in the Fae Realm."

"So?" During our drive, whenever we had slowed down or stopped at a light, Tristan had grilled me about what had happened. I had given him a brief rundown of my time in the Celestial Realm, skipping the part with Regina. I wasn't ready to talk about that yet. And oddly, the dragon. For some reason, my tongue couldn't form words about the dragon. I wanted to talk about it but couldn't. A mystery for another day.

"I didn't know about your ban earlier. We're using a back door into the Fae Realm, one no one bothers to monitor that opens close to the Endless River, but you could be looking at serious consequences if you're caught. I'm trying to figure out if there is a way to do this without you. I need to think." He balled up his cup, threw it in a perfect arc into the garbage can, and stalked off. *Show-off.*

Ten minutes later, we were back on the bike and headed deep into the mountains. Since we were still headed the same direction, I could only assume Tristan had decided I was going with him to the Endless River. His lack of communication made me want to bash him over the head with my purse. Didn't half demons talk?

As the bike climbed, the air cooled, and I burrowed into Tristan to keep warm. I was still mad at him, but not wanting to freeze to death trumped righteous anger. It was already getting dark. Twilight did not seem like the best time to be doing this, but I could feel the poison working its way through my system, and its icy touch scared me. Tristan sped along like it was full daylight, making me even twitchier.

After another hour of pinching myself awake on the motorcycle, my nerves were shot. I was relieved when Tristan turned off onto a path that was hidden on the side of the road. After bumping along the dirt path, he finally stopped. He switched the engine off and then turned to me.

My jaw dropped. His eyes glowed, like Casper's sometimes did. That was why he was driving like it was daytime. He could see in the dark. He tilted his head quizzically, and I realized he didn't know why I was staring.

He waved me off, and I swung my leg over the bike, belatedly realizing I should get off first. He climbed off after me and walked deeper into the shadowy trees, ignoring me. I pulled off my helmet, chucking it onto the ground, and hurried to catch up, grabbing the back of his coat in desperation. I didn't have a flashlight and wasn't sure where we were. Everywhere I looked was darkness. I could walk off a cliff and not know until I was flying through the sky. I checked my phone. Fifteen percent. Damn it. I should be thrilled it survived as long as it had, considering it was a piece of junk and hadn't been charged in days, but I had to fight the urge to toss it against a tree. I really wanted a light, but I needed to keep the last bit of charge for an emergency.

I laughed, a high-pitched, hysterical sound. I was the stupid girl in a horror movie. "Yes, why don't I follow a strange, dangerous man into the dark woods late at night with an almost dead phone and no flashlight? That sounds like a great idea," I muttered under my breath.

"What are you mumbling about?"

Looking around, I kept seeing darkness and shadows and hearing odd hoots and creaks. My heart raced, and I started feeling dizzy. Was it the poison? "I can't see. It's too dark." Rushing on, I babbled, "And I'm getting too sick. This was a bad idea. Maybe you should leave me with the bike. I'll just hold you back. Plus, there is that whole me being banned thing."

Tristan stopped and put his warm hands on either side of my face. "Hey. Calm down. It's going to be okay." His hands moved down to my neck, where I was sure he could feel my pulse hammering away. "You're too worked up."

He was right, but I didn't know what to do. I just wanted to sit down and cry or run away.

"We need to slow down your heart rate, or it will speed up the poison. Take some deep breaths."

Deep breaths. I could do this. I honed in on his smooth voice and let him guide me. He took a deep breath in and then slowly let it out. I did the same. With me shadowing him, we stood there, breathing in sync. It was oddly intimate, standing there, his warm hands on my shoulders, cocooned together in darkness. As the panic dissipated, I became aware of how close we were standing, his breath warm on my face. He was lightly caressing my neck with one of his thumbs. Slow, gentle circles. Tension of a new kind started to build. I met his eyes and his hands stilled, both of us caught in the moment. Was he going to try to kiss me? Did I want him to?

Before I could think too long on that, he dropped his hands and took a step back, clearing his throat.

I looked away, trying to ignore the disappointment. I hadn't wanted him to kiss me, had I?

He walked back to his bike and stooped to get something, but kept his attention focused on me.

Finished, he came back and when he started talking again, voice crisp and businesslike, he was close enough I could see the darker blue flecks in his light eyes. "We are going to go together, and when we're there, I need you to be okay so you can anchor me. They call it the Endless River because you can get lost in there forever. I need someone on the bank to guide me and help me find my way out."

"Wow, no pressure."

Ignoring my comment, he said, "I need you to be okay. Can you do this?"

I nodded.

"Good. Come on." He grabbed my hand firmly and pulled me after him, moving more slowly this time.

The path, if it could be called a path, was rocky and steep. I could see why he had to leave the motorcycle. I stumbled and stubbed my toes more times than I could count. It was so cold my fingers started feeling numb. I wiggled them and tried not to freak myself out with thoughts of frostbite.

As though he heard my thoughts, Tristan stopped and took his coat off, wrapping it around me. The soft fabric was warm from his body, and I wanted to cry with relief. I hadn't realized how cold I was until the warmth made everything tingle again.

"Better?"

I nodded. "Yes, thank you."

He grunted, grabbed my hand again, and led me over the rough, rocky terrain. The hill was steep, and my thighs reminded me I needed to add some inclines to my runs.

Up ahead, there were small bushes lit from behind by a strange blue and green light. As we rounded the hedge, a soft glow radiated from a cave, the opening framed with a gentle luminescence. Tristan led us inside. When we walked in, the dim light intensified, letting us see the rocky floor. Spindly plants glowed, highlighting a wall in the cave with just a trickle of a waterfall.

Picking our way carefully around large boulders, I asked, "What is it?"

"Some algae from the Fae Realm seeped across the gate. There is a spell containing it to the cave, but it's getting a little too bright. I'll have to remember to send someone here to clean it up." Hand on his sword, Tristan headed deeper into the cave and activated a hidden lever. The back wall moved aside enough to slip through. Tristan went first and, when I hesitated, he pulled me through the opening behind him. We had walked into a small room, only ten by ten, with one wall made entirely of light. He closed the opening behind us and then grabbed my hand. "Ready?"

Facing the glowing wall, I nodded. As he started pulling me through, I realized it was another gateway.

Unlike the last one, this one made my stomach drop, and my body felt like it was falling apart. Nothing was where it was supposed to be, everything topsy-turvy. Stepping through took only a second, but felt a lot longer.

Once on the other side, I fell to the ground, vomiting. Thankfully, I hadn't eaten recently, but the healing tea and terrible coffee came up in waves. I hadn't thought the coffee could taste any worse, but that was before I got to experience it a second time.

Tristan rubbed my back, and I growled at him. He ignored me. "It'll only last a minute. The forbidden passages don't have the stabilizers the other routes have. I should have warned you."

Spitting out the vomit, I wiped my mouth. My limbs were weak, like a two-day-old kitten, but I didn't want his help. I didn't need his help. Shaking him off, I managed to stand without falling over. That was promising.

"You good enough to walk? This passage is only open for a few hours every night, so we need to hurry and get back before it closes."

I took a deep breath and nodded. "I'll live. Lead the way." My voice was hoarse, but we both ignored it. My first few steps were shaky, but Tristan was right that the gate's effects faded quickly.

We walked for a while. I tried not to gawk at the strange curling plants that reached for us or the trees that puffed up like puffer fish when we got too close. There were purple butterflies and large, colorful flying creatures. Fairies? Everything had a slight glow about it, which lit up the surrounding area. It entranced and terrified me. I skirted around plants and bent away from the butterflies if they fluttered too close, not sure what was safe to touch.

Then I heard it. A rumbling in the distance.

As we got closer, the roaring got louder. I stumbled over a rock and glanced down for a few moments, making sure of my footing. When I glanced back up, I saw it. The raging river was a deep purple blue capped with white where violent water drove toward a pool of darker water in the distance. But the circle of water wasn't a pond or lake. It got bigger the closer we got. It was enormous and moving faster than the rapids of the river. It was a large whirlpool. The size of a football field, the swirling water made a loud rushing sound, the sides of the bank worn thin from the turning water. There was no wildlife in the pool, but strange tall trees and vines ran up to the edge.

Tristan stopped.

"Why are we stopping?"

"We're here." He nodded toward the swirling water and took off his shirt. His toned arms and back briefly dumbfounded me, and then I realized what that meant.

"Hold on. Wait a second. You said you were going into a river. That's not a river. It's a fucking whirlpool! People don't come back out of whirlpools!"

Tristan ignored me and grabbed a knife from his boot. He cut off a vine and pulled and pulled until he had a long line. Then he tied it around his waist. He pulled more from the trees until it pooled at my feet.

"This is everlasting vine. The vine will keep coming—they're miles long and are very tough to break. Once I go in, if I pull on it, it will keep coming, so I can't use it to help leverage myself out. I need an anchor. Someone to pull me back out against the whirlpool's current." He walked behind a tall tree, creating a natural pulley system by looping the vine around the tree's thick trunk.

"This is a terrible idea. What if I'm not strong enough? Look at the size of you and the size of me. Shouldn't I go instead and have you pull me out?" He was much larger than me, definitely over six feet. I probably couldn't even roll him, let alone pull him from a raging whirlpool.

He didn't even bother to look up from where he was gathering vines, muscles bunching and red runes glowing softly. "Can you hold your breath for over ten minutes?"

"Are you fucking kidding me?" I looked at the

swirling water of the whirlpool and then back at Tristan, desperately searching my brain for other options.

Pulling over more of the vine, he dropped the pile by my feet and put his hands on my shoulders, looking me directly in the eyes. "I am going. You can do this. You won't need as much strength as you think you do, since the vine is wrapped around the tree. Basic physics, right?" He winked at me as he handed me the end of the vine and wrapped it around my wrists.

Tristan bent and took off his shoes. He kept his pants and most of his weapons on, but he removed the large ones, like his sword. I couldn't keep my gaze from roving over his chest and the strange red marks that glowed over his torso, symbols of some kind.

I licked my lips. "What if I'm not strong enough to pull you back up?"

"Then I will die."

"You don't owe me enough for this. Not enough to risk your life."

"I always pay my debts, and I always keep my word. I will get you the algae." His light eyes bored into mine. "And you will be strong enough to make sure I come back out."

"But—"

"You can pull me up. You are stronger than you think you are. You were cold earlier because you expected to be cold. Did you notice that later, the cold didn't bother you as much?"

I shivered, pulling his coat, which I was still wearing, tighter. "It got warmer, and you gave me your coat."

"No, it's been getting colder. It's gone down fifteen degrees since I gave you that coat, but you expected to get warmer with the coat, so your body adjusted. Mythics have some immunity to different extremes of temperature. You were able to tap into that by believing there was a reason for you to be warmer. We are also stronger and faster. Believe in your strength, and you will tap into that as well. Or we will both die. Me now, and you when we can't get your antidote."

The enormity of my part was a crushing weight, bearing me down. If I couldn't tap into my mythic strength, we would both likely die. I took a deep breath and tried for some levity. "That was a cheerful pep talk."

"Take a potion."

"Yes, sir." I couldn't keep the sarcasm out of my voice. He was risking his life for me, even if he said he wasn't, and I still wanted to smack him for being an overbearing ass. I took out one of the small bottles and chugged the dark liquid, the bitter orange taste lingering but my strength returning tenfold. That was powerful stuff.

"Ideally, when I'm at the algae, I'll stop pulling on the vine. Give me a minute to collect it and then pull me up. Ready?"

I tightened my grip and nodded. Before I could take another breath, let alone change my mind, he ran towards the whirlpool and jumped off the edge of the bowl into the deep purple water below.

Chapter 21

Tristan's dive was perfect, barely creating a splash. I loosened my grip on the vine. More and more of the strange dark green plant flowed in after him. After what seemed like hours but was probably only two or three minutes, the thick vine stopped unraveling. Did that mean he'd found the algae? I gave him another minute and then started pulling him back up, wrapping my hands in my shirt to help protect them from the sticky, abrasive surface. There was a tug in the other direction, and then it stopped. I rolled the vine back out. This time I waited for two minutes. My heart pounded. I knew he'd said he could hold his breath for ten minutes, but everything in me screamed that wasn't possible and I was killing him. The unfamiliar vine twisted, and the steady, rushing roar of the whirlpool matched my thundering pulse. As soon as two minutes were up, I pulled the line in again. I didn't let myself look at the pool or see if I could see him. I focused on hand over hand, pulling with all my strength. My muscles burned. The rough surface tore at my skin and my fingers ached, but I kept pulling. As long as I could pull small inches of vine, I kept going. Hand over hand.

There was a *thud* and then another *thud*. I pulled for a few more seconds, hand over hand, and then turned and looked. Tristan's torso was over the ridge. He hung there, unconscious. I pulled faster, unsure where the strength came from. I was sure my arms died in the small rush and I burned the skin off my palms, but I pulled until he was over the ledge and on solid ground. Then I dropped the vine and ran to him.

Turning him over, I listened for a breath and heard nothing. Trying not to panic, I pushed my hands, locked together, into his hard stomach, hoping to dispel the water. One push. Two. Three. After the fourth, a gush of dark fluid poured from his mouth, and I turned him to his side and let the water spew onto the ground.

Wracking coughs shook his body, and I held him and cried while he breathed.

He breathed.

This hadn't killed him. I hadn't killed him. Holding him in my arms, I wept, vowing to make this up to him.

I don't know how long we stayed that way. Me holding him tight, him gasping for air and spitting out water. Eventually, he sat up and grabbed my hand. I sucked in a sharp breath, noticing how raw and red my hands were. Hoarsely he croaked, "I got it, but we have to go." Standing, he cut off the vine and tugged on his shoes and shirt. "The barrier will change soon. We don't have much time."

Stumbling back the way we'd come, we both leaned heavily on each other, exhausted beyond words. We made it to the site. Tristan didn't even hesitate, but pulled us through. Once on the other side, we collapsed to the ground, bodies tangled together. I was so tired this time that the nausea didn't faze me at all. A few moments later, the light went out, plunging us into darkness. It had been close, but we'd made it.

Tristan sat up, and I shivered at the cold as his body left mine. As I reached for him, he grabbed my arm and pulled me to standing. My legs shook. I was so tired, all I wanted to do was curl up on the ground and sleep. I could feel that icy fire in the pit of my stomach growing and spreading. The poison was gaining ground. I debated taking another potion, but knew I should hold off as long as possible. My entire body ached.

"We're going to have to help each other down this hill. We can do it, but we need to work together. No stopping." He cupped my face with his hands. "Got it? Are you with me?" Unspoken was the *we might not get up if we stopped to rest* part.

His words registered…barely. I was in a semi-conscious state. Exhausted and hurt, moving via pure willpower. I was sure he was the same, having almost died. I nodded, or at least I think I did. Together, we stumbled down the hill toward his bike, prickly bushes and thick trees as much help as hindrance as we tripped over one and caught ourselves on the other. When one of us stumbled, the other picked them up. Warm skin getting colder as we trudged down the hill. Him yelling, me yelling. We took turns supporting each other and egging each other on until we reached his bike. Then muscle memory took over. Tristan got on, and I mounted behind him, sinking against his firm back, breathing him in, his unique scent mixing with the brine of the Endless River.

I must have blacked out at some point, because when I opened my eyes again, we were outside the healer's hut. I don't know how I stayed on the bike and could only guess that Tristan must have held me there. Half-dead himself, he somehow got us there together.

Strong arms guided me off the bike and then scooped me up. I didn't have the strength to protest. I heard a murmur or two. Then someone said, "Almost too late."

****

Time was fluid. I had no idea how long we had been there when I was propped up and a warm cup was placed near my mouth. "Drink."

I opened my mouth and swallowed. The contents were thick and bitter. I almost spat it out, but a firm hand covered my mouth and forced me to swallow. They tipped the cup to my lips again, but I turned my head away, avoiding the vile brew that still coated my throat like slime. Strong fingers gripped my chin and held me still, forcing the awful, slimy liquid down my throat until the cup was empty. As I gagged, they lay me back against a pile of soft cushions.

I must have fallen asleep again.

When I woke next, I was warm and cozy, and I snuggled deeper into the covers, only to have my eyes pop open in surprise when the covers were a hard wall of muscle. I was sleeping in a bed. With Tristan. I had never slept with a guy before. I'd never slept next to a guy before. His warm arms around me and light sandalwood scent made me feel safe and yet nervous at the same time. I wanted both to curl up closer and to jump out of bed and run away. Knowing how sick I'd been, I might have drooled on him all night or snored.

I froze, unsure what to do next. Before I could decide, Tristan stirred, awakened by my movement. Eyes wide, he seemed as shocked by our predicament as I was. He tried to jump out of bed and fell back against me, pulled in by the sheet wrapped tightly around us, pressing our bodies together. His hands were warm as he untangled us from the blankets and each other. Did his

210

hand linger on my waist, or was that my imagination?

Stepping away from the bed, he reached down and picked up something off the floor. Pulling the shirt on over hard, smooth muscles, he turned to me and asked, "How are you feeling?"

Blinking dumbly for a moment—yes, his muscles were that distracting—I sat up, pulling the soft yellow comforter with me. I was mostly dressed, but was missing my shirt. I had a bra on, but what the hell had happened to my shirt? It wasn't like I had a stab wound that needed tending. I was poisoned, for goodness' sake. I took stock and realized that the cold pit that had been spreading through me was gone. As well as most of my wounds. "Okay, I guess. Tired and sore, but okay." I searched the floor, a dark oak hardwood, but didn't see it. "Do you know where my shirt is?"

Bending down, he grabbed a shirt and tossed it to me. "No salvaging that last one, I'm afraid. Sorry. The doctor likes to cut off clothes. She said you could have this one."

I took the shirt, muttering under my breath about crazy doctors. Tristan snorted so it's possible I wasn't that quiet. This shirt said, "I want to be a nice person, but everyone is just so stupid." Hot pink again. I shrugged it over my head, feeling flushed with his gaze on me. Once I was clothed, I dropped the blanket. "How are you feeling?"

"I'm fine."

I grinned. "Do you know what FINE stands for?"

He grinned back and said, "Yes. And no, I'm really fine, not *that* fine. I never freak out, and I'm not emotional."

I laughed. "But you might be neurotic or insecure?"

He winked. "I plead the fifth."

The half demon had a sense of humor after all.

He stretched, hands almost hitting the ceiling. "Come on. If you're okay, we should get going, see if we can get a lead on your mom's killer. They might even lead us to the demons who stole the key. I wish I knew where they were going, now that they have it."

I stood too, balancing against the white stucco wall, legs a little shaky. "What if I told you they don't?"

"Don't what?" His eyes bored into me, like a hawk hunting its prey.

I swallowed hard. I hadn't meant to trust him with this, but it'd just come out. He had saved my life. He'd already had what he'd needed—I'd gotten him the water from the Celestial Realm. He almost died curing me when he had no reason to help. Deciding, I said, "They don't have the key. I have it."

He was across the small room in seconds, covering my mouth with his large hand, glancing around like a crazy man. Shaking his head, he whispered in my ear, "Not here. Are you insane? What if the healer heard you? You'd be a target before nightfall, if you even had that long."

I shook his hand away, whispering, "But won't that help? Letting someone know I have it? That is bound to bring out my mother's killer, right? I've been searching for months. I've gotten nowhere. Maybe I should just let them come to me?"

"Don't be stupid, that's too dangerous. Lie low, and I'll help you find the killer. Don't put that kind of target on your back. You'll get yourself killed." He looked uncertain for a minute and then asked, "Do you want me to hold on to it for you? I promise I won't use it until you're ready. We could do a blood oath."

I noticed he very carefully kept calling the key "it." I followed suit. "I can't. It's stuck. I can't get it off."

He picked up my hands, turning them both this way and that. "You're wearing it? I don't see it."

I stared down at the tiny silver ring, the twisting vines glinting around the three stones. "It has some sort of cloaking spell, but trust me, it isn't going anywhere."

He nodded, smoothing his thumb over my fingers. "Interesting." Squeezing my hands, he dropped them. "Finish getting ready. Don't tell anyone. I've got to think." He walked off, way too energetic for having just woken up.

After he left, I stepped into a cozy half bath with yellow cabinets to match the kitchen. I finger combed my knotted dark hair and tried to brush my teeth with a finger and some water, finally giving up and calling it good. Not much I could do without supplies.

Heading to the front, I saw the healer slip Tristan a small bag, and my stomach sank. I remembered him telling me, "Trust no one, not even me. Everyone answers to someone else." He peeked inside the bag, nodded, and then walked away. They had some kind of alternate deal going on. What was it? Did it have anything to do with me? It felt like someone had splashed cold water on my face, startling me awake. I took a deep breath. It was probably just a bag of bagels, and I was jumping to conclusions.

What if it wasn't?

I ducked back into the back room, trembling. Why had I told him about the key? Had I really thought I could trust a half demon? Had I started caring about him? One who had pulverized some guy's hands and killed people for his dad? *No. Just no.* I had told him because I needed help. No feelings involved.

Tristan poked his head around the corner and then came fully into the room, bag still in his fist. "You ready? The healer was looking for you. She wanted to take one last look at your injuries."

Standing straight, I asked point blank, "What's in the bag?"

His lips tightened, and tucking the bag away into a pocket, he said, "Another project. Nothing to do with you, I promise." So, not bagels.

"Sure," I said, but we both knew I didn't believe him. The tension between us was so thick you could cut it with a knife.

"It's not about you." His voice was firm, eyes steady. The problem was that I didn't believe him. When I didn't respond, he shook his head and turned away. "Come out when you're ready. I'll wait out front."

After he left, I banged my fist against the wall. If he was making alternate deals, so could I. I needed to make this work for myself. Taking a deep breath, I headed back toward the front. I was in control of my fate.

The healer smiled at me. "How's the patient this morning?"

"Much better, thank you."

She pulled me to a small curtained off area, sat me down, and looked me over one more time. "Looks like you're a bit worn for wear but will survive." She was looking at my pink hands that had resembled hamburger meat yesterday from pulling Tristan in with the vine. The potion had worked wonders and had healed the worst of the damage. I could move everything, but I was still sore. It had also healed the remaining bug bites but did nothing for the overwhelming exhaustion.

I couldn't hold back. I needed to know. "What was in the bag you gave Tristan?"

She put my hands down, patting them gently, hers frail and cool. "Oh, my dear, I never reveal other people's business. Sorry. If you want to know, you'll have to ask him." Helping me up, she said, "We're all done. Did you need anything else from me, honey? A love spell?" She waggled her gray eyebrows, making me blush.

I was in charge of my fate. I would not wait for Tristan. I was going to get the killer to come to me. Besides, Tristan was wrong. Things were different now. This wasn't like when my mom had the key. I knew others were looking for it and that they were dangerous. I would take precautions. Before I could change my mind, I said, "No, but if I knew how to get information about the key, do you know how I might go about selling it?"

Her gray eyes lit up with curiosity. "Hmm, let me ask around, and I'll see if I can broker a good deal. I get twenty percent. Fair?"

I nodded, and she gave me her card. The information on it was written in a curly italicized script.

"My private number is on the back. Check back later tonight, and I'll let you know if I found anything."

I nodded. "Thank you."

"Pleasure doing business." Watching her rub her hands in glee, I wondered if I'd done the right thing. Oh well. Too late to back out now.

Chapter 22

About ten minutes later, we were all packed up, and I climbed on the bike behind Tristan. I tried to think of a subtle way to ask him about the bag again, but my tired brain produced nothing.

Tristan's secret deal created a tension, like a wall between us, as we rode the wet streets to the shop. A wall neither of us breached.

As soon as he stopped in front of the family store, I got off the bike and headed to the door.

"Wait." He halted me, grabbing my arm and then letting go. Running a hand through his dark hair, he said, "Look, I'm going to spend a few days checking out leads in the Demon Realm. I have to check in—I've been gone too long already—but while I'm there, I'll see if I can help."

I turned back, smile hesitant at the olive branch. "I'll come with you."

"You're not allowed, remember? When we went last night, we went through a back door to the middle of nowhere. Asking questions in the Demon Realm is different. I will contact you if I find anything. Don't do anything stupid." He put his helmet back on, revved his bike, and left. He didn't look back.

"Stupid. Right."

Making my way into the shop, I dropped my stuff

off, plugged my phone into the charger, and then made a beeline for the bathroom. After a long, hot shower and a change of clothes, I made a strong cup of coffee and a sandwich. I curled up on my bed and grabbed the manual. The cover was a soft brown leather. Taking a long drink of the bitter coffee and a bite of my PB and J, I opened the book. I let out a long breath. I could finally read it. The second half of the manual included sections on each of the different realms. I took another sip of coffee, flipping past the introduction chapters. I'd start with the Demon Realm.

My jaw dropped as I read about Chaos time. It was a time once a month when everything was legal. It was barbaric, but it did help explain why Tristan had been so easy to convince to help me check on my mother's death. There was a sanctioned time to kill. Killing outside of that time meant you got a visit from an Enforcer Demon, someone like Tristan. I snorted. I'd stupidly thought he'd been helping me, but he'd just been doing his job, assuming it had been done outside of the regulated killing time. Closing the book, I slammed it against my bed. It did nothing besides bounce, but it made me feel better.

I went to the kitchen to put my dishes away and stopped when I noticed Dad's small black suitcase. I had missed it earlier. Was he home? "Dad? Daddy? You home?" I walked around the apartment and then went downstairs to the shop. There were small signs that he had been there, but panic crept over me when I couldn't find him. "This is stupid. He's probably next door getting a coffee." I grabbed my phone from the charger and sent a quick text. I immediately heard a ding from the reply text, which settled my nerves until I read it.

— We have your father in the Demon Realm. To get him back, give us the key. We know you know where it is. Call this number when you have it. If you take too long, you will get body parts as an incentive. Work quickly. —

I wanted to scream that I didn't have it, but stopped, remembering a demon's ability to tell when I was lying. Would that work on texts? Better not to test that theory. I replied. *—What if it takes longer? —*

— Poor Dad would appreciate it if you didn't take longer. I think he likes all his body parts where they belong. —

My fingers shook as I typed out the question ringing in my head, making me sick. *—How do I know he's not dead already? —*

My phone startled me as it rang, making me jump. Fumbling with it, I answered. "Hello."

"Pumpkin? Are you okay?" Hearing Dad's gruff voice, I got all choked up. Legs weak, I sat on the ground, trying to hold my tears at bay. He was all I had left. No one was allowed to take him from me. No one.

Putting my head on my knees, I said, "I'm fine. Are you okay? What happened? Where are you? I'm going to get you back, you hear me?" I choked the words out, trying to keep my voice light.

"Don't do anything crazy. I am fine. Whatever they tell you to do, don't. There is always a better way."

I hugged the phone to my ear, fingers white. "I love you, Daddy."

"I love you…" His voice faded away.

A stranger's voice came on, clipped and terse. "You have one day. After that, you get your first body part. Good luck." The click echoed in my ear as he hung up.

Tristan could have helped, but he was already gone.

I could have the bubble tea shop try to contact him, but would I have to say why and put an even bigger target on my back? And if I didn't say why, would he even come? He'd been in the Human Realm a lot lately. Would asking him to come get him in trouble? I should probably try to go to him instead.

I chewed on a thumbnail. What was with these crazy people assuming I knew what to do? I was a teenager, for crying out loud. Of course, I already had the key. What I really needed was to find a way to the Demon Realm. Then I could find Tristan and get help getting my dad back. Gracie had been working in the celestial prison. She knew the other realms. Maybe she could help. Before I could think too hard on it, I looked her number up and sent her a quick text.

— *I need help. You free?* —

The reply was immediate. — *I can't help you.* —

My fingers tapped away. — *My dad has been taken. Please.* —

— *I hate you. Meet me at the coffee shop next to your store. I'll be there in twenty minutes* —

— *Thank you* —

I took a deep breath. I needed more sleep, but it seemed like I wouldn't get any today. I walked next door and ordered a mocha with a triple shot of espresso. Sitting in my favorite corner booth, I waited, breathing in the comforting chocolatey scent. Gracie was early, bless her. I somehow managed to wait for her to order a coffee and then come sit with me rather than running up to her like a crazy person.

She plopped down in the seat across from me, her non-glamoured form only slightly different from her glamoured one. I was getting better at controlling my

Sight. As I pinched the magic flow off and on, her eyes got a little bigger, skin a little brighter. The black wings tucked against her back were hardly noticeable, hidden by her oversized black coat.

"You look awful."

"Gee. Thanks." The sarcastic remark tumbled out before I could stop it. I took a deep breath, reminding myself I needed her help.

She took a sip of her drink. "What happened?"

"I got a text telling me they took my dad, and I needed to give them…something they want to get him back." Gracie narrowed her eyes at me and I winced. It was a terrible explanation, but I wasn't sure what else to say.

"Who is 'they' and what do they want?" Gracie's voice was barely above a whisper as she leaned forward over the rough wood table.

I looked at the ground, scuffing my shoe. "I'm not sure on the who, and as to the what… It's better if I don't say. It is valuable, and it seems to have put a target on my back, so you're better off not knowing." I took a deep drink from my mocha, giving her time to respond. When she didn't protest, I continued. "I asked for proof of life, and they called and let Dad talk with me. The caller said Dad was in the Demon Realm. I want to go look for him, but since I'm banned, I need another way in, other than the main gate."

"You can't go to the Demon Realm."

I stared blankly at her. "Why not?"

"It's dangerous. No one goes unless they have to. They don't welcome outsiders. Anything goes in a place like that." She looked haunted, freckles standing out on her pale face.

"I know someone there who could help me, if I can find him…a friend." Remembering that Tristan's nickname was the Hammer, I didn't think telling her I was going to search for him would make her want to help me get there.

"So, let me get this straight. You need someone to sneak you into the Demon Realm, locate your friend, and send them to you so you don't get caught. Then you and your friend are going to find your dad, who's being held by who knows what, who knows where. Then you're going to try to break him out and return here without anyone being the wiser? That about sum it up?"

"Yes. Can you help me?"

She slammed her cup down, coffee splashing through the hole in the lid. "Me? No. What kind of moron do you take me for? That's insane."

"Don't you know where it is and what to avoid once we get there? I just need to get there and find my friend. Then you can leave and not be a part of anything."

"Yes, but I've never been by myself before. I was always with someone else. And how exactly would we find your friend? It would be like searching for a needle in a haystack!" She leaned back in her chair, arms folded. "It's suicide."

"It's not that bad. You won't be by yourself. You'll be with me." I felt stupid even saying it. Like I would be any help. "And my friend will help once we're there." I hoped. "Please? If I don't find my dad soon, they told me they'd start mailing body parts! My mom just died. Please don't make me lose him too." I started crying, unable to stop the tears and not sure I wanted to. She wouldn't help. I wouldn't help in her place. It was hopeless.

"Fine." She spat the word out. "But you will owe me a favor. A huge favor."

"What? Really?" I nodded, sniffling. "I'll do anything." I thought about Tristan crushing that man's hand. "Almost anything. Anything except hurting people."

Gracie chugged the rest of her coffee. "You'll do anything for my help, except hurting someone else, correct?"

I nodded, feeling slightly uneasy at her phrasing.

"Deal. Come on. We have a lot of work to do."

Chapter 23

Gracie took me to a large, out-of-the-way fountain at the edge of town. The water poured down the sides of rectangular concrete blocks, both vertical and horizontal. Kids could jump from one to another and it looked like a fun place for them to frolic in the summer. Another portal near water. Tapping Gracie on the arm, I leaned in close to be heard over the waterfalls and asked, "Are all portals near water?"

"I think so. Something about the water making the energies between realms more flexible. I didn't pay that much attention, sorry." She was hopping from one block to another toward the top of the fountain, and I followed her. Once near the top, she snuck around a block and went behind it, dropping on the other side. I was surprised. From down below, I never would have expected there to be a way to get to the other side. She drew a series of runes on the side of the block, and it started glowing softly.

She hesitated and turned to face me, hazel eyes looking greener than usual. "Are you sure you want to do this? If you get caught, you will be severely punished. The Demon Realm isn't like the Celestial one. They are brutal. They beat people and take slaves."

I'd watched them cut someone's hand off in the Celestial Realm, and she was telling me the Demon Realm was worse? They sounded the same to me. "The celestials have slaves too."

"The Demon Realm is different. The celestials keep slaves, but they have a way to get free. They have hope. It is a small hope, but it is still hope. If you get caught by the demons and sold, you have no hope. Ever. Unless someone breaks you out, and the Pit is almost impossible to penetrate, so even if there was someone willing to try, they'd probably fail. You would need an inside person or a lot of money. We can turn around right now. There are laws against hurting humans. You said your dad is full human. They might just give him back if you don't meet the deadline."

Half of what she said flew over my head, but I caught one very important detail, and it rang in my head, making my blood turn cold. "You said might."

Gracie swallowed. "The laws governing Mythics were made by the Mythical Council, but right now the Council is made up of mostly celestials. A lot of demons ignore the Council's laws and only follow the laws of their realm. They don't like following celestial rules and might do exactly what they said they'd do and just cover it up. Make it look like a burglary gone wrong. A house fire. Something like that."

"I can't leave his life up to chance like that. He's all I have left. I have to do this."

Gracie gave a terse nod. "Okay. Let's go."

I briefly wondered why she'd agreed so quickly and then decided to just trust in my good luck. I needed her help and couldn't afford to look too closely at it. Gracie drew a last symbol on the concrete block, and it shimmered a dark red. When she walked through, I followed. This time I was better prepared for the feeling of my stomach dropping out. The nausea was awful, but

I managed not to dry heave when we walked through to the other side. Barely.

I took a step away from the portal, dark trees on either side. The sky was the same deep blue as the Celestial Realm, but the plants were all in yellows and browns. It was hot here, and I took off my hoodie and tied it around my waist. I leaned against a tree with bark so dark it was almost black. It was huge. Its trunk would take ten people to encircle it with their arms.

"Welcome to the Demon Realm. Don't touch the plants. Many of them eat people."

I jumped away from the tree, brushing at my arms nervously.

She pulled a potion out of her purse and shoved it at me. "Drink this. It will encourage people to look away from you."

I took it and chugged. This one was sickly sweet and reminded me of candy corn. I handed the empty container back to her, and she tucked it back into her black purse.

"Don't look anyone in the eye. They will take that as a challenge, and you don't want to draw attention to yourself. When in doubt, hide. Don't talk to anyone. I will do all the talking. Understood?"

"Yes," I said, nodding. I held back the 'Yes, sir,' sure she'd take offense. The last thing I needed was for her to get snippy and abandon me here. I followed right on her heels, careful not to touch the surrounding plants. I had a mental image of a small plant growing an enormous mouth and swallowing me whole. Sometimes having a vivid imagination sucked.

Trudging forward, she intercepted a wide path. and following it, asked, "How do we get in touch with your friend?"

I swallowed. We were here so I had to tell her, no more putting it off. Hopefully, she wouldn't be too upset. "I'm not exactly sure. He's an Enforcer Demon. Maybe they all hang out at the same place? He told me people call him the Hammer."

She turned, rage on her face. "The Hammer? No one is friends with the Hammer." She was whisper screaming at me, trembling with fury. "Are you trying to get us both killed?"

I took a step back, alarmed. I glanced around, glad we were still the only people in sight. "Okay, maybe not friends, but we have a deal. He'll help."

"I hope you're right. FYI, once we locate him, I'm outta here. You know he's evil, right? He may be handsome, but he's not this bright knight in shining armor. He's a killer and a torturer. He does whatever his father asks. He's dangerous." She stewed in silence as we walked. I could hear her muttering under her breath and was pretty sure it wasn't flattering. I hung back a little, giving her some space.

The ground was made from a rough sand-like substance but was too coarse and dark to be sand. It reminded me of fresh-roasted coffee grounds, dark and grainy. The sky was a beautiful dark blue, deeper than in the Human Realm. "Hey, Gracie."

"What?"

Her bark almost made me say never mind, but I was too curious. "The sky is the same as in the Celestial Realm. Are these the same place?"

"They're different segments of the same place. There was a war a long time ago, and they divided the realm up with magic. They now consider each realm separate. You can't walk from one to the other, so I suppose they are separate in the grand scheme of things. Now be quiet. I can't talk to you right now. I'm too mad, and we don't want to draw attention. It's going to start getting crowded soon. Remember to keep your mouth shut and your head down."

The dusty path was now lined with dark trees. After about fifteen minutes, small huts started showing up between the trees. They were made with the same dark wood, so they blended into the landscape. As we walked, there were more and more crammed together, hundreds of little houses. Soon, the houses gave way to booths and people and strange creatures, yelling out what they were selling.

I didn't understand a single word.

They didn't speak English here. I hadn't even thought of that. I kept expecting Gracie to stop and talk to someone to find out where we were going, but she never did. Instead, she stayed on the same path, moving forward. There were more non-humanoids here than I'd ever seen in one place before. It was disconcerting to see what looked like a gerbil selling something to a slender, sloth-like creature.

I caught up and whispered to her. "Do you know where we're going?"

"Of course. Now shut up."

I closed my mouth and followed. She grabbed a small kid sitting in the street, begging. Short, with human features, he had a coarse coat of fur and wore a pair of baggy shorts which ended a few inches above squat paws with sharp claws. Gracie quickly wrote something on a piece of paper she pulled from her pocket, folded it, and handed both the note and a coin to the boy. *To meet up with Tristan? Does she know how to reach him?* I wanted to ask but didn't want to get yelled at again. I understood that I'd put her in a bad spot. But Tristan wasn't as terrible as she thought. I hoped.

We kept walking as the kid scampered off—presumably to deliver the note, but what did I know? After a while, we passed a large gateway made of obsidian, guarded by creatures that looked like large wolves crossed with Egyptian cats. Twice the size of humans, they had a short fur coat in a deep brown, large ears that perked up as we walked closer, and pointed snouts with sharp teeth. The tails that hung out behind them ended on small barbs. They wore dark armor in some sort of metal material I was unfamiliar with. *Was that another portal?* It looked like it. *Why was it so much more heavily guarded here? Where were the trolls?*

Giving them a wide berth, we walked into a large, open square. Near the front was a raised platform with someone yelling out words in a quick staccato rhythm. Off to the side was another of the strange creatures that had been guarding the gate. Gracie waved and walked over. She talked for a moment in that strange tongue that I didn't understand. She pointed at me a few times. Was she asking about Tristan? I moved closer, walking near the edge of the square, trying to stay inconspicuous.

Before I knew it, they shook hands. The guy she was talking to nodded at someone else who approached me and clasped a cold, hard manacle onto one of my wrists and started pulling me away with an attached chain. I stopped, yanking on the chain. "Wait, what?! Gracie, what did you do?"

She stared at me defiantly, arms crossed. "I took you to the Demon Realm, and you will soon see Tristan. I kept my word. In return, you are doing a favor for me. You will not have to hurt anyone. The parameters of our deal have been met."

I shook the dark metal chain. "Why would you do this?"

"You said you'd do anything for your dad. I'd do anything for my sister. Anything, even if it makes me a terrible monster." She stopped, blinking back tears. "I've been trying to earn the coin to buy her. But it's impossible, so I traded you for her. I wasn't sure I could go through with it, but when you told me who you were here to meet…"

She stepped in close and pulled me into a firm hug. I struggled, wanting to scratch her eyes out, not hug, but stilled as I heard her continue in a soft whisper. "The Hammer can get you out. Easily. I sent a note to him for you. I hope he is a better man than he seems. If it all works out, come find me. If I can, I will help you. I *am* sorry."

Gracie turned, and her face lit up with joy. Tears streamed down her pale cheeks. A young girl, no older than twelve, thin and with rags hanging off her body, followed a guard toward them. Her arms hung listlessly in front of her, and her eyes were glazed over. When the guard took off her manacles, she stared at her wrists in shock, like she'd never imagined in her wildest dreams that this could happen. She looked up, saw Gracie and, for a moment, looked bewildered. Gracie ran forward and swept the little girl into a hug. As they grasped each other tightly, Gracie led the thin waif away.

"I'm sorry," she whispered as she passed, her arms holding the small girl tight.

I was so stupid. One of the first things Tristan taught

me was to trust no one. Why had I thought Gracie could be trusted? Because we'd been passing acquaintances in high school?

The guard dragged at the end of my chain. I pulled back, and he stumbled. Swinging around, I yanked my chains as hard as I could, trying to make a break for it. I didn't know where I'd go, but I definitely wasn't going to sit still and let someone sell me. Before I could get two steps, a zap of electricity jolted me and I fell to the ground, convulsing. Body shaking uncontrollably, I crawled away, coarse sand sticking between my fingers. I was zapped again. I could hear everyone murmuring excitedly in that strange language. A crowd was gathering. *Are they all going to stand and watch as some innocent bystander gets made into a slave? What's wrong with these people?*

Another zap, and my limbs turned to jelly. I couldn't even pull myself along the ground anymore. Faces around me were laughing. Someone poked me with a stick. The murmur was nearing a fever pitch when a loud *thud* echoed throughout the square.

Chapter 24

Everyone froze. Silence rang out as loud as the murmuring had been before. I tried to move my head, but it was too heavy. My muscles weren't working right. The convulsions were lessening, but the effects hadn't worn off yet. A strong baritone rang out, words unintelligible, but the voice was achingly familiar. *Tristan?* Was he here to save me or to tell me he told me so and scold me for being so stupid? Strong hands scooped me up. I tried to fight.

There was a soft whisper in my ear. "Stay still."

Tristan. I relaxed and let him carry me away.

He strode forward, and everyone cleared a path. A covered carriage was waiting. It was made of that black wood and polished to a fine sheen. As he approached, the door opened, and he deposited me inside on smooth, plush seats and then sat down beside me. He whistled a few low notes, and we took off.

Looking up front, I didn't see a driver, just flaming horses pulling the carriage. "What? Who's driving?" My voice was slurred, but I could talk.

"The fire steeds. Careful—you don't want to insult them."

Because of course, fire steeds. *What the heck are fire steeds?* I looked again at the horses that nobody was steering. The fiery horses in front were pitch black, covered in bright dancing flames, with red glowing hooves and dark, bat-like wings. With a lurch, the carriage angled upward, and I realized they were taking off.

Then we were in the air and alone. Well, except for the flying horses. Tristan's strong hand grabbed my chin and turned my face toward his. "That was beyond stupid. Why would you come here? And without me. What were you thinking?" His voice was low and angry.

I swallowed, trying to get my tongue to form words. They were slurred, but I could choke out, "Dad. Someone took my dad. Brought him here. I didn't know how to reach you. I didn't know what to do, so I asked Gracie for help."

He shoved my face aside. "The girl who sold you? Yeah, that was a real solid choice. You're damn lucky the note she sent got to me in time. If they'd have taken you to the Pit, you'd have been lost, even to me."

"What did the note say?" He was clenching and unclenching his fists. *Is he imagining strangling me?*

"She sent a note saying that Zoey was an idiot and was going to be sold today in the square and to get there immediately."

I scoffed. "It did not."

"Pretty close." He pulled something from a hidden compartment in the carriage. "Here." He shoved some yellow leaves into my mouth. "Chew those. They'll help with the aftershocks."

I hadn't even realized I was having them, but now that he mentioned it, my arms and legs were convulsing again. The leaves tasted like dirt. *Why do cures always have to taste so awful?* When the shaking lessened, I asked, "Where are we going?"

"To my place, at least until I figure out how to sneak

you back."

My head jerked up, and I grabbed his arm. "I need to find my father. You have to help me!"

His voice was hard. "I don't *have* to do anything."

"Please. I'll do anything. What do you want?"

Tristan's cool blue eyes were darker than normal but still glowing brightly. There was a fire there. He slammed his fist down, making the carriage rattle. "Never offer anything! I could ask you to cut up your dad and eat him after I save him. This. Isn't. Your. World." He enunciated each word individually, his voice getting louder and harsher.

I swallowed. "I know. I'm sorry. I keep forgetting."

He gestured out the window to the fiery horses. "Look around. How could you forget?"

"I forget around you." I realized what I'd said and blushed, staring down at the dark red upholstery. Rushing on, I added, "You seem so human. It's hard to think you'd even think of asking something like that."

He laughed, and the sound had no mirth. "Ask around. I ask many horrible things. Zoey, I do not belong to myself. You have to remember that. Most of us belong to someone else, and a lot of those who are in power are ancient and…different…than what you know." He paused, thinking. "What happened to your father?"

I sat up and started to tell him, but I got distracted. I hadn't noticed before, but here his runes burned with fire. And he had wings. Huge black wings. He hadn't had them in the Human Realm. Did they retract somehow? My voice trailed off, and I reached out a hand and touched the soft edge of his wing. Tracing it to a sharp barb on the end.

His breath shuddered, and he grabbed my hand.

"Stop."

I pulled my hand into my lap, embarrassed. I was running my hands over him like he was some sort of museum exhibit. My cheeks heated. "I'm sorry, I didn't mean to, I-I was curious. It's not an excuse. I'm so sorry."

His voice was low and husky, and there was a catch in it. "I don't mind, but now is not the time for me to be distracted, and touching my wings like that is…distracting."

Mortified, I stared at my lap, cheeks flaming.

He cleared his throat. "Tell me more about your father. Why did they take him?"

I turned away, looking out the window at the wispy clouds. "I saw the healer give you the bag. I was mad at you for keeping secrets and was stupid and impatient. I told the healer that I may know something about the key and to let me know if anyone was interested."

"You did what?!" His voice was so loud, the carriage shook. "What kind of idiotic—"

I hurried to interrupt him, alarmed at the smoke starting to waft around the small space. "That's it. I didn't say I had it or even that I knew how to get it, just that I might be able to get info. Look, it was dumb. I get it. I made a mistake. I don't need a lecture; I need help. They took him." My voice cracked. "They sent this."

I reached into my pocket and pulled out my phone with the message, handing it over. He read the message and then handed me back the phone, but then clenched his fist as though he were crushing it.

I cradled the sparkly case protectively, glad it was now safely in my possession.

"It could be the Kryjeen. Few Aerellians would have

234

sent a message via text and would have the means to get to your father so quickly. Technology exists but is not as prevalent here. The Kryjeen reside in the…I think the closest translation would be the Poison Pits. In Death Valley. But it could be half a dozen other factions as well. We need more information."

"We could try looking there. The Poison Pits sound lovely. Are they as lovely as they sound?"

He scoffed, the smoke and fire from his runes dying down. Now that they didn't look like they were on fire, I could see they were all symbols of some kind, some cut more jaggedly than others. Were they carved into his skin? "You're joking, right? You would never make it out alive."

"Maybe, but I have to try. If he's not there, please help me find out where. What can I give you? What can I do to get your help? I can't lose my dad. I just…I can't." My voice broke, and I blinked back tears.

"The key. I know you cannot give it to me, but help me find the first of the three artifacts. Do that and I will help you find your father. And before you ask, I do not intend to use it for harm. I want to bring down one of the barrier spells that limit power. It should be distributed equally."

My mind spun with the implications. What would happen if the celestials no longer held as much control over the rest of the Others? "But—"

"That's the deal."

If what Tristan said was true, it was only one of the barrier spells. Assuming each artifact was tied to one, there were three. I could help the fae and the demons and still keep things the same. *I'm a teenager. I can't do any major damage. Can I?* Thinking on Tristan's earlier warnings, I said, "Only if you help get me and my father back to the Human Realm, alive and well."

He gave a wry grin. "You are learning. Fine. Agreed."

I wondered if he'd agreed too easily. I was sure there must be some sort of loophole I'd missed, but I wasn't a skilled negotiator. The deal sounded good to me, and I needed his help. "I agree, too."

Tristan nodded.

I fiddled with a loose thread on the red seat cushion. "Do we need to write it up or anything?" We hadn't with our first deal, but he had with the healer.

He hesitated and then said, "We should. There is a quicker way, if you agree?" He pulled out a knife.

"You going to cut my hand off or something?"

He threw his head back and barked out a laugh. The sound was rusty and all the sweeter since I so rarely heard it. He took my hand, his larger one engulfing mine. "Do you trust me?"

I glanced at the knife, snorting. "No."

"That's my girl." Smiling, he whispered a few odd, lilting words. I jerked my hand at the first touch of the blade, but he held it fast as he scraped lines on my wrist with the tip of his knife. The cold steel burned, but the pain was fleeting. When I looked down, there was a glowing red rune on my skin, like one of the ones he had.

I pulled my hand back, cradling it against my chest. "Why don't other people have runes like this?"

"It isn't a common gift. I know only one other person who can use runes like I do. It's why I was chosen as an Enforcer." He started to draw the same rune on his own wrist. I wanted to ask more, but decided while he was carving into his own flesh probably wasn't the best time. He completed the last line. "It's done. When the terms are met, the runes will disappear."

I traced a finger over the swirling design. It didn't hurt but itched a little when I touched it. "What happens if we don't fulfill our end of the bargain?"

"You belong to the other person."

"What?!" My head jerked up. "Don't I need to agree to that?"

"If you hadn't agreed, the rune wouldn't take." His eyes strayed to the window, not meeting mine. "You would do anything for your dad. The power can read your intentions."

I nodded, a little creeped out that magic could read my intentions. Half the time, *I* couldn't read my intentions. Rubbing the gooseflesh on my arms, I realized he'd manipulated me. This was much more binding than our last deal.

The fire steeds dove, and I had no more time to think on it as I was flung toward the open window. Cold air set my pulse to racing, but Tristan grabbed me and pulled me back toward my seat. Tight grip holding me in place, he sent out a sharp series of whistles. A neigh sounded, and the descent evened out.

A minute later, we landed on a circular stone slab, surrounded by a large open space, in front of what I could only describe as a castle. The building was made of shining obsidian and marble and towered over everything. The sharp edge of a cliff bordered one side, towering mountains hemmed in two others, and a steep winding incline protected the fourth. The castle had battlements and guards and seemed almost medieval in its defense. "You live here?"

Tristan nodded. He bent to open the door and then

237

hesitated. "If anyone asks, you're my new girlfriend, okay? I don't want them to know we're working together."

I lifted my hair and fanned my neck, the heat more oppressive than what I was used to. "What about a new friend?"

He sighed, running a hand through his hair in the way I was learning meant he was getting frustrated or annoyed. I was hoping for frustrated but bet it was a little of both.

"I don't have friends. This is a stretch as it is, but at least it's a believable stretch. No one who knows me would like me. You included. But you are attracted to me. We'll work with that."

"I'm not." My face heated, and I wished I didn't blush so easily.

He raised his eyebrow.

Right. He could tell when I lied. *Arrogant bastard.* "Fine. Let's go."

He opened the door and helped me out, his hand lingering on my waist. I had to stop myself from jumping at the familiar touch. I hadn't realized he'd meant to play up the part so soon. Girlfriend might be the more believable title for him, but him being my boyfriend wasn't more believable for me. I turned to ask him if we could wait to put on a show since no one was here, but then realized that I was wrong. We weren't alone.

A tall, thin man hurried toward us. The man was dressed in a black suit with a dark-gray vest. He looked cool as a cucumber. I would have been sweltering in all of that fabric. He handed Tristan a folder of papers. "Master Tristan, here is the business that needs your immediate attention. And his Lordship is in a tizzy and wants to see you immediately. Should I show your guest to your rooms? I can have someone help her freshen up."

"No, she will stay with me. I don't want her alone in my chambers." The thin man gave a small smile at Tristan's words.

I felt a stab of hurt. He was probably just saying that so we could stay together, but a small part of me wondered if he meant it too. Was he worried someone would kill me, or was he worried I would snoop—which I would—and what I would find?

"Garvin, would you get us some fruit and tea? We can take it in the study. I will wait for Father there. Please warn him I have company."

Garvin nodded sagely. "As you wish, Master Tristan. I'll add some of those pastries you enjoy as well." All of this bowing and catering. Was he some sort of butler?

I followed Tristan as he led me through huge doors that were thicker than my head, to a large courtyard. The walls surrounding the courtyard were all the same thick stone. Once inside, the castle took on a different feel. There was greenery here. So far, I had seen nothing green in this realm. I could only imagine that having green plants was considered a luxury, and that this was Tristan's dad showing off his wealth.

There were small alcoves overflowing with flowering bushes. I smelled roses and gardenias and other scents I couldn't name. Some of the flowers were familiar; others, like a bright-orange one that looked like a teacup with a white border, were not. I reached out a hand to touch it, and Tristan immediately slapped my hand away. I tucked my hand in toward my chest, stung. He pointed out the white border on the flower, careful not to get too close, and said, "If you touch the white part, it will put you into a deep sleep. Try not to touch anything."

I nodded, and we hurried to catch up to Garvin. The path we were following split to either side of a sparkling fountain. In the center of the fountain was a massive, winged beast, reminding me of a cross between a dragon and a griffin. Sparkling yellow eyes gazed out from the lifelike statue as if it were watching me. Behind it were double doors, ornately decorated, which led to a second courtyard. As we passed, I marveled at the details in the carving on the doors. It looked like some sort of epic battle scene, with archers and mounted soldiers fighting great mythical creatures.

The second courtyard had multiple paths that twisted through an immaculate garden. Many plants were tall and flowery. It was a maze. A beautiful maze, but a maze nonetheless. Was everything here geared toward defense?

Once we were through the second courtyard, we reached towering doors that I tried pushing open but couldn't budge, their weight holding them tightly closed. Tristan smirked, opening one of the doors with no obvious effort, and held it for me.

I huffed past him. After walking through a wide-open room with obsidian floors, we took a large staircase, railings made from a dark metal. Midway, it split into two curving staircases in either direction. Garvin took the one on the right. Tristan took the one on the left, and I followed. We went down a hallway, then turned, and then turned again, and then went up more stairs. I was soon lost and focused all of my attention on not getting left behind.

Eventually, he opened a door made of that strange black wood with smooth, dark hardware. This room was large and airy with high ceilings, but the walls were filled with books. Some of the spines were in English, but others were in languages I couldn't read. If Tristan hadn't called it a study earlier, I would have guessed it was a library. The room also had a desk and a few chairs situated next to a large couch and fireplace. The desk had beautiful carvings etched along the sides. At first, I thought they were vines climbing up the side, but upon closer inspection, they had faces that were reaching and crying out for help. It was both beautiful and horrifying. I traced a screaming head. "Your choice?"

His jaw clenched. "It makes an impression. I often do business in this room. It is my public persona. I wanted to make sure people know we are not close, and that I am only seeing you in my public areas." He gestured to the couch. "Have a seat. I'll build a fire." He bent down and tossed some wood in the hearth, and with a whispered word, the flames lit, orange and yellow plumes swirling upward. Was he trying to intimidate me or impress me?

I sat on the edge of the leather couch in front of the fire. The same screaming heads were carved into the armrests. I scooted towards the middle, away from the hollowed-out eyes, and stared at Tristan. "How did you do that? You didn't use fire when you were fighting before." The ability to light things on fire would have been helpful when fighting off our attackers earlier.

"My abilities are muted in the Human Realm. The celestials don't trust us near humans. We're pure evil, remember?" Whispering a soft incantation, he lit a finger on fire and blew it out. Then sat beside me and traced the hot tip up my arm. I shuddered, enjoying the sensation. His eyes caught on mine.

The door opened.

"Splendid timing, as always, Father."

Was that a show for his dad, or had he been coming on to me? Did I want him to? Tristan leaned into me, placing a hand casually on my hip and pulling me into his body. Definitely a show, I decided, and one I could help with. Smiling coyly, I traced a finger over the top of his wing, feathers soft between my fingers. Tristan tightened his hold and then relaxed.

"Are you going to introduce me to your friend?" Tristan's father had a deep, commanding voice.

Tristan kept his gaze on my face, his back to his father. He curled a finger around a lock of my hair, pulling the dark strand forward. "Father, meet Zoey. Zoey, meet Lord Dreydon, my father."

I looked past Tristan's shoulder at the tall, imposing man. He was well built, tan, with the same light-blue eyes as Tristan. One difference was the silver hair. Despite the color of his hair, he looked not a day over thirty. How old was Tristan? His father looked so young. Did half demons age? Did half celestials? Would I stay the same while my father aged?

Tristan's father smiled in my direction. "You are lovely. Make sure he tells you so every day. My boy can get a bit engrossed in his work."

Tristan's hand tightened. He turned so he faced his father, pulling me closer to his side. "Garvin said you wanted to see me. What can I help you with today?"

Lord Dreydon turned his attention back to Tristan. "I have an issue I need your expertise on. Chaos Day comes early this month."

"Understood. Put the information on my desk, and I will see to it."

His father grinned, tossing a folder onto the desk next to a large platter of food. Someone must have brought it in with him. My mouth watered at the pastries oozing something gooey. "Ah, it is good to see you distracted, boy. I was worried you'd become obsessed with getting your brother out. He made his own bed. Best we move on."

Tristan's hand tightened enough that I was sure he was leaving bruises, but I said nothing. The pain helped my mind focus and reminded me of who and what I was dealing with. *What's this about his brother?*

"I'd like to continue distracting myself. Are we done?"

Tristan's father laughed and clapped him heartily on the shoulder, pushing us even closer together, if that was possible. "I'll have Garvin advise everyone that you are not to be disturbed. But son, be sure you don't neglect your duties. My task must be done on time."

Tristan buried his head in my hair. "Yes, Father."

I sat there, with Tristan blocking me from his father, until I heard the door slam shut. Tristan immediately stood, putting some space between us. I rubbed my side where he'd been holding me.

"Sorry about that. Let's get some supplies and get out of here. We should have about a day to search for your father before people notice we're missing."

"Hopefully it doesn't take that long, or I'll be getting body parts. What happened to your brother?"

Tristan stilled. For a minute, I didn't think he would answer. Then he said, "The celestials have him. He did something stupid." He hesitated and then added, "That was what the water was for—and the bag the healer gave me. They're for a finding spell."

I felt immediate guilt that he'd been trying to find his brother and I'd been imagining nefarious plans. I was as bad as everyone else, just assuming the worst. "Thank you for sharing."

He grunted, ignoring me. He walked to a corner of the room and then climbed a moveable ladder to a higher shelf and pulled out a book. Jumping down—I would have never jumped from that high—he landed softly and pulled out a different book. Then he swapped them. Once they were both pushed in, a small alcove opened. My mouth gaped. It was a secret passage. He waved me forward. "After you."

I stood near the couch and peeked inside. This wasn't a passage that was used very often. I could see cobwebs lining the entryway. "Hell no. There are spiders in there. You first."

He laughed and walked through.

I grabbed a pastry, shoved it in my mouth—it practically melted on contact—and followed, the wall closing behind us. I swallowed, throat suddenly dry. It was pitch black. "Do you have a flashlight?"

A hand reached back and grasped mine. "Of course not. I don't need one. Follow me. You'll be fine."

I wanted to comment that yes, I might be physically fine, but I could also run into spider webs and other creepy crawlies, which was a horrifying thought.

Taking a step forward, I shuddered as sticky webs caressed my skin.

There was a soft chuckle in front of me. "Don't worry. The dangerous bugs will need to get through me first." His eyes glowed, lighting up his face as he looked back at me, and I watched him walk through a web, suddenly glad when he turned away and I couldn't see anymore.

I scooted closer to avoid touching them myself. One foot, then another. I willed myself to ignore the brush against my arm and the scurrying by my foot. Must move on.

My grip got tighter and tighter as we walked, but Tristan said nothing. After about five minutes, he pushed my head down. "Duck for a bit. The ceiling is lower here." Creeping through the shorter section of the tunnels, he stopped. *Listening?* He did something, and then there was light.

A fist-size spider stared at me from a few feet away, its multiple beady eyes glittering in the low light. I shoved past Tristan, jumping around like a crazy person, trying to get any residual spider webs off. Dancing around, I noticed this tunnel led to a grassy area. We were somewhere on the grounds, but I hadn't seen this spot before. A group of about eight fiery horses neighed their welcome from where they'd been grazing on straw-colored grass. Tristan stroked one of the fiery beasts, offering it a small crystalline object.

"Sugar?"

Tristan grinned. "Bluebell here has a big sweet tooth." He whistled and led Bluebell and another beast away from their grazing area.

"They can speak, right? Won't they tell your father?"

He lightly stroked the fiery beasts. "These beauties? No. He only knows commands. He never learned their language. Besides, I raised them. They might be his property, but they know I love them. They wouldn't hurt me if they can help it. This is my sneak-out-of-the-house spot, and they know to be quiet about it." He glanced my direction. "Ready?"

"Ready for what?"

Large hands surrounded my waist, lifting me toward one of the horses. A horse covered with flames.

"Tristan! I'm not fireproof." I flailed, working my stomach muscles, doing my best to keep my backside away from the rising flames. "Tristan!"

Chapter 25

"Shh. Calm down. They won't burn you. See, you're fine." My heart was ready to pound out of my chest, run down the hill, and join a parade. *What. The. Hell.* But I could see that he was right. The horse was warm but not lighting my clothes on fire.

"And you couldn't tell me that before placing me on the burning horse?" I hissed. "You are such an ass."

"Yes, I am. But, in this case, I simply forgot you wouldn't know. Everyone knows you can ride these beauties." He crooned to a second one and mounted up. Neither fire steed had a saddle, but we rested between bone ridges, and they both had long manes to hold on to. Tristan whistled to the beasts, and both started walking. My horse followed Tristan's, and I hung on for dear life, wobbling back and forth as I attempted to keep my seat. I was practically plastered to the fire beast's back, fistfuls of its dark mane gripped in my hands. The mane was black, covered with bright-red flames, and had an unusually rough texture, but I kept my death grip anyway.

"Haven't you ridden before?"

I looked up at him, sure my exasperation showed on my face. "I currently live in a city. Did you see any horses nearby when you visited? Where exactly would I have ridden a flaming horse?"

He grunted and turned toward a small path in the

corner.

I kept reminding myself the horse wouldn't burn me as I struggled to stay seated. "Don't mind me falling off back here. I can learn here. Today. While we sneak away from your crazy family and try to rescue my dad from demons." I was muttering and probably sounded like a lunatic.

"Just hang on and stop talking. No one should hear us right now, but we need to go around some more populated areas. When we get far enough away, we'll be flying. Keep hold of the mane and use your legs to hug the sides, and you should be fine. I'll direct them. You just need to stay on."

"Flying? No way. I'm going to fall off and die, you—"

Tristan waved a hand at me, and my voice disappeared. I tried again, but no sound came out. *Did he spell me silent?* I glared, fingers tightening on the fire steed's mane, making the beast step sideways. I took a deep, silent breath and counted to ten in my head. Then twenty. When I got my voice back, that son of a bitch was going to get a piece of my mind. I glared holes in the back of his head as we plodded along.

We saw only a few people as we skirted the more populated areas. Anyone who happened to catch sight of Tristan bolted the other direction. I wondered what it must be like to have everyone run from you in fear. It was probably lonely. I heard a soft whistle and glanced up.

"Time to fly."

That was all the warning I got. My stomach dropped and my grasp tightened as the beast beneath me bunched its legs and launched into the air. I clung to the mane for dear life and screamed a silent scream, mentally cursing Tristan with every bad word I could think of. I looked down, and my stomach flipped. Clutching even tighter, I squeezed my eyes shut, determined not to vomit.

The cool air rushed over me as we flew, drying some of the humid sweat that had been forming on my forehead. It was pleasantly cool in the air, and if I wasn't absolutely sure I was going to die any second, I would have enjoyed the ride. Probably.

Twenty minutes later, when we finally spiraled down to the ground and stopped, the beast under me neighed and pawed at the ground. Likely saying *please get this nincompoop off my back*, but I couldn't let go. I knew we were on solid ground. I knew it was time for me to let go, but I couldn't get my fingers to release. The once terrifying flames were now my lifeline.

Warm hands pried my fingers off the mane and wrapped them around a neck. I started hitting that neck, still unable to speak but wanting him to know how furious I was with him. He pulled me down and put me on the ground, trying to get away from my pounding fists. "Hey, I'm sorry. What did I do?"

I hit him a few more times and then pointed to my throat, where I was still unable to talk.

"Oh, right." He waved a hand, and the spell dissolved.

"You heartless, poopy, crazy ass!"

"Poopy?" His lips twitched, and I swore if he smiled, I was going to deck him.

I looked around at the flat yellow dirt and spindly plants. "Where the hell are we?"

"A place that will be useful for both of us. There is a Seer here. She goes by Madam."

"Madam? That's it? No last name? Is she hiding something?" *Maybe hookers*, I thought, but didn't voice.

"Probably. I don't ask. She can hopefully give you some guidance and help us use your ability to find your dad." He hesitated. "She doesn't like visitors or strangers. You wait here, and I'll be right back. Touch nothing." He looked around as if wanting to say more and then nodded and continued on.

"Wait, Tristan. Don't move? For how long? Tristan!"

He was gone. I decided sitting would be fine and plopped down on the dusty ground. The sun was hot, beating down relentlessly from high in the sky. Fanning myself with the bottom of my shirt, I tried to stay cool while I waited.

And waited.

Does time move differently here? How much time has passed? Is Dad okay, or have they already started sending me bits and pieces? I started digging in the ground, unable to keep my hands from doing something. I didn't notice how deep I had dug until my hands hit the edge of a metal object. I glanced down. It looked like a box. Smoothing the dirt away, I could see a corner with beautiful flowers hand painted on top.

"Stop." The voice was loud, commanding, and definitely higher pitched than Tristan's. I froze. "Do you always dig for buried treasure when visiting people?"

I looked at my hands, covered in yellow dirt, and the deep hole they had dug. What had I been doing? I started burying the box again. "I'm so sorry. I hadn't even realized I was digging. I just—"

I heard a soft chuckle, and an older woman approached, leaning heavily on a cane. Tristan jogged up behind her.

She patted his shoulder absently. "This is the girl you were telling me about? She definitely has the gift. We have a deal."

He nodded.

I looked up, brushing dirt off my hands. "What deal?"

"Nothing you need to concern yourself with, dearie. Follow me, and we'll see what speaks to you, shall we?" She turned back up the path.

I stood, brushing the remaining dirt off my butt, and followed Tristan, taking up the rear. *What kind of deal did he make? And did he leave me behind because he was scared of her reaction to me, or had he wanted to make the deal in private? And how did I end up sitting on top of buried treasure? Had Tristan left me in that exact spot on purpose?* The questions swirled around and around in my mind as we trudged forward.

Knowing I had little choice but to trust him, I followed Tristan and the woman up to her cabin. She walked quickly, and I wondered if she even needed the cane or if it was just part of a disguise. She looked older, with silvery-gray hair swept up into a bun and light wrinkles, but was that who she really was? She definitely had a strong glamour, like Regina. I'd need to touch her to See past it. I wasn't positive on the protocol, but I was pretty sure, if she was anything like Regina, she'd get upset and we'd get kicked out if I tried. I pushed my curiosity down and followed.

The outside of the house had a rustic old cabin charm. There were log walls, flower boxes under the windows, and a cute doormat with a plump, adorable mouse chasing a cat. The actual cat, standing attention at the door, was more big-boned than plump. He stared at us with his bright-green eyes and, as I was about to enter, said, "Take off shoes."

I jumped and gave an undignified squeak. "The cat talked." His voice had been a low rumble, but there were definitely words involved.

Madam poked her head out and smiled fondly at the cat. "Rufus prefers a tidy house."

The large orange tabby started licking his paw and then looked back up and repeated, "Shoes."

I took my shoes off and placed them by the front mat and then hurried in after the old woman, glancing nervously behind me at the large tom. He sprawled out on his side in a warm patch of sun and thankfully didn't follow us.

The front room was a combined family room, eating area, and kitchen. Everything was done in soft blues, greens, and yellows. It was cozy and welcoming. Madam was laying a few things out on a small, round table in the eating area. I was immediately drawn to a deck of cards and a cup. They were set out amongst other odds and ends on the lightly polished wood. When I sat down in the offered chair, I wanted to reach for them. My hands itched with impatience, and the desire to reach out was almost unbearable. I tucked my hands in my elbows and waited, like a polite guest. I'd already gotten chastised for digging up treasure and not taking off my shoes, I didn't need to be called out for anything else.

Madam stared at me, hands on her wide hips. "Hmm, I expected one of those to call to you." Her crackly voice was loud in the silence.

"Uh, they did."

She gestured. "Well, go on then, pick one."

I chewed on a thumbnail. "Can I pick two?"

She grinned, showing a bright-white smile and a few crooked teeth. "Yes, please." She gestured again, and I grabbed the cards and the teacup. When both were in front of me, I felt calmer and less like I wanted to jump out of my skin. I caressed the deck and the edge of the porcelain teacup, oddly soothed by their proximity.

She clapped her hands like a child. "Lovely. Let's pour you a spot of tea, shall we? Which type?" She pointed to the back wall in the kitchen, and standing, I was immediately drawn to a small tub of dark tea leaves. Smelling its warm, fruity scent, I took a small spoon and scooped some into the mug. Then I grabbed a pinch of darker leaves from another tub, and I was done.

Tristan's voice was startling in the quiet. "Does it matter what type of tea she chooses?"

"Yes, and no. A reading can be done with any type of tea, but most practitioners have something they are specifically drawn to that works best for them. Your girl chose rooibos and orange tea."

I looked up at Tristan to see if he'd react to the "your girl" comment. Nothing. Of course not. It shouldn't mean anything to me either, but I found myself wondering what it'd be like to be his girl. I was curious what he'd said our relationship was.

"Quite a tasty combination, if I say so myself. I will pack some of each up and label them so you can buy more at home. Though you might also like to go to a large tea shop and see what calls to you there. I have an extensive selection, but nothing compared to some places."

She turned to me, pouring hot water into my mug, and then sat down in the chair opposite. "Reading tea leaves isn't very complex. Put the leaves in and add boiling water. Let the person drink for whom you are doing a reading. They should think about the question they want to ask. In your case, think about finding your father."

I looked up at Tristan questioningly.

She chuckled. "Yes, he told me what you were seeking."

I swallowed, throat dry. I wasn't thrilled with him telling a stranger about my business.

"Don't be too angry with him. I am old and have learned to never do a session with someone without knowing what they are seeking up front. Money isn't everything, and sometimes I need to listen to my gut and say no." She cocked her head at me. "Does your gut tell you things?"

I looked at Tristan, and he nodded at me. "Yes, sometimes. Not always, though."

"Hmm, that'll get better with practice. Drink your tea, dear."

The tea leaves had sunk to the bottom, so I started sipping the tea. It had a sweet, nutty taste with a hint of orange. It was perfect. I relaxed more with each sip, shoulders drooping, muscles loosening. Madam made herself a cup, something from different bins, and Tristan declined. When I thought I had finished my tea, I stopped.

"A bit more, dear."

Eyebrow raised, I drank the dregs around the leaves until I had sucked out all the liquid. I showed the cup to her.

She clasped her hands. "Wonderful. Now, look at the leaves and tell me what you see."

I stared down at them. They looked like a bunch of wet leaves. Maybe I needed to try harder? I looked at them, concentrating as hard as I could.

I still saw a bunch of wet leaves. They were brown and kind of arranged in an oblong lump. "I see a lump of tea leaves." I tried to squint and see if some of them looked like a map or my father or something.

"Patience, dear. If it was that easy, more of us would do tea readings. Look into the tea leaves and relax. Try to free your mind of anything but the leaves."

We sat there for a good thirty minutes with me staring into the cup.

Nothing happened.

I got sleepy. Drifting off, I dreamed of a cliff. There were large bird-like creatures with snake-like tails perched on it. I could smell a campfire nearby. And then it was gone. I jerked awake.

Wiping my face, glad there was no drool, I said, "I'm so sorry, I must have drifted off. I had the strangest dream."

"Those were the tea leaves. What did you see, my dear?"

I told them about the cliff and the strange birds and the smell of a campfire. Tristan was writing it all down.

Madam nodded at Tristan approvingly. "Tea leaf readings disappear quickly. It is good to get all the details written out. Tell us more about the birds."

"They had golden feathers and strange long tails with heads on the ends, like snakes, but flatter." I tried to remember more, and suddenly my memories were gone. I didn't have a picture of them in my mind at all. "They're gone. I'm sorry."

"The vision lasted longer than I thought it would.

Very good for your first time. Most don't get any vision at all, and those who do can barely hold on to it for a minute. Would you like to try the cards?" She caressed them lovingly.

I was drawn to them. I touched them, and my pocket warmed. It was the card I'd gotten from the Seer who'd turned me in. It wanted me to pull it out. I did, and Madam started.

"Oh my. He's lovely. Did he choose you?" She gazed at the card in wonder. "So few from that deck are still around." She pushed the deck on the table closer to me. "Take this deck. I gift it freely to you. Shuffle it with your King."

"Should I remove the King of Cups from this one since I'm adding one?"

She shook her head. "No, your King will set things to rights."

A cognizant card. That's not creepy at all. I tentatively grabbed the deck. The cards were stiff and new.

Tristan spoke as I shuffled, his low voice a surprise after so much time. "Did you know we were coming?"

She laughed a smoker's laugh. "No. I train a lot more than I used to and make sure I have at least one new deck on hand. I got this one last week."

"Why? Is it difficult to get a new deck?"

"A new deck of playing cards, no. But a new deck of hand-painted tarot cards is much harder to come by. The hand-painted ones work best, and I commission one every year or two. To work well, a deck needs to be gifted to you. You can't buy one, and it should be handcrafted, if you can get your hands on one." She waved a hand at me encouragingly. "Shuffle, girl. Stop when it feels right."

I shuffled. The cards were stiff at first, but then they came to life. I could feel the pictures changing as I shuffled. Then they stopped. "They're good."

"Now cut the deck. We'll start with a simple three card draw. Pull three cards and place them in front of you. Never forget to think about the question you are asking."

I laid out the cards. Thinking about finding my dad, I turned over the first card. It had a man with a long gray beard carrying a lantern.

"The Hermit. This card represents your past. It speaks to isolation. Likely signifying your time spent outside the Mythic world. Seeing it but not a part of it."

In the card, I Saw my childhood and time spent yearning to play with the pixies and other magical beings. I turned the second card, not wanting to See any more. This card had two people holding each other.

"The Lovers. This card represents your present. Lovers is not literal but speaks to a need to work with others in order to achieve your goal. It represents tough decisions that depend on your relationship with other people."

As I stared at the card, I Saw Tristan and I kissing. Then we stabbed each other in the back with sharp, glittering knives. Quickly, I turned over the last card. A skeleton wearing a shroud.

"Death. The third card represents the future. As with the Lovers card, it does not mean literal death but represents an ending and a new beginning. Good or bad is yet to be seen."

I Saw large groups fighting and a dragon breathing fire over everyone. I blinked my eyes and tried to focus on the room and the present. I'd decided I hated tarot. Clearing my throat, I said, "I don't think that helped much."

"No, but the tea reading did. The snake hawks are in the Blood Canyon. Your description matches the east end. The cards did tell us that you need to work together. Did you See anything when you looked at the cards? Sometimes Seers will get visions."

"No, sorry."

Tristan growled softly.

Madam laughed. "You should know better than to lie in front of one of his kind. They can always tell." She glanced at the Lovers card. Then cocked her head as if listening. "I think this one might be personal to you two. Not about your father." Tapping a finger on her lips, she smiled. "I will give you two a few minutes alone."

Her chair scraped across the floor. The sound was loud in the utter silence. When the door closed, Tristan advanced expectantly. He pulled a chair out, turned it backwards and sat down, arms folded across the top. "What does the Lovers card mean? What did you see? Did you see us?" He looked at the card and the entwined bodies. "As lovers?"

"No."

He nodded, then said, "But you did See something. Something you don't want to share. Zoey, this could be important. What was it?"

I could feel my cheeks heating. "Fine. I saw us kissing."

"What else did you See? That's not what you were afraid to tell me."

"While we were kissing, I saw us stab each other in the back. Then we watched as we each bled out and died." The image kept repeating on the card, and I scooped it up and shoved it back into the deck, wrapping them up. "I don't know what it means. My best guess would be that we become close, betray each other, and both die for it."

"That sounds like a very literal meaning. The cards are not usually literal."

"Well fine, Mr. Expert. What is your interpretation, then?" My voice was snappy and waspish, but I was getting sick of him pushing.

"I can't interpret it. Dig deeper. What are the cards telling you?"

I jumped up, the chair toppling behind me. "I don't know, okay?"

He nodded. Bending to pick up my fallen chair, he said, "Okay." After a moment he said, "Let's take what we know and go find your dad."

I nodded.

Madam walked in as if called. Tapping her cane on the ground, she said, "All sorted, then? I have some hot biscuits for you to take on your journey. Zoey, dear, you are welcome anytime you'd like to visit."

Pushing in my chair, I said, "Thank you." I walked over to the door to put my shoes back on. The big orange cat, now sleeping in front of the door, opened an eye and stared at me, but stayed silent.

Tristan bent and kissed Madam's cheek before turning to go.

"Before you go…I was eavesdropping. An alternative interpretation of those cards might be that you will need each other to survive. Keep that in mind. Gods be with you both."

Neither of us said anything as we walked back to the

horses. Once there, Tristan lifted me up so I could mount. I almost put up a fuss but realized we'd be stranded and my father would die, so I bit my tongue and let him guide me into place. The fiery horse shifted lightly beneath me. Hands still wrapped around my waist, Tristan stilled. I turned to look at him, but he was positioned so I couldn't see his eyes, just his profile and ebony wings. He held me there, warm hands too hot in this humid weather.

"I can't trust anyone. I can't rely on anyone. Not with what I do."

"I understand." And I did, but if Madam's interpretation of the cards was true, that meant we'd fail. *Or did it mean that the only way we would succeed was if we learned to work together? We could learn, couldn't we?*

He leaned in against my leg, his voice soft. "I will try to trust you."

"I will try to trust you too." And I meant it.

Chapter 26

Tristan let go and mounted his horse. He whistled a few notes, and both mares burst into a canter. I knew what they were going to do and braced for it, watching the edge. My stomach dropped as they jumped off the cliff face, flapping their wings and climbing. I hung on for dear life, fingers tangled in the horse's coarse mane, trying to pretend my hands didn't look like they were covered in flames. It would be okay. *I* would be okay.

I squeezed my eyes shut. Holding tight to the horse's mane did nothing to keep my stomach from churning with every dip in the air currents. I wanted to peek, look at the strange new landscape below, but the glimpses I got just made the nausea worse. Everything was just a little off. The canyon had sharp edges instead of soft worn sides, and the landscape was full of deep reds and blacks instead of the browns and greens I was used to seeing.

Eventually, we evened out and I could breathe, the air cooler now that we were high in the sky.

Lulled by the quiet, I was surprised when, a short time later, there were flashes of light as the sun glinted off something bright. "What's that?"

"Hmm?"

A shining, golden blur dove at me, screeching. Plunging down, my horse evaded. Another flash of bright light. Then two more. I wrapped my hands tighter.

We twisted left then right, the horse making acrobatic maneuvers that were decidedly un-horse-like. I could see now that the attacking golden lights were, in fact, huge bird-like creatures. They were large, half the size of the beasts we were riding. Their long, curved talons glowed gold.

A shriek of pain cut through the air, and we turned sideways. Bluebell was losing altitude. *Had she been hit?* I slid to the side as she tried to keep us in the air. Flames danced over my hands as I tangled them in her long black mane, desperately hanging on to anything I could grab. My legs were dangling free, and I knew at any moment I could lose my grip. *Would* lose my grip. How long could I hang on?

"Tristan!" My scream echoed throughout the canyon. I was slipping. "Help!"

Rough hands grabbed my waist and pulled. There was a strong, almost painful, pressure around my middle as Tristan tore me from Bluebell's back. Strands of her mane caught on my fingers as my hands released.

I screamed in terror as I dangled in the air for a moment, Tristan's hands the only thing keeping me from plummeting to the ground. Trembling, I screamed again as my body collided with the rounded back of his horse.

I burrowed into Tristan's chest, wrapping both arms and legs around him, sobbing in fear, babbling about how awful he was, barely able to catch my breath between sobs. "Horrible, crazy…I'm never riding that thing again. So stupid."

"Shh, you're okay. I've got you. It wasn't her fault." He was sending out blasts of fire toward the birds while holding me close.

"S-She d-dropped me!"

"We entered their territory, and she got surprised. They're not usually nesting this far out. Protecting their eggs is what makes them so aggressive. We're going to fly a little closer, and then we can go on foot."

I could barely talk around my tears. "Wh-Who's territory?" I was pleased I'd put together words and made a coherent sentence. I squeezed my eyes shut as we dodged another enormous bird, its golden feathers glinting in the sun.

"The snake hawks. That's why this is called Blood Canyon. They bloody anyone who comes here."

"You couldn't have warned me?"

"Why?"

Argh! He was so infuriating! If my arms weren't permanently wrapped around his body, still clinging for dear life, I would have beaten him senseless. Or tried, anyway. I was sure I was squeezing way too tight, but I was unable to loosen my grip. I sat there fuming while he dodged the snake hawks and threw the occasional fireball toward them, making them back off.

Tristan searched the ground below. "Hold on. There's a good spot." We dodged another dive-bombing bird and circled around to the side of a cliff. There was a small open area before the rocky slab gave way to large black and red trees. Tristan's horse dove, taking us in for a rough landing, but we landed. My breath left in a huge rush. We were finally on the ground. Bluebell limped in afterward, bleeding from a deep gouge to her side, eyes wide with pain.

I didn't feel bad. That crazy horse almost killed me. I looked over again, and my anger melted as she gave a soft snuffle, struggling to keep up, dark head drooping.

Okay, I felt a little bad. *Poor thing.*

Tristan guided us deeper into the cover of trees. The snake hawks circled above as we disappeared into the vegetation, but thankfully didn't attempt to land. After a few minutes, I could breathe again and suddenly realized I was crying and wiping snot all over Tristan. I mean, I'd been doing it for a while, but now that we were safe, my cheeks heated with embarrassment. I straightened, wiping my eyes with the back of my hand. "Thank you. I'm sorry."

"It's okay. You were scared." He dismounted and went to the injured beast, ignoring me and letting me pull myself together. He coaxed Bluebell to lie down and then said a few words, and the mare passed out.

I slowly lowered myself off Tristan's horse, my landing less than graceful. "Can I do anything to help?"

"Blue likes sugar cubes. Can you find a few from my bag?" He tossed me a small bag I hadn't noticed, and I rummaged around until I found a few. I suspected he'd given me the task to make me feel useful, and I was grudgingly grateful. Not that I'd tell him that.

"Put them in front of her. She'll see them when she wakes up."

After cleaning out the wound, he glued the edges of skin together. Once glued, he smoothed on a thick white paste that smelled strongly of peppermint. After that, he added a pale-pink paste that had a light rose scent and made me sneeze.

Rubbing my nose, I asked, "What're those for?"

"The first one fights infection, and the second one helps with pain."

"Can't you just 'magic' it closed?"

"Not everything needs magic." He kissed the horse's mane and ruffled her ears. Then he found some plants for her to eat and placed them next to the sugar cubes.

I stared at him blankly as he cared for the sick horse. *Fire steed*, I reminded myself, eyes drawn to her flaming mane. How could he be so caring one minute and so brutal the next?

When both beasts were settled, he grabbed his bag and stood. "Come on. We have some walking ahead of us."

"We're just leaving them?" For all that I wasn't a fan of flying right then, riding sounded infinitely better than walking.

"They'll find their own way home and would be too obvious where we're headed. We don't want to be noticed."

Teeth gritted against what I was sure would be more horrible things, I followed.

****

"Some walking" was the understatement of the century. We walked for over an hour, over rough terrain. Tristan cut his way through odd twisty vegetation, none of it green. I got slapped in the face by branches and stumbled over rocks and uneven ground, which did not help my mood. He finally let us rest when I put my foot down and said I wasn't moving another step without a water break. We couldn't rescue Dad if we passed out. Or if I murdered him due to how hangry I was. He took out the biscuits and split one with me—they were huge—and gave us each some water. The biscuit was buttery and flaky and filled with a sweet berry jam, although I couldn't place the berry. "What type of jam is this?"

"Riddleberry." He stared at me, a small smile on his face. That's when it hit me—a sharp, tart aftertaste that made me pucker up like I'd sucked on a lemon, mixing with the sweet. It kind of reminded me of sour candy gummies.

"It is native to this realm and isn't something you would have come across in the human one. It's a favorite of mine, but not everyone appreciates it." He stared at me with a raised eyebrow, awaiting my verdict.

I took another bite, licking my lips. It was delicious, sweet but tart at the same time. I winked at him and said, "Their loss."

When we'd finished, Tristan said, "We have another hour of hard hiking, and then we'll come to the flats. Based on your tea reading, that is likely where the raiders are camping and where they are holding your father. There are caves there, which are great to hide out in. When we get close, we won't be able to talk. I'm going to teach you a few hand signals." He held up his hand.

"Wait?"

"Yep. Just sit tight and wait." He walked his fingers and pointed to me and then pointed in a direction.

"You want me to walk that way?"

"Yes, as quietly as possible."

I rolled my eyes. Like I needed a reminder that I walked like a rampaging dinosaur. "I will do my best. Any others?"

He held out a fist and put his other, open hand, on top.

"I have no idea."

"Hide. Don't come out until you're sure they're gone. I will find you. Okay?"

I nodded.

"Last one." He moved two fingers in a circular pattern.

I shrugged.

"Go back to home base. When we go silent, I'll designate a safe place, and that is where we both go back to if anything goes south. Got it?"

I nodded. "Got it."

After about forty-five minutes of walking, he designated a spot as our safe place. I looked at the stack of rocks under a wider-than-normal tree until I had it firm in my memory. Then we each had another sip of water and took off again. This time, silently. Or at least as silently as possible. Unfortunately, I was not used to sneaking. He was, and I could barely tell he was moving. I, as expected, stepped on every crunchy leaf and breakable stick there was.

Tristan gave me the stop signal, and I stopped and waited. He crept ahead, scouting the area out. Coming back, he used his fingers to walk me to an area farther away. I backtracked, and then he signaled to stop and hide. I stopped and hid in some black bushes with sharp leaves.

The bushes pricked my skin, and I hoped they weren't some strange form of poison ivy. That would be just my luck.

I waited.

And waited.

My legs were cramping from the crouched position, so I lowered myself to the ground, careful not to make too much noise. After about ten minutes, I started panicking. What if he had left me here to die? Was he really helping? Why had I trusted him, almost a complete stranger? A different species, even. What if "wait" to him meant a day instead of ten minutes? We should have spent more time discussing the plan.

I debated going off on my own, but quickly

discarded that thought. I didn't know where I was and had no way of getting to my father or back home without help.

I was trapped.

Time passed. I tried to ignore my twisting stomach. The sky grayed. It must be dusk. Was he going to leave me here, by myself, all night?

My anxiety grew as I watched the slow deepening of the reds and purples of the sky. My heart raced as I tried not to hyperventilate, jumping at every small sound.

Fixated on the darkening sky, I didn't hear Tristan until he was right next to me, touching my arm. I jumped a mile, screeching. His hand covered my mouth, silencing me.

"Quiet! It's me. I found your dad."

"You did? Where were you?!" I smacked him on the arm, trying to convey my freak-out in one mediocre hit.

He cocked his head, his black hair casting shadows on his face in the low light, and then said slowly, as though speaking to a small child, "There are quite a few camps out here. It took a while to find him."

He pointed back the way he'd come. "He's a few miles to the northeast. His captors made camp in a large flat area, so it will be impossible to sneak up, but I came up with a distraction. Come on. I'll tell you on the way."

Chapter 27

The camp was larger than I expected. Twenty demons milled around with swords, bows, and even the occasional mace. What was it with all the medieval weaponry? The demons were all different sizes—some with horns, others with thick fur. Some even walked on four legs. One had feathers sticking out of its head and looked like it might be molting. *Gross.* Most were moderately humanoid. A few tentlike structures were up, but most of the demons were gathered in small groups around a cook fire or were lying wrapped in blankets on the ground. Dark smoke rose from the roasting spit and smelled faintly of chicken, although it looked very much like an enormous snake. At the edge of the camp, there was a slumped form tied up between two guards. A small glowing ball cast a faint red light on his face.

Dad.

My breath caught, and I strained my eyes for any small sign that he was okay. He appeared to have all of his limbs, but he was filthy and too still. Was he breathing? He was leaning against a pole, tied by his arms. Part of his face was swollen, and he had a black eye.

He moved, shifting position.

He's alive.

My body tensed with the urge to run to him, but I didn't. I waited. Tears of relief streamed down my face.

I couldn't mess this up. I'd have one shot.

Tristan's plan was simple, but dangerous. He was going to start a stampede of wild beasts—I couldn't remember the name he called them—and drive them through the camp. He would ride in on one of them and create a distraction. I would rush in, untie my dad, hope he was well enough to move on his own, and rush out. I had a dart gun filled with a sleeping potion to use if anyone tried to stop us, but Tristan warned that its effects wouldn't last long, so we'd have to run.

So many things could go wrong. What if the animals ran over Dad before I got there? What if he was unconscious and couldn't run with me? What if the guards figured out the stampede was a diversion and didn't leave?

Heart pounding, I waited. It was dark out, only a sliver of moon visible. Darkness would add to the confusion. The raiders had more of those balls of magic lighting each corner of the camp, but there remained plenty of shadows. A few demons meandered along the perimeter, but they were doing a halfhearted job, and Tristan had placed me well away from their route.

Off to my left, a deep rumble was coming from a small rise. *Is this it?* I strained to see what was happening, but saw nothing. Crouching behind a bush, I noticed a flickering in the distance. A movement flowing over the ridge and across the flats. As they got closer, I made out hundreds of bodies stretching thick limbs as they tore across the land. One of the lookouts sounded an alarm, and everyone in the camp was immediately up and moving.

Now that they were almost upon us, I could see the creatures galloping across the plains, deep-red fur covering large buffalo-like bodies. I hunched lower, waiting for the signal from Tristan, and wiped sweaty palms on my jeans.

Scattering, the demons ran away from the stampeding herd, grabbing items as they went, not even stopping to get dressed. I hunched as low as I could and let out a soft breath when none of the raiders came too close to my hiding spot.

The thundering grew louder. Then the animals were tearing through the camp.

Dad stood up with the sound, looking around, eyes wide, ropes pulled taut.

To the left of him, an arrow pierced a guard's throat, and he dropped. Then an arrow flew at the second guard, and he went down too. Neither uttered a sound. That was my cue. I ran straight for Dad, eyes on nothing else.

My feet pounded the dusty ground. Thirty yards. Twenty. The sound of my footsteps seemed as deafening as a pounding waterfall, but were likely drowned out by the stampede. Ten yards. Then I was there in front of him. I used the knife Tristan had given me to cut Dad's bonds. It slid through the rope like butter. Grabbing his arm, I yelled, "Come! Now!"

He blinked, taking a moment to process. "Zoey?"

I tugged harder. "Move!"

He stumbled off in the direction I indicated, legs tangling in the ropes I'd cut. I yanked his arm up and shoved him forward, following close behind.

Then, out of the corner of my eye, I saw him.

The demon who had killed Mom.

I froze, my hand letting go of Dad and curling into a fist. The burn of rage overtook me, and I could barely see straight.

He was looking away from us, his face in profile. Same large build, dark skin, spikes, and horns. When he turned to watch the stampeding animals, his red eyes filled my vision. I could never forget those eyes. I wanted to go over and empty my dart gun into his face. I wanted to beat him bloody and make him feel the pain I had felt.

But that would draw attention.

He hadn't noticed us. I needed to get Dad to safety, or I could lose Dad too. Shuddering, I took a deep breath. Then another.

It was the hardest thing I'd ever done, but I forced my feet to move. Dad had kept moving while I was frozen. He was now far ahead. How long had I stood there staring?

I ran, kicking myself for getting distracted. *This is about Dad. Dad is alive. He needs to be my focus right now.*

There was a whistling near my head and I spun to the side, narrowly evading a thrown axe. I threw myself to the hard ground as I heard another whistling sound.

"Fuck!" Someone had noticed me. I rolled, stirring up more dust. The air was thick with it. Dad had stopped up ahead. "Keep going! I'm coming!" Looking around, I couldn't see the attacker, but I Saw a person-sized dome of magic in the darkness and fired in that direction.

Jumping to my feet, I ran smack into a hard, wide chest.

A deep, harsh voice, one burned into my memory, said, "What have we here?" A large hand grabbed my hair, pulling it to his face and breathing in my scent. He let go and smiled, a baring of teeth. "So much like your mother. I'll make it quick for you too." Those burning red eyes bored into mine.

I pulled the trigger on my dart gun as fast as I could. Shot after shot. He took a step back, attempting to deflect my shots. I turned and ran, still firing behind me. If he caught me, he'd kill me. I ran like the wind. Shot after shot, until I was empty. Glancing back, I saw him on the ground.

My mother's killer on the ground. My steps faltered.

One of my shots had hit him. I could run back and kill him, and he'd be gone. I'd never have to fear him again. This was my opportunity. I might never have another chance.

Then Dad was there, running toward the downed demon, face contorted with rage. "I'll kill you!" He was not in good shape, cuts and bruises everywhere. No weapon. Going against a demon. A demon who was twice his size. A killer for hire.

"Dad, no!" I grabbed him before he could get past me, hugging him tight. "Please, don't leave me!"

"That thing killed your mother! I heard it!" He was shaking with rage, but in no shape to break out of my grasp.

I looked back, and the demon twitched. The dart was wearing off.

"We don't have time. Let's go. Now!" Turning him back around, I grabbed his hand and ran. He resisted for a second, but then followed.

We needed to get out of there. We might already be too late.

I'd already lost Mom. I couldn't risk losing Dad, too. Tears spilled down my face. Taking one last glance back at the downed demon, I bottled up my rage and let it go. I'd had my chance, but it was time to move forward.

I ran, leaving my mom's murderer—and my revenge—behind.

Chapter 28

I gripped Dad's hand, his large one enveloping my small one, and we ran. No words were spoken. Tristan had made me memorize the route, and I was glad for the repetition. I thought I'd had it firmly in my head, but now it was a little fuzzy. I activated the tracking charm Tristan had given me and headed in the right general direction. I used the meager light cast from the glowing trees to not fall on my face. When I started gasping for air, I slowed and pulled Dad to a stop. *Tristan will find us.*

Tears streamed down my face. I hurled myself at my dirty, bruised father, falling against him like a wilting flower. "Are you okay?" I asked in a wobbly voice.

He squeezed me tight, making it hard to breathe. "I'm fine. You brave, foolish girl. I can't believe you would come here."

"But—"

He squeezed me tighter. "Now isn't the time. We'll talk about this after we get back. Are you okay? Why did we stop?"

"I'm fine. Just tired. We're waiting for someone." I helped Dad sit. Leaning beside him, I put the spare clip in the dart gun. Looking at him sitting on the strange terrain, I whispered, "I'm so glad you're okay."

I kept alert, ears open for any sound that could mean pursuit. Dad grabbed my hand and squeezed it, not letting go until we heard a rustling behind us. Both jumping to our feet, I shot at the dark trees. Tristan stepped out with a raised eyebrow, holding the dart pinched between two fingers. *Did he catch it midflight?* "Look before shooting next time."

Dad pushed the gun tip down so it pointed at the ground. "Maybe I should take the gun." I ignored him, and after a moment he let it go, asking, "Is this who we were waiting for?"

Putting the gun away, I wondered what Dad thought of the strange runes glowing on Tristan's skin and his faster-than-normal reflexes. His wings weren't currently visible, but he was definitely part Other. *Will it bother him that Tristan isn't fully human?* I nodded. "Tristan, Dad. Dad, Tristan."

Dad held out his hand and said, "It's Terry. Nice to meet you."

Tristan briskly shook his hand, then said, "Follow me. No sounds."

Dad hesitated. "Where are we going?"

Tristan whispered, "Back to your realm," before trudging forward.

Before following, Dad turned to me and held out his hand. "Gun. Now."

"They're just sleeping darts." I grudgingly pulled it out and handed it over. I didn't want to, but now wasn't the time for an argument, and I *had* just shot at Tristan.

Tristan led our small group, and we walked single file through a thicker part of the woods. I had to resist the urge to glance back every few feet and make sure Dad was still there. I could hear him stumbling and muttering the occasional curse. I couldn't believe we'd actually found him and that he was okay. As time passed, the strange dark trees started glowing brighter around us.

Unable to contain my curiosity, I whispered to Tristan, "Why are they glowing?" I was glad for the light, but it was odd.

"They're charged by the sun and glow at night. The glow usually fades by the early morning. True darkness doesn't happen until right before dawn, when the plants have used up all the energy they absorbed during the day and go dark."

I reached out and gently traced a glowing leaf, the color changing as I put pressure on it. I opened my mouth to ask another question, but Tristan stopped me with a finger over my lips. "Quiet. We may have put some distance between us, but they won't give up easily."

We crept through the phosphorescent trees and bushes for a long time. I recognized nothing. It was like *Alice in Wonderland*, just as topsy-turvy. I half expected a Cheshire grin to float above us in the trees.

I thought we would leave the same way we had come in, but everything looked different. I wasn't sure if it was a different route, or just the glow of night making everything strange and unfamiliar. I wanted to ask about the yellow plants we passed, the odd hoots off in the distance, the strange hum of energy in the air. I wanted to ask how much longer before we could rest, but I kept my questions to myself.

As the night wore on, the darkness grew more pronounced, and I realized that the glow from the plants was fading. I started stumbling, unable to see where I was going. I was exhausted, and my legs were like rubber. I was only moving through pure force of will. Tristan must have realized this, because he stopped. Before I could sink to the ground, he grabbed my hands and placed them on his shoulders. "Up."

"For real?"

He nodded, and I wrapped my arms around his neck and jumped up on his back. He adjusted me to a good position and kept walking, not even glancing at my dad, who was also stumbling.

"Shouldn't we rest?" I whispered in his ear.

"Soon. In about another hour, we should reach the safe zone I planned on. We can sleep for a few hours and then go through the gate tomorrow. This is a dangerous area to stop, or I would give your father some rest. We're still too close to the raiders, and this area isn't defensible at all. Your dad will be okay. He, at least, has been sitting all day instead of hiking up the mountain."

I nodded, trying to situate myself to be as unobtrusive as possible. While I wanted to walk and show Tristan that I was capable, my legs were trembling in his grip, and I knew there was no way I would convince him I was fine to walk. I *wasn't* fine. I needed him to carry me. It was embarrassing to be so helpless. I remembered him saying that I should be able to regulate my temperature and be stronger and faster. I just had to access it. If only I'd found the time to learn how. I vowed to make that a priority when we got back to the Human Realm.

I rested my head on Tristan's broad shoulder, breathing in his warm, spicy scent. In the growing darkness, I could still make out faint touches of light. Sometimes they outlined the tops of plants, the parts that had received the most sun. Sometimes they were eyes, glowing menacingly and tracking our group. Nothing attacked. Were they scared of Tristan, or was it luck? We weren't an especially large group, and we were tired and injured.

Whatever the reason, I felt safe enough that I found myself mesmerized by the fading glow around us and started drifting off.

When we stopped, I jerked awake, realizing it had somehow become full dark. Tristan lowered me to the ground, holding on until he was sure I was standing on my own. My cheeks heated. *How long was I asleep?*

Tristan gently pushed me into a dark opening. I reached around and touched something cold and hard above and to the sides of me. As I walked farther, it opened up, and I realized we were about to enter some sort of cave. My mind immediately panicked at the thought of bats or spiders or bears. I paused. Tristan sighed and squeezed by me, hard body squishing me up against the cave wall as he passed in the tight space.

A minute later, a light lit up a wall sconce and then three more. The entrance had been narrow, but the actual cave was huge, ceilings reaching farther than I could see. "We'll be safe here for a few hours. Rest up. We have a long trek tomorrow."

I went straight for Dad and hugged him tightly, not wanting to let him out of my sight. I looked him over again, noting he wasn't missing any fingers or ears. I knew he was fine. I didn't know why I kept having this compulsion to check, but I couldn't help it. "Are you sure you're okay?"

"Just some bruises. I'm fine. You're exhausted. Sit down." He pulled me down beside him on the smooth stone floor.

I leaned against him, happier just knowing he was there and safe. "What happened?"

"I came home from my trip and found some men

waiting for me inside the shop." His hand went up to his neck. "They shot me with something, and when I woke up, I was here. Wherever this is." Dad looked at Tristan. "Thank you for your help."

Tristan nodded. Then, ignoring us, he walked deeper into the cave. Maybe to check the rest of it?

"Where are we?"

I turned my attention back to Dad and the stubble covering his jaw and bruises coloring his face in some sort of odd paint by number design. "Dad, what did you know about Mom and the Mythics?"

Dad paled, eyes on his feet. "Not as much as I wish I did. I knew they existed, but not much outside of that. Your mother didn't like to talk about it. Said it was safer to pretend magic didn't exist." He looked up. "Which of the Other realms are we in?"

"The Demon Realm." Tristan was back and dug into his pack and handed everyone some type of jerky. Dad tore into his like he hadn't seen food in days—which, maybe he hadn't. He hadn't been kidnapped that long, but he did sometimes forget to eat.

Tristan cocked his head, listening. "I have a friend coming to help us. She is…unique. Please do not insult her."

Into the light flew a shape, which then landed and shook out its wings and folded them in. It looked like a giant fruit bat, arms covered in a soft brown fur, brown leathers covering its body, and large, leathery wings. The wings were covered with thick scars, making them fold in unevenly. Turning toward us, her face was decidedly human, but most of the rest of her was…not.

"This is Bea. She's going to help us get back to the gate. Bea, this is Zoey and her dad, Terry."

Dad nodded, but didn't seem able to form words.

"Nice to meet you." I held out my hand, and she took it, shaking it firmly. Her skin was soft and supple, like a fine leather wallet.

"Likewise. Tristan doesn't bring many people here. Any friend of his is a friend of mine." She looked over at Tristan, her yellow eyes glowing.

Tristan said, "They're not friends."

"Sure." Her voice was curt. "How do you want to do this?"

"We can't go back the way we came. We'll have to use the gate in the snake pits. It's the closest. We'll rest for a bit first and then buddy up. You take Zoey, and I'll take her dad."

She snorted. "I am stronger and should take the heavier one. I can smell his fear, but he's going to have to get over it. If you try to take him, you might not make it."

Tristan glanced at my dad, considering.

Dad straightened and cleared his throat. Seated, you could still tell he was almost twice my size. "A lot of this is new to me, and yes, I am scared, but I have no qualms about accepting help when I need it. I need help. My daughter needs help. We would both be grateful for whatever you can offer, and I'm sorry for my fear. I've never seen anything other than humans before today, and it's all been a bit…much."

She nodded, yellow eyes not blinking. "I'll go scout. You all rest. I'll be back in a few hours, and then we will leave." She took off and was gone, fading into darkness like a wisp of fog dissipating on a breath.

After a moment, I heard my dad's low rumble. "What is she? If you can tell me."

"It is rude to ask and even ruder to discuss it without the person here," Tristan said.

I could almost hear Dad backing up, hands in the air. "Never mind. I meant no disrespect."

"I know. I am telling you so you know not to ask again. She grew up here and is one of the best guides we could ask for to get us safely to a gate."

"Will we owe her?" My debts were starting to add up. Would I end up a slave? Would I be *his* slave? How did that work? If you had debts to multiple people, did the person you owed the most get you?

"She owes me. This does not add to your debt. It is part of our deal. I must get you both to the Human Realm safely to satisfy our bargain, and I can't do that without her help." He looked side-eyed at me. Lips quirked up in the barest of smiles. "I noticed you met the demon you wanted to find. That debt has been met."

I sighed, wanting to be mad at him, but the anger wasn't there. The inferno of rage that was usually attached to thoughts of Mom's killer had dampened. I still wanted to get justice for what he did to Mom, to our family, but it no longer consumed me. I thought back to all the dangerous situations I'd put myself in. I had been so reckless. *What if I'd failed and died? What would that have done to Dad?*

I gave Tristan a wry smile. "Yes, that debt has been met."

"Are you going to look on your own?"

"No." As I said it, I realized it was true. I was done chasing the past.

He nodded. "Good. Get some rest. We will leave in a few hours." I heard him rustling in the dark.

I scooted closer to Dad. "You okay? Can I get you

anything?'

"A steak sandwich?"

We both chuckled, and I gave him another tight hug. He hugged me back, solid and safe and smelling a little ripe, but with the familiar hints of ancient texts and coffee and home. He said, "I'm okay. Thank you for saving me. Although, I never ever want you to do something so stupid ever again. You hear me?"

The stern tone of his voice sounded just the way it always did. I nodded, smiling. He was going to be okay.

"I love you, pumpkin."

"I love you too."

We both made up beds on the hard stone floor with the pile of blankets Tristan had dropped nearby, courtesy of Bea. I looked one last time at Dad, assuring myself he was still there, before closing my eyes and falling into a fitful sleep.

Chapter 29

When I woke, I couldn't tell how much time had passed. Out of the darkness, silvery blue eyes stared back at me. I sat up and moved closer to Tristan, being quiet so I didn't wake my dad. "How long did I sleep?" I whispered.

Tristan's voice was a low rumble. "Not long enough. Go back to bed. Bea won't be back for another hour, and you need the rest."

My body ached something fierce, and I knew he was right, but I couldn't get myself to scoot away. My mind was too fired up for the exhaustion to take over. Instead, I inched closer and laid my head against the wall of the cavern next to him.

"The place we're going to sounds…spooky." Anything I could think of with the title *snake pits* wasn't good.

"It is dangerous. Hundred-foot anacondas with poisonous fangs live there. We will take a path well above them, but if they detect us, they might swarm. We will have to be silent."

I thought back to my tramping through the woods. "That's not good."

"No, it isn't your strong point."

I punched him in the arm. "Not necessary. Is there an antidote? If we get bitten?"

He chuckled. "If we get bitten, blood loss will get

you before the poison does. They have big teeth. If they get close, Bea and I will fly you up."

"Why don't we just fly the entire way?"

"My wings aren't as strong as hers, and I can't fly that long carrying someone. Get some rest, Zoey."

There was a light touch on my arm, and exhaustion closed over me again and my limbs turned to lead.

****

When I next woke, I was more rested, but an angry pit burned in my stomach. *Did he use magic on me again? To make me sleep?* I was lying on something soft and warm. I was too comfortable to move, but I'd get up in a minute and yell at him. The jerk.

A few minutes later, I opened my eyes. Long legs stretched out in front of me. I jerked up. I'd been sleeping on Tristan. My head had been pillowed on his lap. I could feel my face getting warm. I looked over and saw my dad glowering at us disapprovingly and was glad the semidarkness hid my blush. I avoided looking at Tristan and heard a soft chuckle. My anger came rushing back, and I turned and glared. "You put a sleep spell on me. Isn't it against the rules to put a spell on someone against their will?"

"You going to report me? Look, you needed the rest and were too worked up to sleep without it. Let it go, Zoey."

"No. Next time, ask first."

"Really?"

"Next. Time. Ask. First." I enunciated each word, anger boiling in my gut. Controlling what someone did was not a small thing. He needed to know that was a line he couldn't cross again with me.

He sighed. "Next time, I will ask first. Satisfied?"

I nodded and crawled over to where my dad was sitting. He looked pale, but it could have been the weird lighting from the cave. "How're you feeling?"

He gave a grunt, then said, "Confused. And tired. And hungry. Your mom called herself a Mythic, but she was nothing like these people. I knew there were other realms, but didn't realize how intertwined they were with ours. I thought it was a lot more regulated than it is. It's hard—" he cleared his throat, eyes shiny, "—realizing how different she was. How much I didn't know her and this world she was more a part of than I realized."

I looked away, giving my dad a moment to compose himself. "Neither of us knew the real her, but I'd like to think we were the escape she wanted. That she showed us the best parts of herself. That we were her paradise."

He kicked a pebble, and it rolled across the hard floor. "Maybe. She told me you had magic too. That's why we never saw a doctor for your…" He waved a hand vaguely, like it was a bad word and he couldn't quite say it.

"Visions?"

"Yeah. She told me you could see magic, and that she was going to give you something to help. When you stopped seeing things, I never questioned it. I never looked into what you had been seeing and if those visions were real. I didn't want them to be real. When you were three, you told me about a huge monster in the backyard. Now I wonder, was that a real monster? How much danger did I put you in by not questioning more?"

Tristan's quiet voice came out of the dark. "If you didn't acknowledge them, it is against the law for us to interact. Pretending the monsters didn't exist likely saved her. It was the right choice."

Dad paused in thought and then nodded. His shoulders relaxed.

Warmth built in my chest. I was thankful for Tristan and his words. Thankful that they could ease my dad's guilt. The more time I spent with him, the more confused I got. Everything I heard about him suggested he was a monster, but the more time I spent with him, the harder it was for me to reconcile that truth with the guy I was slowly getting to know.

****

When Bea returned, she had more food, and odd harnesses and ropes. I picked up one of the ropes, pulling on it and testing its strength. "What's this for?"

"The mountainside will be tough. You and your dad will each be harnessed to one of us so we can help you across." She tossed me a hard roll. I caught it and stared at the strange, orangey roll.

"Thank you." I sniffed it warily. "What is it?"

"Food. Eat it." She huffed off.

I glanced up at Tristan, who was already eating his roll. "Did I offend her? If I did, I'm sorry."

He looked at the orange roll. "Tahla bread can be scarce. It packs lots of nutrients and can help you feel full for a long period. It was a great kindness for her to get it."

"So, I was rude. Damn it. I'm sorry."

He shrugged. "Tell her, not me."

I nodded, taking a bite. The roll was dense but bready and had a sweet aftertaste. I licked up every crumb and then went over to Bea. "Thank you for the bread. It was delicious." I had an old chocolate mint from a restaurant in my pocket. On instinct, I took it out and offered it to her. "This is from the Human Realm. Would

287

you like to try it?"

She nodded.

I unwrapped the chocolate and handed it to her. "You can chew it, but it is better if you suck on it."

She put it in her mouth, and her eyes lit up in delight. She put her hands together and bowed. Perhaps her way of saying thank you? I did the same back and then walked back to sit next to Dad.

Tristan stopped me before I got there and started fitting the harness to me. We were all tired and injured, and now we were going to climb a cliff and evade monster snakes. *What could go wrong?*

****

Dangling hundreds of feet in the air, I wished I hadn't thought that last thought. Clearly, it had been bad luck. Strong arms pulled me back up, and I glanced over the side at the red and orange scales writhing below me. Being back on the "platform" that ran along the side of the deep chasm didn't make me feel much safer. It was about six inches wide and was not meant for anyone afraid of heights.

"You okay?"

I clung to the side of the cliff, arms shaking. "I hate you so much right now."

Tristan chuckled. "You're okay. We're almost there." Up ahead, I could see Dad and Bea waiting for us on a blissfully large platform.

When we reached it, Dad pulled me into a tight hug. "Stop scaring me like that."

Bea's soft voice interjected. "The gate is close. Once we're through, I can bring you to a safe house and give you both a chance to figure out your next steps."

Dad nodded. "That sounds lovely. Thank you."

"Let's take a minute to catch our breath, and then we'll be off."

I looked out over the chasm. It was beautiful, in a dark, creepy way. My gaze kept being drawn back to an odd bird-shaped rock on the other side. There was something familiar about it. What was it?

I touched the gray stone on my ring and whispered the incantation. A map appeared. When I held my hand just so, it aligned perfectly.

It was here. The artifact was here. I had promised Tristan that I would help him find one of them for his help with Dad. But right now, I was tired and sore. Every muscle ached. I was almost out of this realm and free. The thought of climbing more made me want to sit down and cry. But he had saved my dad. I owed him.

There was a light tap on my shoulder. "Come on. It's time." Tristan was already striding away after Bea and Dad.

I took a deep breath and called out, "Wait."

Chapter 30

Tristan jogged back, feet kicking up dark dust. "What's wrong? Are you okay?" I could feel his gaze checking me for signs of injury, likely assuming I'd hurt myself on my latest stumble.

Dad was up ahead with Bea, and he looked back, face showing concern as well.

"We're here," I whispered.

Tristan looked around at the deep canyon surrounded by sturdy-looking plants, a puzzled look on his face. "Where?" He put his hand on my forehead. "Are you feeling okay?"

I shrugged his hand off, annoyed. "The map." Shoving my hand in his face, he looked even more concerned, until I got out the words. "My ring. The key." I'd briefly forgotten he couldn't see it.

Understanding dawned, and then concern lit his ice-blue eyes as they trailed up and down my body. "How far? I don't think you can make it if we need to travel much farther."

I jutted my chin out and said, "I owe you. You saved my dad. And I'm not a weakling. I'll be okay."

"Are you sure? You're exhausted. I'd hate to have gone through all the trouble of saving you for nothing." His dry tone made me want to smack him.

"We need to go now. Unless you want to wait another few weeks while I learn the handbook Regina gave me, so I'm no longer banned."

Tristan looked torn. Dad and Bea had turned back and were almost to us. "What's wrong? Why did you stop? Are you injured?"

I turned toward Dad, wanting to reassure him. "No, I'm fine." I decided to be blunt. "I owe Tristan a favor. You go on ahead. We have a slight detour, and then we'll be right behind you."

Turning to Bea, Tristan said, "Take her dad to the safe house. We'll catch up later."

Dad interrupted. "Favor? Absolutely not. There will be no favors."

My face turned bright red. "Dad, it's not that kind of favor. Chill out."

It was his turn for his face to go crimson, but he stayed resolute. "You're not going anywhere without me. I'm coming."

Bea piped in, "You're exhausted, dehydrated, and were limping earlier. You need to see a medic. You're going to the safe house. Tristan will not harm her, I promise."

"It's okay, Dad. I'll be fine. I need to do this. I'll see you soon, okay?"

Dad looked like he was going to argue, but before he could, Bea shot him with a sleeping dart. She caught him as he fell and threw him over her shoulder like he weighed nothing, despite the fact that he was bigger than she was. At my open-mouthed look, she shrugged and said, "He wasn't going to leave you." She resettled him, then turned to walk away. Glancing over her shoulder, she said, "Tristan, just so we're clear, you owe me. He's going to be a pain when he wakes up."

Tristan nodded. "Agreed. See you soon."

I stared after them, mouth hanging open. "I can't believe she did that."

After Bea had rounded the bend, Tristan said, "I can. Bea is a little dart-happy sometimes, although this time I'm glad it was her and not me. Which direction?"

I pointed across the chasm we'd just climbed, where the canyon backed up into a large rocky area. "See up there? That rock formation that looks like a bird's head? We need to go that way. It looks like there might be a path. Hard to tell from here though."

Tristan nodded, then looked at me and said, "Looks safe enough here. Rest. I'll go scout it out, see if there's an easier way up." He spread his wings and flew off.

Rest where? On the big expanse of rock? Under a sparse tree? Where was safe? I grumbled and then sat down and leaned back against a small tree. If I got eaten by a strange animal, I was coming back to haunt him.

****

My mind had been wandering when a sudden presence made me bang my head against the tree. Shaking, I stared into large orange eyes in a black reptilian face. A scream froze in my throat. I scooted as close to the tree as I could, getting as far as possible from the massive wolf-like body in front of me. "Shit, shit, shit."

Tongue hanging out between his teeth, the large animal's nostrils flared as he sniffed me. I relaxed as my tired brain noted that it was a *familiar* wolf-like body. I'd seen him before, with Tristan.

As if on cue, his warm baritone interrupted my racing thoughts. "BC, bad boy. Down."

Tristan grabbed the large animal and pulled it away. "I told you to watch over her, not traumatize her." He handed the triangular head something small and patted it like a dog.

My eyes widened. "Did you just give him a treat for scaring me?"

"No, it was for watching you. Which he's done a really good job of, didn't you, boy?" he said while scratching the creature's ears. "Outside of scaring you."

I crept up to a sitting position and hesitantly reached out a hand, patting the soft black head. BC leaned into my hand, his big orange eyes half-closed. "BC? Is it yours? Like a dog?"

Tristan ran a hand through his hair sheepishly. "Yeah, sorry. I was gone longer than I intended, so I sent him to make sure you were safe. He's been popping in and out. He doesn't like to leave me alone. He can teleport."

I stared at him, momentarily speechless. With his dog, he almost seemed human. And young. It was the first time I'd seen him truly relaxed. I wondered how old he was but didn't think he'd answer, so I stuck with a safer question. "What does BC stand for?"

BC seemed to know we were talking about him and flared his wings, tongue out.

Tristan grinned. "Bone Crusher."

I smirked, but couldn't contain my giggles when BC jumped up, licking Tristan's face.

"Down boy." Tristan wiped off his face, laughing. "Don't judge. I named him when I was ten. Come on. Let's get going before it gets any later. I'll fly us there."

I looked at him and didn't See his wings. "How do your wings work? I don't See them."

He muttered a few words under his breath and his wings burst out behind him. "I can fold them back or use a spell to retract them." He pointed to a series of interlocking runes on his wrist. "I usually keep them out around other demons. They help people recognize me, since wings like mine aren't common, but they're a bit unwieldy otherwise. Hence, the spell."

Walking forward, I reached out to touch his wings and the soft-looking black feathers. Then I remembered what that meant and blushed, putting my hand down guiltily.

His stare intensified. "I don't mind."

My face got even hotter.

He chuckled and then reached out and scooped me into his arms. I squealed and hoped he couldn't hear my racing heart.

"Hold on." Gripping me firmly, Tristan spread his wings.

Squeezing my eyes shut and clinging to his wide shoulders, the ground dropped away.

When I opened my eyes, we were gliding along the side of the canyon. While terrifying, it was much easier than climbing had been. He pulled his wings in as we reached a rickety bridge that I hadn't noticed earlier and landed on a moderately firm surface. It was probably the only firm surface on the rundown bridge. He put me down gently, hand lingering on my waist, setting off butterflies in my stomach. Reluctantly stepping away, I clung to the side ropes and tapped a foot on the boards experimentally. The wind made the bridge sway and I tightened my grip.

"Don't worry. It's not as rundown as it looks. Just hold on to the railing and test each step before putting your weight down."

Railing. *Did he actually call the worn rope a*

railing? Staring ahead, the beak of the bird's head rose in front of me. We were here. I could do this. My foot shook as I inched forward and tapped on the next board. "Why did we land on the bridge and not the nice, firm ground over there?"

"Sorry. It was the best landing spot I could find with a good view of where we're going so you can direct us." Tristan looked behind me. "BC, go home."

I turned. I hadn't noticed the large animal following us. A soft growl escaped the gigantic head as he landed, his wings tucking into his sides. His large body spread across the entire width of the bridge, his landing creating a wave of movement.

"I mean it. Now!" After a pause. "You're going to break the bridge."

The growl got louder, and the large animal lowered its head in challenge.

Tristan threw up his hands. "Fine. Break the bridge. See if I care." A soft chirp accompanied the words, and Tristan shook his head and started forward. "Idiot."

I was clinging with both hands to the rope railing, knuckles white, I was squeezing so hard. "Uh, I don't want him to break the bridge."

"I was exaggerating. He's a menace, but it'll be fine."

That did not make me feel better. As we moved across, me taking very small steps, I was surprised that the large beast somehow stayed on the bridge behind us. I kept expecting his huge bulk to crash through the bottom. The bridge *was* sturdier than it looked.

My stomach dropped when I glimpsed the abyss below, and I momentarily closed my eyes to let out a long breath. *Note to self, don't look down.* We were about two-thirds of the way across, so I stopped and checked the map. This time when I checked, I could see extra lines and details leading into the side of the cliff off a narrow trail.

Working our way closer, I heard a shout and glanced back. BC appeared in front of me, biting an arrow in half, one that had been headed straight toward me, wings flapping to keep himself airborne. Growling, he charged at the shooters, wings carrying him swiftly. The demon raiders had found us.

"Run!" Tristan threw fireballs, hitting the demons across the way and forcing them back. I ran, praying with everything in me that I didn't fall to my death or get shot with an arrow. *Who uses arrows?* I was almost at the end of the bridge when my foot found a weak board and crashed through. I grabbed the rope railing and clung for dear life as a chasm opened up beneath me. Feet dangling in the air and arms weak from climbing all day, I slipped.

Screaming, I fell, and my life flashed before my eyes. Then something was suddenly underneath me, shoving me up. Using the momentum, I hauled myself forward, scrambling for purchase until I reached a solid plank.

Black wings shot out from below, and BC's massive body charged some shooters, distracting them. I owed him a big bone when we got back, or whatever it was the demon dog ate.

I used all my strength and resolve to crawl along the final boards. "I don't want to die, I don't want to die, I don't want to die." When I got to the other side, I ducked behind an outcropping, limbs shaking so much I had to sit, lest my legs give out. *I almost died.* I took a deep breath. Then another. I had to pull it together. Tristan and

BC were still fighting. *I can do this.*

With a shaky hand, I checked the map again. I Saw that the lines went into the wall. Literally into it. There was no path, just a wall of dirt in front of us. Trusting the ring's projection, I put my hands in front of me and walked into what should be a solid wall of dirt and rock. Instead, I pushed straight through the powerful illusion. "Tristan, this way!"

Tristan followed me, but BC balked.

Tristan didn't even hesitate. "BC, home. Now!"

BC whimpered, but left, disappearing instantly. Keeping the map open, we wound our way through illusion after illusion. There were multiple paths, but with the map I was able to keep us going in the right direction.

Moving quickly, we worked to lose our pursuers as we traversed deep into the stone, following a path that only a Seer with the map could follow. We were moving so fast that the first trap almost got us.

I barely stopped in time and almost fell into the open pit with spikes that were hidden with illusion. Heart racing, I slowed down and tried to ignore the sounds of yelling behind us as the demons tried to follow.

When the sounds of pursuit had faded, Tristan whispered, "You okay? Did they get you?"

I pulled up my arms and couldn't tell. It was completely black, outside the glow of the illusions. Deep within the mountain, the light of day was lost to us. Tristan wordlessly produced a glow ball and sent it flying above us. The soft glow highlighted the scrapes I'd gotten clinging to the bridge when the plank had fallen, but other than the scrapes, I was fine. "I'm okay. You?"

Tristan grunted. *Really, is it that hard to give an actual worded answer?*

The path was tight, the walls closer than I would have liked. Water dripped down the sides, and I wondered exactly how deep we were going. I imagined water rushing all around us and, for the first time since pushing through the illusion, I felt claustrophobic. To distract myself, I studied the map again and realized we were almost there. A large, cavernous room was just ahead. Hurrying forward, we stepped into a wide, open space. In the center was a pedestal with a knife sticking into the stone. "It's the *Sword in the Stone*," I mumbled.

"Huh?"

Hard to use pop culture references with a demon. "Never mind." Using the map, I noticed that, below the pedestal, words were written out, but they were in another language, one I didn't understand. "If I write out some words, can you read them?"

"I won't know until you try."

Using a finger, I traced out the foreign letters into the dirt.

"Only those who do not want the dagger for themselves may attempt to remove it. To do so without a pure heart will lead to your death. Twist counterclockwise three times and then twist clockwise and pull."

"Lovely. Guess that means I'm pulling it."

Tristan stopped me. "Are you sure you don't want it? There is no personal gain for you?"

"Aw, you almost sound like you care."

"I don't," he said a little too quickly. He rushed on and said, "I'd just never find this again without you, so if you think you might die, we'll find someone else to remove it."

"Uh-huh. Don't worry, I'm good." Despite my bravado, I was nervous. Stepping up to the dagger, I thought hard for a minute. *Do I want it for self-gain? Do I care about taking down the shield and breaking the imbalance of power? The revolution*? I did, but I didn't associate myself with those who had been subjugated. I wanted it for Shield and Carrion and the others who had been hurt. I wanted this for Tristan. I didn't want this for myself. I grasped the handle, made three turns counterclockwise, one clockwise, and pulled.

Chapter 31

For a moment, nothing happened. And then a pure-white light shot from the dagger, up my arm, growing to touch every nerve. It was invading my very pores and my mind. I couldn't move, couldn't release the dagger, couldn't even blink as it worked through my system like lightning. It burned through me, making me scream as it spread.

The magic was growing, using me to focus the spell as it built in power. I understood now why death would come to one who had wanted to use the power. I was a tool to focus and contain it. If I had tried to use it, I would have ruptured the fragile workings. I did not understand all of what was happening, but I could See the hundreds of workings tied together. One wrong move, and the entire thing could collapse.

In my periphery, Tristan was beating at a shroud of light that now surrounded me. Time stopped. I couldn't breathe. The magic burned as it filled me. I was overflowing with power. I couldn't take much more. *Did I make a huge mistake? Is this how I die?*

I hadn't had a chance to really see Dad again, to explain about the registration and tell him how sorry I was for everything.

My skin felt like it would burst open any second. Tendrils of light shot out, the force of the spell activating, throwing Tristan across the room. Slowly, as the light sped out, the pain lessened. The pressure on my chest faded, and I could breathe again. I collapsed on the ground, gasping for breath, shuddering as I felt the first barrier fall. I was still connected, and through that magical connection, I felt the magic rebounding to its owner, Gabriel, the leader of the Mythical Council. I heard Gabriel's voice roar in my head as his careful shield took its first hit. I felt his challenge. His promise.

"You. Will. Pay."

Shuddering, I let go of the knife, ending the spell.

Sitting there on the floor, I didn't feel any different. *Aren't I supposed to be stronger?* Bending over, I picked up a rock and squeezed.

Nothing happened.

Tristan had gotten up and was by my side. He reached for me and then dropped his arms. Had he been about to hug me? I grinned and pulled him into my arms. He hesitated and then buried his face in my hair, hugging me back tightly before letting go.

Holding me at arm's length, he reached a hand out, and a warm glow lit up my arms. The cuts from scraping against the bridge knit together and healed.

I ran a hand over my healed skin. "Thank you."

His warm voice was husky. "Thank you. It feels wonderful. The extra power. I feel more…me."

I remembered hearing that the key would take down a spell. Something that was holding back access to magic, but I didn't feel any different. "Why don't I feel that way?"

He shrugged. "Celestials were never bound by the veil. It's why the demons and fae don't usually get along with celestials. Not your fault, but it can be hard to watch someone every day who has everything you want. It's hard not to be bitter."

Bending over, I picked up the dagger. The dagger glowed softly, but otherwise seemed like a normal dagger. I handed it to Tristan, who took it reverently. "What happened?"

"When you pulled the dagger, the first of the three veils went down. Each veil cuts us off from some of our power. Remember how I almost collapsed after healing you at your home?"

"My broken neck. How could I forget? I would like to never talk about that again."

He gave a small half smile. "I almost passed out afterwards. It drained me dry. I just healed you, and I still have reserves. Admittedly, this isn't as big a healing and I am always going to be stronger in the Demon Realm, but this is a huge win for us."

"Great. Now, how do we get me home?"

"I think I can get us out without running into the raiders, but they know who you are. I can go back for them later, but if even one gets away…You're going to have to go into hiding. They've already shown they know where you live."

"I know. I knew when they took Dad. He's probably already starting the process."

"Now that you're registered, it will be harder. Let me help."

I thought about it and asked, "What would I need to give you in return?"

"A favor."

I thought about all the things a favor could mean, and about his warnings not to trust him. I wanted to trust him, but an open-ended favor was probably a bad idea. "We'll be okay, but thanks."

"The offer stands, if you change your mind."

I nodded, a little concerned over the fact that I was already tempted to change my mind.

****

We'd circled around most of the raiders. Thankfully, they were loud, and the brush was thick enough they weren't too hard to avoid. The few we'd run into were quickly dispatched by Tristan. I'd been worried about BC, but when we'd finally found him, he'd been prancing around with joy. BC hadn't gone home like he'd been told. He'd been leading some of the demons on a wild-goose chase and seemed to have enjoyed himself immensely. Tristan scolded him, but it had been half-hearted. He'd finally sent BC off with a few rough pats on the head and a promise of a treat later.

Tristan grabbed my hand and brought us to the bushes surrounding the portal. We knelt and watched, looking for...I didn't know what. There was a rustling above from some small animals jumping from tree limb to tree limb. The movement made a few dark leaves fall. An odd movement caught my eye, and a pool of sludge slid over the fallen foliage. When it moved past, the leaves were gone. In fact, the entire ground in that area was bare. Mouth dropping open, I looked around, glad the sludge was nowhere near us. Was it some kind of Venus fly trap mud? "Did you see that?"

Tristan nodded. Warm breath tickled my ear as he whispered, "The slurries aren't native here. Someone must have brought them to guard the portal. The psychics probably spread word about the key being used somewhere in this area, and everyone is scurrying to thin the competition."

"Them?" I looked around to see if I could find more.

"That looks like one, but there are usually at least two or three all connected."

"Can we go around them or move them or something?"

"No, but we passed some berries a short way back. We need to feed them. Once they are full, they will take time to process the food and we can pass without getting eaten."

I turned wide eyes toward him and swallowed hard. Nodding, I followed as he led me toward a patch of berries about a half mile back down the path. I filled the base of my shirt with berries and then turned to Tristan. He'd taken his shirt off and had filled the makeshift container. I had to work not to stare. He looked at what I'd gathered and nodded, then took off back through the woods. While there was no discernable trail, Tristan picked out a path that wasn't too hard to get through.

He slowed me with a hand before we got to the clearing. I stopped behind him, careful not to spill any berries and trying hard not to stare at his perfectly defined back. The runes glowed red and swirled in weird patterns across his shoulders to the center of his back. Runes concealed slightly raised skin where his wings likely came out, and he had three spikes poking out at the top of his spine. The spikes were short. I had never noticed them before.

As if he noticed my gaze, he said, "They're retractable claws of a sort. It is dangerous here, and I don't want to be caught unawares."

My face flushed that he caught me staring. He tossed his berries at the slurry. It slurped them up, separating so you could see the one slurry was actually four distinct bodies. Tristan motioned me forward, and I followed suit, trying not to stumble as I tossed my contribution. He steadied me with a tight grip on my shoulder, and then we went back for more. After we dumped the second haul, I stopped him. "Why don't we try?"

He stared at me and said simply, "That is how people get killed."

After the third round, he told me I could sit and wait, and he went back for more by himself. The area was spooky, and I could hear the slurries' bellies gurgling as they digested their food. When he tossed in a last pile, the berries finally fell to the ground and just sat there. None of the slurries moved to gobble them up. Tristan grabbed my hand and pulled me forward, carefully steering clear of the slurries. They didn't move our way—just sat there like big blobs. At the portal, he clutched my hand tightly and walked us through.

The world fell away and rushed toward us at the same time, making my stomach flip. When we stopped, I wrenched myself away from Tristan and hurled. His hand was cool on my neck, and there was a gentle tug as he pulled my hair away from my face. He waited quietly while I puked my guts up. After my last spit, I wiped my mouth and then stood up. He let my hair go, and I whispered, "Thanks," my voice hoarse. Someday I'd get used to that.

He nodded curtly and handed me a water bottle. "Drink that. We've got to go."

I looked around and found us in a dark corner of what seemed like a basement. I could hear rushing water, but it was too dark for me to see anything but large shapes. When I handed the water bottle back, he gripped my hand and led me forward to a ladder. The dank, wet smell reminded me more and more of a sewer. Were we in a sewer tunnel? Climbing the slick ladder after Tristan, I tried to focus on each rung and not on falling to my death. When he pushed open the lid and pulled himself out, I could see the faint glow of the moon. It was dark out. The trees were green, and the air smelled fresh. A horn honked in the distance. We were in the Human Realm.

****

After we got to the safe house, we explained everything to Dad and slept. The safe house was a small wood cabin. Nothing too fancy, but it was cozy and safe. When my head hit the pillow, it was the best sleep I'd had in a long time.

The next day, when I was cleaned up, refreshed, and ready to face the day, I saw a stack of papers by my bed. Neat, block handwriting. At the top was written, "*Study Guide.*" Below that was: "*Mythic Rules. Rule number one. Never trust a Mythic.*"

I smiled. Tristan had written me a study guide. Shaking my head, I wondered when he'd found the time. Didn't half demons sleep?

Putting the pages under my pillow and away from prying eyes, I tiptoed out back, closing the screen door softly behind me. Dad was a bit overprotective right now and had been upset last night when I'd gone to the kitchen to get a snack and told him he couldn't come with me. I snuck as quietly as I could, hoping to avoid him on my way outside. The hovering was sweet, but I needed some space.

I found Tristan out back, walking along a narrow creek. I headed toward him, fingering the area on my wrist that once had his rune. The rune he'd added when we made our deal; him helping me get my dad and me helping him get the first artifact. It had disappeared after we stepped through the portal. Once I passed Regina's test, my last deal with Tristan would be done. Our time together was almost up.

Tristan turned at my approach, catching me touching where the rune had been. "Our bargain is complete."

"Almost complete. I haven't passed the test yet."

He smiled sadly. "You need to work on your wording. The bargain was to help you read the book. I have done that." At my slack jawed look he said, "I'm not disappearing. If you have questions, just ask."

Walking closer, he took my hand and smoothed his thumb over my wrist. "We could make another. My protection for you and your dad in exchange for your help taking down the next veil?" His eyes bored into me as he touched my bare skin.

Pulling my hand away gently, I said, "No. No more bargains. You said yourself I was terrible at making them, and I don't want to mess up any more than I already have." I wrung my hands together, staring at my intertwined fingers. "I think things turned out okay, but I need to see what taking down the first veil did before I look at taking down a second one. I don't know enough about the different realms and what the veils do. I need to learn more. I can't just go blindly into it this time."

"I understand."

I may have been reading him wrong, but he seemed disappointed. He started walking again, and I joined him. "What are you doing next?" I remembered the conversation he'd had with his dad. "Looking for your brother?"

"Yes."

I rolled my eyes at his short answer. "Do you want help?"

He glowered at me. "You can't give something freely. Our world doesn't work that way."

I smiled, choosing to ignore his posturing. "Good thing we're not in your world."

"I don't work that way." He grabbed a stone and chucked it out across the water. It skipped three times before sinking.

I'd been thinking about him and his inconsistencies all morning. I decided that, while he wasn't the kindest person, he wasn't bad either. "You know, you're not the monster you think you are."

He growled, "Yes, I am."

I stared down at the soft grass beneath my feet as I decided what to say. "You kill people to protect those you love and to help protect your home. That is not evil. That is survival."

"And using you? Getting you caught? I didn't think Gabriel would hurt you for taking the water, but I knew it was possible. I could have gotten you killed." He threw another stone into the water, and we both watched as it sank.

"But you didn't. You were trying to save your brother. You were trying to save me." I caught his arm, stopping him, and looked him in the eye. "I would have done it anyway, knowing the risks, if you'd just explained."

His icy-blue eyes held my gaze, neither us blinking. Finally, I spoke. "If this is some sort of weird staring contest, I have to warn you, I'm really good at these."

A loud snort erupted, and I watched as he tried to

tamp down his laughter.

"It's okay to laugh. It's good for you."

He sobered, grin fading. "We aren't friends."

"Yes, we are. I may not trust you completely, but we are friends. You helped me when I needed you, and I would do the same for you."

"No, we're not." His voice had a harsh finality to it that was troubling. "I can't have friends."

"Sure, you can."

"Do you remember Bea?"

I nodded.

"Did you see her wings?"

I remembered the veined, mangled wings. They worked but weren't pretty. I nodded again.

"We were friends once. We used to go on adventures as kids. When we were older, someone was mad at me, and rather than hurt me, they took her and tortured her for three days."

My throat grew dry. "I'm so sorry."

He picked up a stick and broke it in half, throwing the pieces into the water. "She never told me what happened. Her wings were salvaged, but she had been the best flier in our area, and afterward, it took her two years to fly again." He paused, letting the silence speak for him. "Because she had been friends with me. I don't have friends. Understand?"

I swallowed and sat down on a flat rock facing the creek. "I hate to break it to you, but you and Bea are still friends."

"We're not—"

I interrupted him. "Look, I understand you want to keep me safe. But I'm part human. We have friends. I can try to pretend we're not, like you pretend that you and Bea aren't friends, but I'll be here if you need me. And I'll help you not because we have a bargain, but because that is what friends do."

He slumped down next to me. "You're an idiot."

"Maybe. But I can't let you try to rescue your brother by yourself. You need me. If for nothing else, to make you less of a grouch."

"I don't need you." We both stared out at the stretch of water, and I almost missed his quiet response. "But thank you."

I smiled, butting his shoulder lightly with mine. He butted me back, and my heart sped up as I tried not to think about how much I liked being next to him. I leaned against him as we sat there, shoulders touching, staring out at the quiet water.

Closing my eyes, the creek made a soft trickling sound, and I thought of Mom. Thinking of her still hurt, my chest still tightened, but the burning rage was gone. I was still angry at her killer, but I had made a choice to focus on the living, not the dead, and I wanted to continue doing that. I knew now that I had to let go of the past and focus on moving forward.

Dad was safe, and the first veil was down. I was registered and on my way to passing the registration test. I had made a lot of mistakes and I still had a lot of decisions to make, but for today, right now, next to Tristan, I felt like Mom was smiling down at me and everything was going to be okay.

A word about the author...

C.E. Brown has lived most of her life in the Pacific Northwest, close to family and friends. She loves to travel, always searching for magical places to help inspire creativity. She attests that she has a very patient and understanding husband, a wildly creative son, and three crazy cats—one steals her shoes, another steals her food, and the third is a sweetly neurotic old man who can't decide if he'd prefer to be pet or left alone. C.E. Brown didn't find her passion for writing until she began wrangling kids as a school counselor, but then the writing bug bit and she's been writing ever since. Please visit her website for updates: http://www.cebrownauthor.com

Thank you for purchasing
this publication of The Wild Rose Press, Inc.

For questions or more information
contact us at
info@thewildrosepress.com.

The Wild Rose Press, Inc.
www.thewildrosepress.com

Printed in the USA
CPSIA information can be obtained
at www.ICGtesting.com
LVHW020809041024
792846LV00039B/823